Láadan

A Third Dictionary & Grammar of

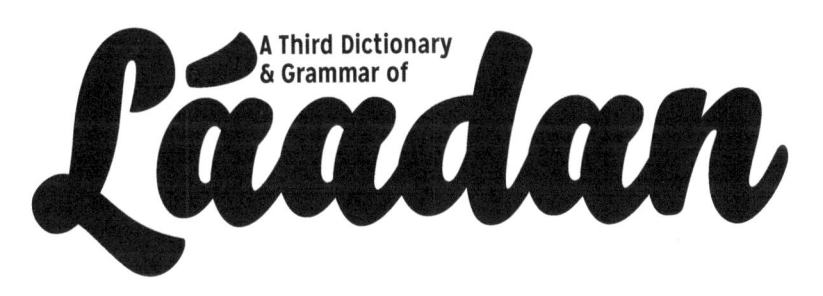

Suzette Haden Elgin

Láadan

A Third Dictionary & Grammar of

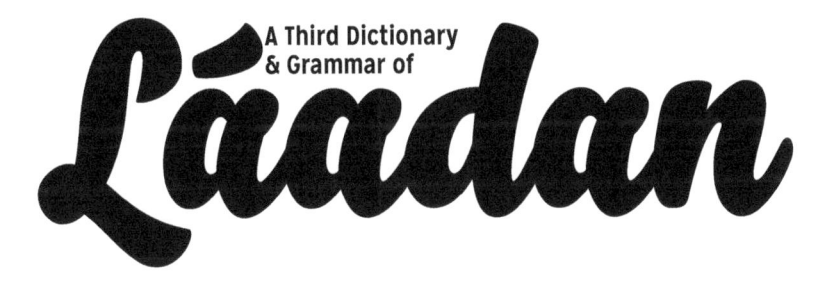

Suzette Haden Elgin

Edited by Jeanne Gomoll
and Diane Martin

UNIONSTREET**PRESS**

Dedicated to
Suzette Haden Elgin
November 18, 1936–January 27, 2015

A Third Dictionary & Grammar of Láadan
Copyright ©2020 by Jeanne Gomoll & Diane Martin

extensively revised from
A First Dictionary & Grammar of Láadan
Copyright ©1985 (First Dictionary) and 1988 (Second Dictionary),
by Suzette Haden Elgin

This book contains additional material from the Láadan website
https://laadanlanguage.com

"Teach Yourself Alien," by Suzette Haden Elgin
was published in *Aurora*, whole number 19, Vol 7, No. 1, Summer 1981.

Permission granted from the estate of Suzette Haden Elgin.
All rights reserved

First Edition, May 2020

Cover and book design by Jeanne Gomoll

A Third Dictionary & Grammar of Láadan
can be purchased here: tinyurl.com/LaadanDictionary

ISBN 978-1-71614-612-1

Selected Works by Suzette Haden Elgin

Fiction (novels)

The Communipaths
Furthest
At the Seventh Level
Star-Anchored, Star-Angered
Yonder Comes the Other End of Time

Twelve Fair Kingdoms
The Grand Jubilee
And then There'll be Fireworks

Native Tongue
The Judas Rose
Earthsong

Peacetalk

Non-Fiction

The Gentle Art of Verbal Self-Defense
More on the Gentle Art of Verbal Self-Defense
The Gentle Art of Verbal Self-Defense Workbook
The Last Word on the Gentle Art of Verbal Self-Defense
Language in Emergency Medicine
Growing Civilized Kids in a Savage World
The Gentle Art of Verbal Self-Defense for Business Success
Success with the Art of Verbal Self-Defense
Staying Well with the Gentle Art of Verbal Self-Defense
GenderSpeak
The Gentle Art of Written Self-Defense
The Gentle Art of Written Self-Defense Letter Book
Language in Law Enforcement
Linguistics & Science Fiction Sampler
BusinessSpeak
"You Can't Say That to Me!"
The Gentle Art of Communicating with Kids
How to Turn the Other Cheek and Still Survive in Today's World
The Gentle Art of Verbal Self-Defense at Work
The Gentle Art of Verbal Self-Defense: Revised and Updated
A First Dictionary & Grammar of Láadan

Contents

How to Use this Book 5

Preface by Rebecca E. Haden 7

Introduction by Suzette Haden Elgin 11

The Sounds of Láadan 15

Lesson Set One: Patterns 19
   Lesson 1 21
   Lesson 2 25
   Lesson 3 29
   Lesson 4 33
   Lesson 5 37
   Lesson 6 41
   Lesson 7 45
   Lesson 8 51
   Lesson 9 55
   Lesson 10 59
   Lesson 11 65
   Lesson 12 69
   Lesson 13 73
   Lesson 14 75

Lesson Set Two: Going to the Con 77
   Lesson 1 79
   Lesson 2 83
   Lesson 3 85
   Lesson 4 87
   Lesson 5 91
   Lesson 6 93
   Lesson 7 95
   Lesson 8 97
   Lesson 9 99

Dictionaries 101
   English to Láadan 103
   Láadan to English 139
   Affixes 205

Exercises 213
    EXERCISE 1: Birth Song 215
    EXERCISE 2: The Lord's Prayer 217
    EXERCISE 3: Sháam 100 221
    EXERCISE 4: Sháam 23 223
    EXERCISE 5: Wohíya Wodedide Shósho Bethu 227
    EXERCISE 6: Aranesha Bethu 231
    EXERCISE 7: Wolaya Wohilub........................ 237
    EXERCISE 8: A Nativity Story Written from Mary's Point of View.. 241

Essays by Suzette Haden Elgin 247
    Can a Language Be Owned? 249
    Láadan, the Constructed Language in *Native Tongue* Books 253
    Language Construction 101........................ 257
    The Link Between Language and the Perception of Reality 261
    Frequently Asked Questions 265
    Láadan Made Easier—How It Works, part 1 269
    Láadan Made Easier, part 2 273
    Myths About Láadan.............................. 277
    Just One More Láadan Myth 279
    Teach Yourself Alien 283

Appendixes 291
    APPENDIX 1: Rules of Láadan Grammar 293
        A) Auxiliaries 293
        B) Case Markers 293
        C) Degree Markers 294
        D) Doer/Agent Marker 295
        E) Duration Markers 295
        F) Embedding Markers 296

- G) Focus Marker 297
- H) Pejorative Marker 297
- I) Plural Marker 297
- J) Evidence Morphemes 298
- K) Repetition Morphemes 299
- L) Speech Act Morphemes 299
- M) State of Consciousness Morphemes 300
- N) Other Speech Act Suffixes 300
- O) Speech Acts. 301
- P) Noun Declensions. 305
- Q) Word Order 306
- R) Morphology 306
- S) Adverbial Dependent Clauses. 307
- T) Grammar Facts About the Láadan Affixes 308
- U) The Láadan Passive. 311
- V) Adjectives 312
- W) Time Auxiliaries 312

APPENDIX 2: Miscellaneous Additional Information 313
- A) Days of the Week, with English Equivalents 313
- B) Months of the Year, with English Equivalents 313
- C) Set of "Love" Nouns 314
- D) Numbers, Numerals 314
- E) Pronouns. 315

APPENDIX 3: Notes on Adding to the Láadan Vocabulary . 317

APPENDIX 4: Pattern Practice Answers. 325

APPENDIX 5: Resources. 327

About the Author 329

About this Book 331

About the Contributors. 333

How to Use this Book

LÁADAN IS A LANGUAGE CONSTRUCTED BY A WOMAN, for women, for the specific purpose of expressing the perceptions of women. This grammar and dictionary are intended to introduce you to the language and give you an opportunity to see if it is of interest to you or could be useful to you. Each grammar unit ("Lesson") has both a core section and a supplemental section that expands on the core. You might find it best to read through all the core sections first to get the feel and weight of the language, and then return to the supplemental sections.

The first set of lessons ("Patterns") appeared in *The First Dictionary and Grammar of Láadan*; the second set of lessons ("Going to the Con") was originally posted on the Láadan website.

Vocabulary is listed in the Dictionaries section, which is divided into an English-to-Láadan section, a Láadan-to-English section, and a section listing affixes, which are additional elements placed at the beginning or end of a root, stem, or word, or in the body of a word, to modify its meaning.

Following the Dictionary section are a set of exercises originally published in *Hot Wire* magazine. Following the Exercises section, you will find essays about Láadan and language construction by Suzette Haden Elgin. And finally, you will find useful information in the Appendixes.

Preface

by Rebecca E. Haden

MY MOTHER, SUZETTE HADEN ELGIN, was a feminist all her life. She did not live to see the #MeToo movement, Pantsuit Nation, or the Women's Marches for resistance. She probably would not have joined in, though, because she sincerely believed that language determines perception, and perception determines reality.

When we use a word, that word defines our understanding of its referent. If we have no word for a concept, it doesn't exist. Láadan was designed to make it practical and even possible to express women's feelings and experience well. English, Suzette hypothesized, just can't do this.

Or not without destroying the patriarchy.

My mother believed in the power of language to shape reality so strongly that she generally considered political action pointless. She voted as a matter of civic duty and had strong political opinions, but her writing was her action.

She wrote novels intended to increase people's awareness and change their minds, self-help books about using language to change one's health and career and

Suzette (center) with daughters Patricia and Rebecca, 1974. Photo by George Elgin.

other aspects of life, and letters to prisoners which were supposed to infuse those prisoners' lives with lovingkindness. This great torrent of words was, to Suzette, the most powerful kind of action she could take, because of the great power of language.

She would have seen plenty of evidence that she was right in our current political reality. If tweets can influence our elections and the words of our leaders can be blamed for mass shootings, language is clearly very powerful.

She would also have noticed that Láadan's ability to convey emotional data and information about the source of the speaker's knowledge could be extremely useful in today's public discourse. One of the strengths of Láadan is that it prevents claims of "I only said…" or "I only meant…" by making it crystal clear what the speaker presupposed and intended. It's not a language for manipulation; it's a language for revolution.

We have not seen Láadan creating revolutions, or even being used in daily life. Suzette officially declared it a failure in reaching that goal. But it has caused people to think about women's perceptions. It has caused people who wouldn't otherwise have thought much about language to do so. It has caused people who have never read the novel it sprung from to think about and talk about this language as something other than a literary device.

In order to see the power of Láadan, however, we probably have to think about the woman who created it. While she was a respected linguist and teacher, she retired young and went to live off a dirt road in the Arkansas Ozarks, on unimproved land, very much in the middle of nowhere. From that time on, she rarely left her home. Special occasion visits to small nearby towns and family members' homes and weekend trips to science fiction conventions were her primary connections with the outside world. She welcomed family members into her home, but the rest of her relationships were long-distance.

Neighbors knew her as a nice lady who grew enormous tomato plants in her greenhouse and crocheted toy dragons for her grandchildren.

As she moved into the 21st century, Suzette sent her language out into the world in blogs and a website. Google "Láadan" and you will find more than 83,000 mentions from around the world. People continue to write about Láadan with strong emotion.

They probably do not guess that Suzette crocheted toys for her grandchildren.

The influence that Suzette and Láadan have had, so far beyond the number of people she touched directly, is a testament to the surprising power of language. With this new edition of the Dictionary, more people may meet and be influenced by Láadan. It might cause more of us to think about nuna (contentment for bad reasons), about positive and negative states of bewilderment, or the relationship between storing and squandering.

At the very least, reading through the lessons, the vocabulary, and the essays brought together in this book invites us to think in new ways about the experiences of our daily lives. If it is not a radicalizing experience for all readers, it can at least be a refreshing one.

Rebecca Haden
August 2019

Crocheted toy dragon. Photo by Diane Martin

Introduction
by Suzette Haden Elgin

The Construction of Láadan

IN THE FALL OF 1981, I WAS INVOLVED in several seemingly unrelated activities. I had been asked to write a scholarly review of the book *Women and Men Speaking*, by Cheris Kramarae; I was working on a speech for the WisCon science fiction convention scheduled for March 1982, where I was to be Guest of Honor; and I was reading—and re-reading—Douglas Hofstadter's *Gödel, Escher, Bach*. I had also been reading a series of papers by Cecil Brown and his associates on the subject of lexicalization—that is, the giving of names (words, in most cases, or parts of words) to units of meaning in human languages. Out of this serendipitous mix came a number of things.

1. I became aware, through Kramarae's book, of the feminist hypothesis that existing human languages are inadequate to express the perceptions of women. This intrigued me because it had a built-in paradox: if it is true, the only mechanism available to women for discussing the problem is the very same language(s) alleged to be inadequate for the purpose.

2. There occurred to me an interesting possibility within the framework of the Sapir Whorf Hypothesis (briefly, that language structures perceptions): if women had a language adequate to express their perceptions, it might reflect a quite different reality than that perceived by men. This idea was reinforced for me by the papers of Brown et al., in which there was constant reference to various phenomena of lexicalization as the only natural and self-evident possibilities. I kept thinking that women would have done it differently, and that what was being called the "natural" way to create words seemed to me to be instead the *male* way to create words.

3. I read in *Gödel, Escher, Bach* a reformulation of Gödel's Theorem, in which Hofstadter proposed that for every record player there were records it could not play because they would lead to its indirect self-destruction. And it struck me that if you squared this you would get a hypothesis that for every language there were perceptions it could not express because they would lead to its indirect self-destruction. Furthermore, if you cubed it, you would get a hypothesis that for every culture there are *languages* it could not use because they would lead to its indirect self-destruction. This made me wonder: what would happen to American culture if women did have and did use a language that expressed their perceptions? Would it self-destruct?

4. I focused my Guest of Honor speech for WisCon on the question of why women portraying new realities in science fiction had, so far as I knew, dealt only with Matriarchy and Androgyny, and never with the third alternative based on the hypothesis that women are not superior to men (Matriarchy) or interchangeable with and equal to men (Androgyny) but rather entirely *different* from men. I proposed that it was at least possible that this was because the only language available to women excluded the third reality. Either because it was unlexicalized and thus no words existed with which to write about it, or it was lexicalized in so cumbersome a manner that it was useless for the writing of fiction, or the lack of lexical resources literally made it impossible to *imagine* such a reality.

Somewhere along the way, this all fell together for me, and I found myself with a cognitive brew much too fascinating to ignore. The only question was how I was to go about exploring all of this.
A scientific experiment and a scholarly monograph would have been nice; but I knew what the prospects of funding would be for an investigation of these matters, and I was without the private income that would have let me ignore that aspect of the problem. I therefore chose as medium the writing of a science fiction novel about a future America in which the woman-language had been constructed and was in use. That book, called *Native Tongue*, was published in August 1984 and was the first book of the *Native Tongue* trilogy, published by DAW. *Native Tongue II: The Judas Rose*,

appeared in February 1987; *Native Tongue III: Earthsong* came out in 1994.

In order to write the book, I felt obligated to at least try to construct the language. I'm not an engineer, and when I write about engines I make no attempt to pretend that I know how engines are put together or how they function. But I *am* a linguist, and knowing how languages work is supposed to be my home territory. I didn't feel that I could ethically just fake the woman-language, or just insert a handful of hypothetical words and phrases to represent it. I needed at least the basic grammar and a modest vocabulary, and I needed to experience what such a project would be *like*. I therefore began, on June 28, 1982, the construction of the language that became Láadan.

Because I am a linguist, I have studied many existing languages, from a number of different language families. In the construction of Láadan I have tried to use features of those languages which seemed to me to be valuable and appropriate. This method of construction is often called "patchwork," and is not looked upon with great favor in the Patriarchal Paradigm that dominates contemporary science. I would remind you, nonetheless, that among women the patchwork quilt is recognized as an artform, and the methodology of patchwork is respected.

My original goal was to reach a vocabulary of 1,000 words—enough, if well chosen, for ordinary conversation and informal writing. I passed that goal early on, and in the fall of 1982 the journal *Women and Language News* published the first writing in the language, a Nativity story written from Mary's point of view.[1]

There was one more factor that entered into my decision to construct Láadan, and I saved it for last because it was not there originally but developed out of the work that I was doing. I found myself discussing the idea of the woman-language, proposed need for it, etc., at meetings and conferences and among my friends and colleagues. And I found that it was possible to get the necessary concepts across, if I was patient. (There was, for example, the useful fact that English has no word whatsoever for what a woman does during the sexual act…this generally helps to make some points

---

[1] See page 15.

more clear.) But I got thoroughly tired of one question and its answer. People would ask me, "Well, if existing human languages are inadequate to express women's perceptions, why haven't they ever made one up that is adequate?" And all I could ever say was that I didn't know.[1] This became tiresome, and frustrating, and it was a relief to me when I was at last able to say, "Well, as a matter of fact, a woman did construct such a language, beginning on June 28, 1982, and its name is Láadan."

This book is a teaching grammar of Láadan, with an accompanying dictionary. It is only a beginning, and for all I know, the beginning of a failure, something that will never be of interest to anyone but the collector of linguistic exotica. But because this book exists, it will be very hard to "lose" Láadan in the way that other languages have been swallowed up by the History of Mankind. For that, I am most grateful to the members of SF³, who thought the work was important enough to justify publication.

Suzette Haden Elgin
near Old Alabam, Arkansas

---

[1] At that time I had not yet had the opportunity to read Mary Daly's book, published in May 1984, called *Pure Lust*. In that book Daly tells us that St. Hildegarde of Bingen, who lived from 1098–1179, constructed a language consisting of 900 words, with an alphabet of 23 letters. She was a distinguished scholar, with publications to her credit in a number of fields; as Daly says, it is impossible for us to know how much of value was lost to us when this language was lost. And I now have an alternative answer to that persistent question, although I have no way of knowing whether St. Hildegarde's motivation for the construction of her language was a sense that no language adequate to express her perceptions was available to her.

The Sounds of Láadan

Láadan was constructed to be simple to pronounce. This description is tailored for speakers of English, because the material is written in English; but the sound system has been designed to present as few difficulties as possible, no matter what the native language of the learner.

Vowels:

a	as in **f**a**ther** and **w**a**nder**	i	as in b**i**t and b**i**g
		o	as in h**o**me and h**o**pe
e	as in b**e**ll and b**e**st	u	as in s**oo**n and m**oo**n

Consonants:

th as in **th**ink and **th**ree—two letters, but just one sound

zh as in plea**s**ure and gara**g**e—two letters, but just one sound

sh as in **sh**ine and **sh**are—two letters, but just one sound

b, d, h, l, m, n, r, w, y
    For speakers of English, these sounds (and **th**, **zh**, **sh**) are pronounced as in English.

lh There is one more consonant in Láadan; it is "**lh**" and it has no English equivalent. If you put the tip of your tongue firmly against the roof of your mouth at the point where it begins to arch upward, draw the corners of your lips back as you would for an exaggerated smile, and try to say English "**sh**," the result should be an adequate "**lh**." It is a sound with a hissing quality, and is not especially pleasant to hear. In Láadan it occurs only in words that are themselves references to something unpleasant, and can be added to words to give them a negative meaning. This is patterned after a similar feature of Navajo, and is something so very handy that I have always wished it existed in English.

Tone

An accent mark over a vowel (or, when your keyboard doesn't offer accents, a vowel that's a capital letter) means that the vowel has high tone.

For English speakers, this means that you should give the high-toned vowel slightly higher pitch and a bit more emphasis. The word "**wáa**" has a sound-pattern like English "*uh*-oh!" The word "**waá**" has a sound-pattern like English "ah-*ha*!"

Láadan Grammar Facts

1. Láadan has two kinds of words: content words, and function words.

   Content words are words like "house" and "cat" and "eat" and "run."

   Function words are words like "of" and "and."

2. Most Láadan content words can be used as both verbs and nouns.

   This is like the way any English verb ("swim," for example) can be used as a noun if you add the "-ing" MORPHEME to it, as in "Swimming is fun."

   Notice that in Láadan you don't have to add anything to the word to make it a noun or a verb.

   Definition: A MORPHEME is any part of a word that has a meaning of its own and cannot be divided into smaller parts. For example, the English word "walking" has two MORPHEMES: the MORPHEME "walk," which can be used all by itself, and the MORPHEME "-ing," which cannot stand alone.

3. Láadan doesn't have any words like English "a, an, the."

4. In Láadan, verbs and adjectives are the same class of words, and they are only one class, the way conjunctions or pronouns are only one class of words in English.

   The word for "red" can mean the name of the color red, or it can mean "to be red." Which means that in Láadan you don't need "is/are" or any other form of "be" in sentences like "Roses are red" and "Jane is a linguist" and "This is the bus stop."

5. Láadan has a group of function words called "SPEECH ACT" words.

   For example, the word "**Bíi**" means "I say to you as a statement," while the word "**Báa**" means "I say to you as a question."

   English can do the same thing; we can say "I ask you" and "I promise you" and "I warn you," and so on. The difference between the two languages is that in Láadan the SPEECH ACT words are required, while in English they're optional.

   A SPEECH ACT word will always be the first word in a Láadan sentence.

   NOTE: We'll be discussing SPEECH ACT words in more detail as we go along.

6. Láadan has a group of function words called "EVIDENTIALS" that English doesn't have; many other languages do have them.

   An evidential tells you why the speaker feels justified in claiming that the words being said are true.

   For example, "**wa**" means "The reason I claim that what I'm saying is true is that I have perceived it myself" and "**wi**" means "The reason I claim that what I'm saying is true is because it's self-evident; everybody can perceive that it's true, or everybody is in agreement that it's true."

   The evidential will always be the last word in a Láadan sentence, and—unlike the situation in English—it's required to be there.

   NOTE: We'll be discussing evidentials in more detail as we go along.

Lesson Set One: Patterns

Lesson 1

Pattern

[VERB (NEGATIVE) CASE PHRASE – SUBJECT]

NOTE: Don't be concerned about the notation above; it will be useful in the long run. A "CASE PHRASE" is the same thing as what traditional English grammars call a "prepositional phrase." In English this means a preposition and its following noun phrase, as in "with a hatchet" or "to the beach," most of the time; in Láadan it usually means a noun phrase and its ending. This will become clear as we go along, and each of the sentence patterns explained will use the notation, with "CASE PHRASE" abbreviated to just "CP" in future to save space. "CASE PHRASE – SUBJECT" will be written "CP-S." The parentheses around "NEGATIVE" mean that it is an optional element in the sentence.

Vocabulary

Bíi	declarative	**ben**	they, many
ra	no, not, negative	**ro**	weather
i	and	**with**	woman, person
izh	but	**wa**	SEE NOTE, NEXT PAGE
be	she, he, it	**thal**	to be good
bezh	they, few	**hal**	to work

Examples

1. **Bíi thal ro wa.**
   The weather's good.
2. **Bíi thal ra ro wa.**
   The weather's not good.

NOTE: A Láadan sentence begins with a word that tells you what sort of sentence it is—statement, question, request, etc. The most common of the words is "**Bíi**," which begins declarative sentences, ordinary statements. A Laádan sentence ends with a word that states why the speaker considers the sentence to be true; in the example it is "**wa**" which means "claimed to be true because the speaker herself perceived whatever has been said." "**Wa**" is probably the most common of these words, which are called "EVIDENCE MORPHEMES" or "EVIDENTIALS."

3. **Bíi hal with wa.**
   The woman works.

   Bíi hal ra with wa.
   The woman doesn't work.

4. **Bíi hal be wa.**
   She works.

   Bíi mehal bezh wa.
   They work. (2 to 5 persons)

   Bíi mehal ben wa.
   They work.
   (more than 5 persons)

5. **Bíi hal with wa.**
   The woman works.

   Bíi mehal with wa.
   The women work.

Rules

1. The basic sentence begins with a SPEECH ACT MORPHEME to indicate what the sentence does, and ends with an EVIDENCE MORPHEME. (When several sentences are used together by one person, and these remain the same, they don't have to be put on every single sentence—this will become clear.)

2. The verb comes before the noun phrase in Láadan.

3. To make a sentence negative, just put "**ra**" immediately after the verb.

4. To make a verb plural, put the prefix "**me-**" at the beginning of the word. (Notice that the shape of the noun phrase doesn't change in the plural)

5. Láadan doesn't divide adjectives and verbs into two classes as English does. Thus "**thal**" means "be good" without any need for a separate word "**be**" in the sentence.

Supplemental Section

1. **Bíi hal**   omid   wa.   horse
               háawith   child
               omá   teacher
               thul   parent
               ábedá   farmer

   The _____ works.

   NOTICE: Láadan has no separate words for "a" or "the."

2. **Bíi hal ra**   áwith   wa.   baby
                   rul   cat
                   mahina   flower
                   ezha   snake

   The _____ doesn't work.

3. **Bíi**   áya   be   wa.   beautiful
            balin   old
            lawida   pregnant
            wam   still, placid
            shóod   busy
            lath   celibate by choice

   She is _____ .

4. **Bíi**   amedara   be   wa.   dances
            yod   eats
            ada   laughs
            ma   listens
            osháana   menstruates
            wéedan   reads
            wod   sits
            rúu   lies down

   She _____ .

NOTE: For this (and all the other) supplementary sections, it would be good if you would practice combining the patterns you know—make the positive sentences negative by adding "**ra**," make the singular verbs plural by adding "**me-**" and so on. Láadan is a language that works to maintain a pattern of alternating consonants and vowels, for ease of pronunciation; for this reason, you can't put "**me-**" directly on a verb that begins with a vowel. In such a case, you insert an "**h**" to keep the pattern.

Examples

Bíi hal ra omid wa.	The horse doesn't work.
Bíi mehal ra omid wa.	The horses don't work.
Bíi áya mahina wa.	The flower is beautiful.
Bíi meháya mahina wa.	The flowers are beautiful.
Bíi mehada ben wa.	They laugh.

Lesson 2

Pattern
[(AUXILIARY) VERB (NEG) CP – S]

Vocabulary

Báa	question	**dala**	plant, any growing thing
eril	PAST	**wíi**	to be alive
aril	FUTURE	**owa**	to be warm
le	I	**híya**	to be small
ne	you, one	**óoha**	to be weary
em	yes		
mid	creature, any animal		

Examples

1. **Bíi eril wíi mid wa.**
   The creature was alive.

   Bíi eril wíi ra mid wa.
   The creature wasn't alive.

2. **Bíi aril mehóoha with wa.**
   The women will be weary.

   Bíi eril mehóoha with wa.
   The women were weary.

3. **Bíi híya dala wa.**
   The plant is small.

   Báa híya dala?
   Is the plant small?

4. **Báa owa ne?**
   Are you warm?

   = **Em, owa le wa.**
   – Yes, I'm warm.

   – **Ra, owa ra le wa.**
   = No, I'm not warm.

Rules

1. When you need to indicate time in a sentence, put an auxiliary immediately before the verb. Auxiliaries never change their shape in any way, even if the verb itself is made plural.

2. When you ask a question, you aren't providing information but are asking for some. Therefore, you don't need an EVIDENCE MORPHEME at the end of a question.

NOTE: If you speak English, you may find all these remarks about parts of the sentence being optional, only being used if needed, etc., very confusing—or annoying. Please don't be concerned. If you prefer, use as your rule that you will always put a SPEECH ACT MORPHEME at the beginning of your sentence, or that you will always use an auxiliary to make your sentence time clear. The result may be very formal Láadan, but it will be grammatical.

Supplemental Section

1. | **Báa eril** | **wóoban ne?** | give birth |
   |---|---|---|
   | | **mime** | ask |
   | | **lothel** | know |
   | | **bedi** | learn |
   | | **benem** | stay |
   | | **ulanin** | study |
   | | **om** | teach |

   Did you _____ ?

(Remember that the plural of "**ulanin**" will be "**mehulanin**" and the plural of "**om**" will be "**mehom**." So, "**Báa eril mehom nen?**" is the sentence for asking a group of people "Did you teach?")

2. | **Báa eril** | **sholan be?** | alone |
   |---|---|---|
   | | **loyo** | black |
   | | **leyan** | brown |
   | | **aba** | fragrant |
   | | **liyen** | green |
   | | **sho** | heavy |

   Was it _____ ?

3. | **Báa** | eril | hal ne? | PAST: Did you work? |
|---|---|---|---|
| | aril | | FUTURE: Will you work? |
| | ril | | PRESENT: Are you working (now)? |
| | eríli | | FAR PAST: Did you work long ago? |
| | aríli | | FAR FUTURE: Will you work sometime far ahead? |
| | rilrili | | HYPOTHETICAL: Would you work? |
| **Bíi rilrili hal ne wo.** | | | You might work. |
| | | | Let's suppose you worked… |

Lesson 3

Pattern
[(AUX) VERB (NEG) CP-S CP – OBJECT]

Vocabulary

rana	beverage	**den**	to help
ana	food	**di**	to say, speak
áana	sleep	**wi**	EVIDENCE MORPHEME "**wi**" means "self-evident to everyone."
nezh	you, few		
nen	you, many		
-(e)th	OBJECT ENDING		
néde	to want		

Examples

1. **Bíi owa ana wa.**
   The food is hot. (said because the speaker perceives it)

   Bíi owa ana wi.
   The food is hot. (said because it is obvious to everyone)

2. **Bíi aril néde with áanath wa.**
   The woman will want sleep.

   Bíi eril menéde ra with anath wa.
   The women didn't want food.

3. **Bíi eril den with neneth wa.**
   The woman helped you.

   Bíi eril den be witheth wa.
   She helped the woman.

4. **Bíi aril di le Láadan wa.**
   I will speak Láadan.

NOTE: Example (4) is a good illustration of what is meant by "if you need it." It would not be ungrammatical to put an object ending on the word Láadan and say "**Bíi aril di le Láadaneth.**" But it is impossible for a language to speak a person, and the subject always comes before the object in Láadan sentences. This means that the object ending is not really needed and can be left off, and it is more natural to do so. Also, just as Láadan allows two vowels together only if one of them is a high-toned vowel, it does not allow two consonants together in most cases. (Although "**th, sh, zh, lh**" are written as two consonants, each of them is only one consonant sound—like English "**sh, ch.**") If you added the object ending "**-th**" to "Láadan" or to "**nen**" you would break that rule—the "**e**" is inserted to keep that from happening.

5.	**Bíi eril**	**di**	**be**	**Láadan wa.**	She spoke Láadan.
		ndi	**bezh**		They (few) spoke Láadan.
		ndi (or **medi**)	**ben**		They (many) spoke Láadan.

Rules

1. To mark a CASE PHRASE as an object, add "**-th**"; if the word ends in a consonant, use "**-eth.**" Notice that there is no ending for the CASE PHRASE that is a subject.

2. When a verb begins with "**d**" the plural prefix is "**n.**" This is what is known as a "SYLLABIC N," and English has syllabic "**n**" at the end of words like "button." Speakers that find the syllabic "**n**" uncomfortable often use "**me-**," and that is perfectly all right; it is just less formal. (There are no other rules for making verbs plural.)

Supplemental Section

1. **Bíi eril néde le** | esheth wa. | boat, **esh**
   | | áabeth | book, **áabe**
   | | yobeth | coffee, **yob**
   | | losheth | money, **losh**
   | | lotheth | information, **loth**

   I wanted _____ .

2. **Bíi eril yod be** | baleth wa. | bread, **bal**
   | | ódoneth | cheese, **ódon**
   | | thilith | fish, **thili**
   | | yuth | fruit, **yu**
   | | medath | vegetable, **meda**
   | | anadaleth | (a) meal, **anadal**

   She ate _____ .

3. **Báa aril meden with** | áwitheth? | baby, **áwith**
   | | obetheth | neighbor, **obeth**
   | | babíth | bird, **babí**
   | | romideth | wild animal, **romid**
   | | shamideth | domestic animal, **shamid**
   | | bediháth | student, **bedihá**
   | | eháth | scientist, **ehá**

   Will the women help the _____ ?

Lesson 4

Pattern
[(AUX) VERB COMPLEX (NEG) CP – S]

Vocabulary

balin	old	**wáa**	EVIDENCE MORPHEME
áya	beautiful	**wo-**	a prefix; explained below

NOTE: When "**wáa**" is used, the speaker is stating that the source of the information is one she trusts, even though she has no personal perception of that information to rely on.

Examples

1. **Bíi néde hal with wáa.**
   The woman wants to work.

   Bíi eril néde hal with wáa.
   The woman wanted to work.

   Bíi eril menéndi mehal with wáa.
   The women wanted to work.

2. **Bíi néde hal ra with wáa.**
   The woman didn't want to work.

3. **Bíi balin with wáa.**
   The woman is old.

   Bíi áya with wáa.
   The woman is beautiful.

   Bíi áya wobalin wowith wáa.
   The old woman is beautiful.

   Bíi meháya mewobalin wowith wáa.
   The old women are beautiful.

d) Bíi néde hal wobalin wowith wáa.
The old woman wants to work.

Bíi néde hal ra wobalin wowith wáa.
The old woman doesn't want to work.

Rules

1. The sequence: "to want + to VERB" in Láadan forms a single unit called a VERB COMPLEX, which is used just like an ordinary verb. The auxiliary goes before it, the negative follows it, and nothing can go between its two parts. Since two verbs are used, both must be marked plural if either is. As always, the auxiliary does not change its form.

2. Láadan has a form that is much like an English adjective + noun sequence, as in "green tree" or "small child." You can take any sequence of verb and subject (remembering that "adjectives" are only ordinary verbs in Láadan) and put the marker "**wo**" the beginning of each one. "Beautiful woman" is thus "**woháya wowith**." This is very useful, but it is a bit different from English, because it can only be used if you have just one verb. You cannot use this pattern to translate an English sequence like "little red brick wall."

3. The plural marker is always the first piece in any verb; thus "beautiful women" will be "**mewoháya wowith**."

4. You will have no trouble with combining the parts of the words in these patterns if you just add the endings before you add "**wo-**." So, "I helped the woman" is "**Bíi eril den le witheth wa**"; "I helped the weary woman" is "**Bíi eril den le wohóoha wowitheth wa**." You would not put an object marker on a verb, you see.

Supplemental Section

1. **Bíi eril yod be worúsho   wohanath wa.**   bitter, **rúsho**
	wohéeda	sacred, **héeda**
	womáanan	salty, **máanan**
	womeénan	sweet, **meénan**

   She ate the _____ food.
   (**yod** = eat; **wo+ana** (food) + object ending = **wohanath**)

   NOTE: "**Wa**" is used in the example, meaning that the speaker knows from her personal perception that the food is bitter, salty, etc. If she knows that only because she has been told that it is so and trusts the source, she will use "**wáa**" instead. If everyone present can obviously see or otherwise perceive the characteristic of the food, she may use "**wi**."

2. **Bíi néde le worahíya   woháabeth wa.**   big, **rahíya**
	woleyi	blue, **leyi**
	woleyan	brown, **leyan**
	wolula	purple, **lula**
	wolaya	red, **laya**
	wolíithi	white, **líithi**
	woléli	yellow, **léli**

   I want the _____ book. (**áabe** = book)

3. **Báa néde   lith   withid?**   think
	lothel		know
	en		understand
	dom		remember
	wéedan		read
	thod		write
	lishid		sign (as in sign language)

   Does the man want to _____?

   NOTE: The masculine ending is "**-id**," so that if it is necessary to specify that a person is male, you can do so by adding "**-id**" to the basic form. Here "**with + id**" means "man."

Lesson 5

Pattern
[(AUX) VERB (NEG) CP-S (CP-O) CP – GOAL]

Vocabulary

wida	to carry	**lezh, len**	we-few, we-many
sháad	to come, to go	**nezh, nen**	you-few, you-many
ban	to give	**-di**	GOAL ENDING
beth	home	**du-**	try to VERB
weth	way, road		

NOTE: The verb prefix "**du-**" is very useful. You have the verb "**wida**," meaning "to carry"; make it "**duwida**" and you have "try to carry." As always, the plural marker comes first; thus, if many people are involved in the act, the word is "**meduwida**."

Examples

1. **Bíi aril sháad le bethedi wa.**
   I will go home.

   Bíi aril mesháad lezh bethedi wa.
   We (few) will go home.

   Bíi aril mesháad len bethedi wa.
   We (many) will go home.

2. **Bíi aril sháad le wethedi wa.**
   I'll go to the road.

   Bíi aril dusháad le wethedi wa.
   I'll try to go to the road.

3. **Bíi eril wida le anath wethedi wa.**
   I carried the food to the road.
4. **Báa eril ban ne anath withedi?**
   Did you give the food to the woman?

Rules

1. To mark a CASE PHRASE as a GOAL, use the ending "**-di**." As always, if the word ends in a consonant, use "**-edi**."

2. You may not be used to talking about the CASE of noun phrases. CASE is the term that refers to the role the noun phrase has in a sentence—that is, whether it is something that acts, something acted upon, something used to act, etc. The three cases we have used so far are SUBJECT, OBJECT, and GOAL; a GOAL CASE PHRASE is the one to which or toward which something is directed. (A CASE PHRASE is just a noun phrase plus its case-marker ending; a noun phrase is any sequence that can fill a case role, such as a noun or a pronoun.)

Supplemental Section

1. **Bíi eril ban le beth oninedi wa.**   nurse, **onin**
                       hudi   boss, **hu**
                       ebadi   spouse, **eba**
                       háawithedi   child, **háawith**
                       zhilhadedi   prisoner, **zhilhad**
                       haládi   worker, **halá**
                       duthahádi   healer, **duthahá**
                       lanemidedi   dog, **lanemid**

   I gave it to the _____. (**be** + **th** = it, OBJECT)

NOTE: The suffix (ending) "**-á**" is like English "-er, -ist." You see it here in "worker." You can use this piece to form many words from verbs. It is worth looking at the word for "healer" in the example. "To heal" is "**dutha**"; to add "**-á**" you must insert an "**h**" even though a sequence of two vowels is allowed when one of them is high-toned, because the second vowel is a meaningful piece (a MORPHEME) all by itself.

2. | **Báa eril sháad ne** | **hozhazhedi?** | airport, **hozhazh** |
	oódóodi?	bridge, **oódóo**
	áathamedi?	church, **áatham**
	shéedi?	desert, **shée**
	ábededi?	farm, **ábed**
	olinedi?	forest, **olin**
	bothedi?	hotel, **both**
	maridi?	island, **mari**
	belidedi?	house, **belid**
	hothedi?	place, **hoth**
	miwithedi?	town/city, **miwith**

Did you go to the _____?

Lesson 6

Pattern
[(AUX) VERB (NEG) CP – S (CP-O) CP – SOURCE]

Vocabulary
bel	take, bring	**thel**	get
dan	language	**-de**	SOURCE ending
edaná	linguist	**ná-**	continue to VERB
menedebe	many		keep VERBing

Examples

1. **Bíi eril sháad le wethede wa.**
   I came from the road.

   Bíi eril mesháad with wethede wáa.
   The women come from the road.

2. **Bíi eril sháad ben wethede.**
   They came from the road.

   Bíi eril násháad ben wethede.
   They kept coming from the road.

3. **Bíi eril bel le anath edanáde wa.**
   I took the food from the linguist.

   Bíi eril bel le anath edanáde menedebe wa.
   I took the food from the many linguists.

4. **Bíi eril thel le anath withede i edanáde wa.**
   I got the food from the woman and the linguist.

NOTE: The two examples in (2) above do not have any EVIDENCE MORPHEME at the end, and they are not in a series of connected sentences that would indicate what the speaker intended. This is possible in Láadan, but it can mean only one thing: that the speaker does not wish to state the reason why she considers what she says to be true.

Rules

1. To mark a CASE PHRASE as a Source, use the ending "**-de**." If the word ends in a consonant, you'll need to use "**-ede**," of course.

2. There are times when you need to indicate a plural, but you have no verb to take the plural marker, as in the second sentence of (3) above. You can then put the word "**menedebe**" ("many") immediately after the noun phrase you want to make plural. The same thing is done with numbers, and with the words "**nedebe**," meaning "few, several" and "**woho**" meaning "all, every." These words never change their form, never add prefixes or suffixes; thus, if those "many linguists" up there were OBJECT CASE PHRASE members you would use "**edanáth menedebe**." The CASE MARKER would never appear on "**menedebe**."

3. You will notice that a sentence such as "**Bíi eril sháad le wethedi wa**," meaning "I went to the road," is exactly like "**Bíi eril sháad le wethede wa**," meaning "I came from the road." You can only tell the direction of the motion verb by the case ending on "road." Speakers of some languages are not comfortable keeping the vowels "**i**" and "**e**" separate, because in their languages they are only one sound. In such a situation, and if no other information is available in the sentence to make things clear, it is correct to use "**-dim**" as an alternate form for the GOAL CASE PHRASE. Such a speaker could say "**Bíi eril sháad le wethedim wa**" for "I went to the road."

Brief Reading

Bíi eril methi[1] with menedebe dosheth[2] wa. Medi with, "Bíi methi ra len daneth wa. Methi withid daneth, izh len—ra. Menéde medi len, izh methi ra len dáaneth[3] menedebe. Menéde medi, izh methad[4] ra len." Id[5] medi edaná, "Bíi aril meden len neneth wa."

[1] **thi**	= to have		[4] **thad**	= to be able
[2] **dosh**	= burden		[5] **id**	= and then
[3] **dáan**	= word			

Free Translation

There were many women who had a burden. The women said, "We have no language. Men have a language, but as for us—no. We want to speak, but there are many words we don't have. We want to speak, but we can't." And then the linguists said, "We will help you."

Notes on the Reading

Notice that once the speaker has established that she is offering declarative sentences and is speaking on the basis of her own perception—by beginning with "**Bíi**" and ending with "**wa**" in her very first sentence—she does not have to keep doing that. If there were a change, if she wanted to ask a question or to offer information based on her trust in a source or something other than her perceptions, she would have to add the words that specify those things. Otherwise, listeners will assume that there is no change. The same thing holds for the auxiliary "**eril**" that indicates past time; it does not have to go into every sentence in a connected sequence. However, if you are not sure whether to use any of these sentence pieces, you will always be safe putting one in.

Supplemental Section

1. Bíi eril bedi le Láadan **lanede** wa.   friend, **lan**
                                         omáde   teacher, **omá**
                                         lebede   enemy, **leb**

   I learned Láadan from a/the _____ .

2. | Báa eril masháad nen | wéehothede? | library, wéehoth |
|---|---|---|
| | bode | mountain, bo |
| | melade | ocean, mela |
| | wilide | river/creek, wili |
| | ulinede | school, ulin |
| | yedede | valley, yed |

Did you (many) come from the _____ ?

Lesson 7

Pattern
[(AUX) VERB (NEG) CP – S (CP – O) CP – INSTRUMENT]

Vocabulary

oya	skin	**ílhi**	disgust
oyu	ear	**el**	to make
oyi	eye	**láad**	to perceive
oma	hand	**loláad**	to perceive internally
ili	water	**thad**	to be able
zho	sound	**-nan**	INSTRUMENT ending
thena	joy		

Examples

1. **Bíi el le beth omanan wa.**
   I make it with (my) hands.

2. **Bíi láad le neth oyinan wa**
   I see you.

   Bíi láad le neth oyunan wa.
   I hear you.

   Bíi láad le zhoth oyunan wa.
   I hear a sound.

   Bíi láad le ilith oyanan wa.
   I feel the water.

3. **Bíi eril loláad with thenath wáa.**
   The woman was joyful.

   Bíi eril loláad with ílhith wáa.
   The woman was disgusted.

Rules and Explanation:

1. To mark a CASE PHRASE as an Instrument (as that which is used to do something), use the ending "**-nan**." Insert an "**e**" if necessary.

2. Láadan handles perceptions and emotions rather differently than English does. In Láadan you perceive things externally, with your eyes or your ears or your nose or your skin. Emotions are something you perceive internally, inside yourself. The first sentence in (2) says that the speaker perceives "you" and that the speaker's eyes are the instrument for that perception. We could translate it as "I see you with my eyes" in English, but that is a little superfluous—English "see" includes the information that it is done with eyes. In Láadan you could add an INSTRUMENTAL CASE PHRASE to the examples in (2), using "with (my) mind" or "with (my) heart or something of the kind, but it would be considered as odd as saying "I hear you with my ears" in English; the organ or organs of internal perception are assumed.

3. You could translate the examples in (3) as "The woman felt joy" and "The woman felt disgust" if you preferred, or if that phrasing seemed better in the context of your sentence.

4. In Láadan there are a number of different forms for the names of emotions, rather than a single word "joy" or "love" or "hate" and so on. The word translated as "joy" here is the most neutral form, meaning "joy for good reasons."

5. Finally, the object marker has been used in all the example sentences, and it is correct. But it is far more common to omit the object suffix on emotions (since love or disgust cannot "perceive" living things); similarly, it is much more common to say "**Bíi láad le zho oyunan wa**," than to use "**zhoth**"; a sound cannot "hear" anything. This is a matter of personal choice and style, so long as the meaning cannot be misunderstood.

Brief Reading

Bíide[1] eril meloláad with menedebe shalath[2] wáa. Eril methi ra ben daneth. Id mesháad edaná i medi benedi, "Bre[3] menéde nen daneth, ébre aril mehel len daneth wa." Medi with, "Báa methad nen?" I medi edaná benedi, "Bíi aril meduthad len wa." Eril meláad with beneth oyunan i menahul[4] ben wáa.

[1] **Bíide**	= I say in narrative, as in telling a story		something can be done about the situation
[2] **shala**	= grief for good reasons; grief for which there is cause and someone is to blame but	[3] **bre…ébre**	= if…then
		[4] **hul**	= hope; this form is the verb stem "**hul**" plus the prefix "**na-**" which means "to begin to VERB" plus the plural prefix

Free Translation

Once there were many women who felt grief, and for good reasons. They had no language. And then the linguists came and said to them, "If you want a language, then we will make a language." The women said, "Can you do that?" And the linguists said to them, "We will try." The women heard them and began to hope.

Notes on the Reading

In this example the speaker has established that she is telling a story by adding "**-de**" as the SPEECH ACT MORPHEME at the very beginning. If it were a completely imaginary story, she would close her sentence with "**wo**," the hypothetical EVIDENCE MORPHEME; by using "**wáa**" instead, she is telling the listener that this is a story she considers to be true because she trusts the source of it. There is a whole set of other endings for "**Bíi**" to indicate the speaker's feelings, by the way; here are examples using the other ones:

Bíid	= speaking in anger	**Bíida**	= speaking in jest as a joke
Bíith	= speaking in pain	**Bíidi**	= speaking as a teacher
Bíili	= speaking in love	**Bíiya**	= speaking in fear
Bíilan	= speaking in celebration		

Supplemental Section

1. **Bíi eril láad le**

lalith oyanan wa.	rain, **lali**
hisheth	snow, **hish**
rosheth	sun, **rosh**
yuleth	wind, **yul**

I felt the _____.
(The object endings are optional here.)

2. **Báa eril láad ne**

nith oyinan?	cup, **ni**
bodeth	dish, **bod**
onidath	family
shidath	game
déelath	garden
binith	gift
shinehaleth	computer, **shinehal**

Did you see the _____?
(Notice there's no need for me to write out the basic form for words like "**onidath**"; the "a" has to be part of the base word, because only "e" is inserted before endings.)

3. **Bíi eril láad ra le**

zhazheth oyunan wa.	airplane, **zhazh**
ohamedith	prayer
deleth	radio, **del**
dedideth	story, **dedide**
loroloth	thunder
ditheth	voice, **dith**
limlimeth	bell, **limlim**

I didn't hear the _____.

4. **Bíi eril loláad with am wáa.** love, for one related by blood

	sham	love, for a child of her body
	ad	love, for one respected but not liked
	ab	love, for one liked but not respected
	bala	anger and blame, for good and not futile reasons
	maha	sexual desire
	heyi	pain
	lash	indifference
	shara	grief and blame, for good reasons, but futilely; that is, nothing can be done

The woman felt _____.

Lesson 8

Pattern

$$\left[(\text{AUX})\ \text{VERB}\ (\text{NEG})\ \text{CP - S}\ \left\{\begin{array}{l}\text{CP - ASSOCIATE}\\ \text{CP - BENEFICIARY}\end{array}\right\}\right]$$

Vocabulary

wil sha	Hello, Greetings	**-da**	BENEFICIARY ending
áala	thank you	**-den**	ASSOCIATE ending, neutral
dóo	Well…		
bóo	request, polite command	**-dan**	ASSOCIATE ending, with pleasure

Examples

1. **Bíi aril hal be witheden wáa.**
   She'll work with the woman.

   Bíi aril hal be withedan wáa.
   She'll work with the woman with pleasure.

2. **Bíi hal be witheda wa.**
   She works for the woman.

   Bíi hal be wobalin wowitheda wa.
   She works for the old woman.

3. **Bíi eril el le anath witheda wa.**
   I made food for the woman.

Rules

1. To mark a CASE PHRASE as a Beneficiary (that for whom, or on whose behalf, something is done), add the ending "**-da**."

2. To mark a CASE PHRASE as an Associate (with whom something is done, as in English "I danced with her"), add the ending "**-den**." If you want to indicate that there is pleasure in the association you may use the alternative Associate marker "**-dan**"; "**-den**" is a neutral form.

3. The Beneficiary marker given above is the one used when something is done voluntarily. There are three alternative forms:

    -**dá**   against one's will when forced or coerced
    -**daá** accidentally
    -**dáa** not because of force or coercion, but because of an obligation of law or duty that one accepts.

    In any other situation, use "**-da**."

Brief Reading

Bíide eril láad with háawitheth[1] oyinan wo. Eril delishe[2] háawith. Di with, "Wil sha, háawith! Bóo delishe ra ne!" Izh nádelishe háawith. Eril di with, "Báa loláad ne heyi?" "Ra," di háawith. "Bíi loláad ra le heyi wa. Delishe le bróo[3] aril di rawith[4] leden." Di with, "Dóo, ril[5] di le neden. Ril di le neden i nedan wa." I di háawith withedi, "Áala!" I eril nodelishe[6] háawith wáa.

[1] **háawith**	= child	[4] **rawith**	= nobody
[2] **delishe**	= to cry, to weep	[5] **ril**	= now
[3] **bróo**	= because	[6] **nodelishe**	= stop + to cry

Free Translation

Once a woman saw a child. The child was crying. The woman said, "Hello, child! Please don't cry!" But the child kept crying. The woman said, "Do you hurt? Do you feel pain somewhere?" "No," said the child. "I don't hurt. I cry because nobody will talk with me." The woman said, "Well, I am talking with you right now. I am talking with you and I do so with pleasure." And the child said to the woman, "Thank you!" And the child stopped crying.

Supplemental Section

1. **Bóo aril lo leden.**   rejoice
   - **edethi** — share
   - **lishid** — sign
   - **alehala** — music (that is, make music)
   - **amedara** — dance (notice that no EVIDENCE MORPHEME is used after "**Bóo**.")

   Please _____ with me.
   Or Would you _____ with me?

2. **Bíi néde le dizheth laneda wa.**   kettle, **dizh**
   - **dínidineth** — toy, **dínidin**
   - **bineth** — bowl, **bin**
   - **idoneth** — brush, **idon**
   - **doneth** — comb, **don**
   - **odeth** — cloth, **od**
   - **oweth** — garment, **owe**
   - **dimilineth** — ornament, **dimilin**

   I want a/the _____ for a friend.

3. **Bíi eril eb le beth laneda wa.**   buy
   - **ri** — record
   - **nori** — send
   - **redeb** — find
   - **déedan** — interpret
   - **héedan** — translate

   I _____ it for a friend. (all in past tense)

NOTE: the verb "**lishid**," which means "to sign" as in a sign language, may have added to it the same set of endings that are allowed with the SPEECH ACT MORPHEMES like "**Bíi**." This is also true for the verb "**dama**," which means "to touch."

Lesson 9

Pattern

$$\left[(\text{AUX}) \text{ VERB } (\text{NEG}) \text{ CP - S} \begin{Bmatrix} \text{CP - TIME} \\ \text{CP - PLACE} \end{Bmatrix}\right]$$

Vocabulary

aril	Goodbye	**obée**	during
e…e	either…or	**náal**	night
o	around	**-ya**	TIME ending
		-ha	PLACE ending

Examples

1. **Bíi aril mesháad ben bethedi náaleya wáa.**
   They will go home at night.
2. **Bíi eril mehal ben betheha wáa.**
   They worked at home.
3. **Bíi hal le betheha o wa.**
   I work around home.
4. **Bíi hal le náaleya obée wa.**
   I work during the night.
5. **Bíi aril hal e with e withid wáa.**
   Either the woman or the man will work.

Rules and Explanation:

1. To mark a CASE PHRASE as Time, add the ending "**-ya**."
2. To mark a CASE PHRASE as Place, add the ending "**-ha**."
3. These two endings specify an event or state as being at a particular location in space or time. English has a wide variety of prepositions which are used in such CPs to make the information more precise; thus, something will be said to be not just "at" a particular location but "inside, between, underneath, before," and so on. In English these prepositions are used as the first element in the phrase and could be said to be used instead of a more general case-marking preposition. In Láadan the general marker is always used, but there is a set of more narrow forms that can be added to the phrase to make its meaning more precise. We can say that "**-ya**" and "**-ha**" mean "at" some time or place; if more precise information is required, the speaker puts an additional locational word at the end of the CASE PHRASE as in example (4) above. "**Bíi hal le náaleya wa**" is grammatical and means "I work at night"; "**Bíi hal le náaleya obée wa**" adds "during" to the sentence at the speaker's option. The set of words like "**obée**" (called postpositions) is made up of words which never change their form in any way; they take no affixes at all.

Brief Reading

Bíide eríli násháad Dumidal[1] wetheha wo. Eril láad be éelen[2] oyinan. Lith be, "Womemeénan wohéelen!' Eril nahoób[3], be; duthel be éeleneth. Izh eril dúuthel[4] be beneth. Eril mehíthihal[5] éelen. Id eril di Dumidal, "Dóo, néde ra le éelheneth! Néde ra rawith éelheneth! Bíi meyemehul[6] éelen wa!"

[1] **dumidal** = fox
[2] **éelen** = grape(s)
[3] **oób** = to jump
[4] **dúu-** = try in vain to VERB; it is a prefix
[5] **mehíthihal** = to be very high
[6] **meyemehul** = to be extremely sour

Free Translation

Once, a very long time ago, a fox was going along a road. He saw some grapes. He thought, "Sweet-tasting grapes!" He started jumping; he tried to get the grapes. But he tried in vain to get them. The grapes were very high. And then the Fox said, "Well, I don't want the darned grapes! Nobody wants those old grapes! I can tell that they're horribly sour!"

Notes on the Translation

In this reading you see the use of the Láadan sound "**lh**" to add a negative meaning. The Fox calls the grapes "**éelen**" as long as he has only positive feelings about them. But when he becomes upset because he can't reach them, he calls them "**éelhen**," translated here as "darned grapes" and "those old grapes." You can always, in Láadan, change an "**l**" to "**lh**" or add an "**lh**" to a word to give it a negative meaning. And of course, the Fox is deliberately lying in this story. Notice that in the last sentence he uses "**wa**" as his EVIDENCE MORPHEME, indicating that he claims the grapes are horribly sour because he has personally perceived them to be so—this has been translated as "I can tell…" The reader is able to determine from the context that the Fox is making this up.

Supplemental Section

1) **Bíi hal with**

loshebelideha wa.	bank, **loshebelid**
shodeha	room, **shod**
duneha	field, **dun**
áatheha	door, **áath**
sheniha	intersection, **sheni**
weheha	store, **wehe**
duthahotheha	hospital, **duthahoth**
sheshihotheha	beach, **sheshihoth**

The woman works at/in the _____ .

2) **Báa hal ne**

sháaleya?	day, **sháal**
Henesháaleya	Monday, **Henesháal**
Aleleya	January, **Alel**
wemeneya	spring, **wemen**
wumaneya	summer, **wuman**
diidineya	holiday, **diidin**

Do you work on/in _____ ?

Lesson 10

Pattern

$$\left[(\text{AUX}) \; \text{VERB} \; (\text{NEG}) \; \text{CP - S} \begin{Bmatrix} \text{CP - IDENTIFIER} \\ \text{CP - MANNER} \\ \text{CP - CAUSE} \\ \text{CP - PURPOSE} \end{Bmatrix} \right]$$

Vocabulary

lothel	to know, not said of people	**héeya**	to fear
an	to know, of people	**-nal**	MANNER ending
lóolo	to be slow	**-wan**	PURPOSE ending
		-wáan	CAUSE ending
		Ø	IDENTIFIER ending

Examples

1. **Bíi le with wa.**
   I am a woman.

   Bíi le wothal wowith wa.
   I am a good woman.

2. **Bíi eril hal withid lóolonal wa.**
   The man worked slowly.

3. **Bíi eril sháad be bethedi halewan wáa.**
   She went home in order to work.

   Bíi eril sháad be bethedi héeyawáan wáa.
   She went home because of fear.

Rules and Explanation:

1. To mark a CASE PHRASE as an Identifier (that which identifies the subject by profession, sexual gender, nationality, etc.), add the zero ending— that is, add no ending. This is identical to the rule for Subject CASE PHRASES.

2. To mark a CASE PHRASE as Manner (the way in which something is done), add the ending "**-nal.**" This ending is much like English "-ly" as in "patiently" and "thoroughly."

3. There are two endings used to mark a CASE PHRASE as the Cause of what is in the statement. One is "**-wan,**" which means "in order to, for the purpose of"; the other is "**wáan,**" which means "due to, because of."

4. As you can see from the examples in (3) above, you can turn a verb of Láadan into a noun phrase by giving it a case-marker ending. English does the same thing, forming "abandonment" from "to abandon," "carelessness" from "to be careless," and so on; any English verb can be used as a noun if "-ing" is added, as in "Swimming is good exercise."

Brief Reading

Bíide eril melothel with nedelotheth[1] menedebe wáa. Eril medam[2] ben wotheth.[3] Medi ben edanádi, "Bre aril mehel nen daneth leneda, ébre aril loláad len thenath. Izh aril memíi[4] len woho." Eril medi edaná benedi, "Bíi mehan len neneth wa. Nen with, len with. Bre medúuhel len daneth witheda, ébre aril meloláad len shamath."[5]

[1] **nedeloth** = fact
[2] **dam** = to show, to manifest
[3] **woth** = wisdom
[4] **míi** = to be amazed
[5] **shama** = grief for good reasons, but grief for which nobody is to blame and about which nothing can be done

Free Translation

Women knew many things. They showed wisdom. They said to the linguists, "If you make a language for us, we will be joyful. But we will be amazed, every one of us." The linguists said to them, "We know you. You are women, we are women. If we fail to make a language for women, we will be sorrowful—but that will just be the way things are."

Notes on the Translation

There are of course many ways to translate the end of the reading. For example, "We hope we can do it, and we will be sorry if we can't, but all we can do is try. And if we fail that's how it goes sometimes." It's not that you cannot express in English what is expressed in Láadan by "**shama**," but it is extremely cumbersome to do so.

Supplemental Section

1. Bíi eril di with **shóodenal** wáa.   busy, **shóod**

	rahowanal	cold, **rahowa**
	lirinal	colorful, **liri**
	menanal	compassion for good reasons, **mena**
	balanal	anger with valid cause, someone to blame, not futile, **bala**
	ohenanal	respect, for good reasons, **ohena**
	bishibenal	sudden, **bishib**

The woman spoke _____ ly.

2. **Bíi eril di with balanal wa.**	anger, for good reasons and blame, not futile
baranal	anger, for good reasons, and blame, futile
hananal	anger, for good reasons, no blame, not futile
bamanal	anger, for good reasons, no blame, futile
binanal	anger, no cause, blame impossible, not futile

The woman spoke _____ ly.

3. **Bíi le**	**ewithá wa.**	anthropologist
ehashá	astronomer
emidá	biologist
eloshá	economist
edutá	engineer
hena	sibling
belidá	carpenter
lilahá	lover, one who carries out the female sexual act; not of males
yodá	diner, one who eats
yodálh	glutton, one who eats too much

I am a(n) _____.

NOTE: You can form many useful words with the suffix "-á" and the prefix "e-" shown above. ("E-" means "science of," something like English "-ology.") For example, you can begin with "**shon**," the word meaning "peace"; "**shoná**" means "peacemaker," "**eshon**" means "peace science," and "**eshoná**" would then be "peace scientist." Similarly, from "**om**," "to teach," we have "**omá**," teacher, and "**ehom**," education, and "**ehomá**"; the last refers to a specialist in education who is not herself necessarily a teacher.

4. | **Bíi ril sháad be** | **áanawan** | **wáa.** | sleep, **áana** |
	imewan		travel, **im**
	róowan		harvest, **róo**
	rúuwan		lie down, **rúu**

She's going now in order to _____.

5. | **Bíi eril delishe be** | **olobewáan wáa.** | blow, trauma, **olob** |
	ibewáan	crime, **ib**
	doshewáan	burden, **dosh**
	ludewáan	debt, **lud**
	ozhewáan	dream, **ozh**
	lodewáan	household, **lod**
	uhudewáan	nuisance, **uhud**
	éeyawáan	sickness, illness, **éeya**

She wept because of the _____.

Lesson 11

Pattern
[(AUX) VERB (NEG) CP – S CP – POSSESSIVE]

Vocabulary

-tha	POSSESSIVE ending, by birth
-the	POSSESSIVE ending, for no known or acknowledged reason
-thi	POSSESSIVE ending, by chance
-tho	POSSESSIVE ending, other, by law or custom or gift, etc.
-thu	POSSESSIVE ending; this is the "false" possessive, and is explained below

NOTE: Because the explanation of the possessive takes so much space, no other vocabulary is added in this section.

Examples

1. **Báa eril ma lan netho?**
   Did your friend listen?

   Báa mehóoha oyi netha?
   Are your eyes tired?

   Báa aril yod eba netho?
   Will your spouse eat?

   Báa thal ana nethe?
   Is your food all right?

(In these sentences, your friend and your spouse are asserted to be "yours" by law or custom or something of the kind; your eyes are yours because you were born with them; and the speaker who mentions "your" food is stating that she either does not know or will not acknowledge why it should belong to you.)

2. **Bíi eril meláad len beth nethoth wa.**
   We saw your home.

   Bíi eril mesháad len beth nethodi wa.
   We went to your house.

Rules and Explanation

1. To use the Láadan possessive, you must first decide what sort of "ownership" is involved. Is it because of birth, as with "my arm" or "my mother"? If so, add the ending "**-tha.**" Is it for no known reason—for example, a task that you just ended up with somehow, inexplicably, and that is now "your" work? Then the proper ending is "**-the.**" Is it a phony ownership, marked in English by "of" but really involving no possession, as in "a heart of stone" or "a collection of books"? If so, use the ending "**-thu.**" Is it by luck, by chance? Use the ending "**-thi.**" In any other situation, when ownership is due to law or custom or anything not included in the other forms, use the ending "**-tho.**" You would use "**-tho**" if you were not certain of the reason but were quite sure there was one and that it was legitimate.

2. Next, realize that the Possessive will always be part of some bigger CASE PHRASE. When you say "He stole the jewels of the Queen," the Object is the whole sequence "the jewels of the Queen," of which "of the Queen" is only a part. This means that except for those case categories which have a Ø (null) ending in Láadan (Subject and Identifier) you will first add the possessive ending and then the case-marker ending of the larger CP. When "your house" is the Goal, and English would show that by the sequence "to your house," Láadan uses "**belid**" plus the ending "**-tho**" plus the Goal ending "**-di.**" to give you "**belidethodi.**" The possessive marker will always come before the other ending.

3. Finally, you cannot add the Possessive markers directly to the name of a person or animal. Instead, you add a pronoun to carry the case ending—like this:

    A) **Bíi eril eb le belid withethoth wa.**
    I bought the woman's house.

    B) **Bíi eril eb le belid Meri bethoth wa.**
    I bought Mary's house.

    The sequence "**Meri bethoth**" is literally "Mary she-of-OBJECT," you see. You cannot say "**Merithoth**" to mean "Mary-of-OBJECT." (Note that this rule does not apply to names of places and of times—only living or once-living beings.)

Brief Reading

Bíide eril el edaná daneth wa. Eril thi dan zhath[1], Láadan. Bíi ril di le nedi, "Ril nawéedan ne Láadan, dan withetho nede[2]." Eril el edaná Láadan, izh ril ra dan edanátho wa. Bre menéde with Láadan, ébre Láadan dan withetho witheda.

[1] **zha** = name
[2] **nede** = one

Free Translation

Once a linguist made a language. The language had the name Láadan. I say to you, "You are beginning to read Láadan now, one woman's language." A linguist made Láadan, but it is not the linguist's language now. If women want Láadan, then Láadan is a language for women and of women.

Notes on the Translation

There might be disagreement about the choice of the possessive ending in "**dan withetho nede**." Like any human language, Láadan has possible ambiguities, and this is one of them. You cannot tell from these few sentences if "**dan withetho nede**" means "one language of a woman" or "one woman's language"; nor can you tell why "**-tho**" has been chosen. You know only that the speaker or writer is claiming that the ownership is not because of birth, that it is not unknown or unacknowledged, and that it is claimed to be real ownership rather than the "house of wood" sort. It may be like the situation in English when we speak of "Emily Dickinson's poems" or "the novels of Jane Austen"; there is a sense in which such things "belong" to those who make them, but it is a restricted sense. To make this reading quite clear on the subject, it would have to be longer. (The word "Láadan," by the way, is formed from "**láad**," to perceive; and "**dan**," language.)

Supplemental Section

1. **Bóo dama ra ne**

oda lethath.	arm
oba lethath.	body
ona lethath.	face
óoda lethath.	leg
óoyo lethath.	mouth
oyo lethath.	nose
thom lethoth.	pillow

Please don't touch my _____.

2. **Bíi eril lámála beye rul nethoth wa.**

	caress, stroke
wem	lose
bel	take, bring
she	comfort
doth	follow
bóodan	rescue
naya	take care of

Somebody (VERBED) _____ your cat.

NOTE: "**Beye**" means "somebody"—just one somebody. Like all the other pronouns, it can take the ending "**-zh**" to mean two to five persons, and the ending "**-n**" to mean many persons. It can also mean "something" and is made clear by the verb used with it.

Lesson 12

Pattern

This is a lesson about embedding one sentence inside another sentence. In the examples, the embedded sentence will be enclosed in parentheses to help make the process clear.

Vocabulary

lali	rain, or to rain	**lith**	to think
rahowa	to be cold	**bróo**	because
na-	to begin to VERB	**-hé**	statement embedding marker
nó-	to cease to VERB	**-hée**	question embedding marker

Examples

1. **Bíi lith le (rahowa lalihé) wa.**
   I think that the rain is cold.

2. **Bíi lith ra le (rahowa lalihé) wa.**
   I don't think that the rain is cold.

3. **Báa lith ne (rahowa lalihée) ?**
   Do you think that the rain is cold?

4. **Bíi lothel ra le (rahowa lalihée) wa.**
   I don't know whether the rain is cold.

5. **Bíi lith le (nalalihé) wa.**
   I think that it's starting to rain.

   Bíi lith le (nólalih) wa.
   I think that it has stopped raining.

NOTE: Láadan does not require any "it" in the sentence to do the raining, although one will appear in the English translation.

Rules and Explanation

1. To embed a declarative sentence, add the ending "**-hé**" to the last word in the sentence.

2. To embed a question, add the ending "**-hée**" to the last word in the sentence.

3. It's true that the embedded sentences in the examples above are all Objects of the verb "to think." However, it is impossible for a sentence to be doing the thinking, and there can be no misunderstanding; no "**-th**" ending is required here. No case marker of the embedded sentence precedes the embedding marker. A case marker reflecting the embedded clause's role in the sentence will *follow* the embedding marker. If you should ever have a sentence that could be misunderstood in this way, the embedding marker will follow the case-marker ending—this is the *only* piece that can be added to a case-marker ending, and it will very rarely be necessary.

Brief Reading

Bíide eríli násháad lanemid[1] wetheha óobe wo. Eril láad be anath oyinan doniha; di be, "Wu[2] wothal wohana! Néde le beth!" I bel be anath i nawida be beth. Eril nosháad lanemid ilidi. Eril láad be lanemideth i anath oyinan iliha yil.[3] Di be, "Bíi néde le beth wa!" Id eril wem[4] be anath, bróo u[5] óoyo betha. I bróo eril lanemid yodalhá[6] wi.

[1] **lanemid**	= dog	[4] **wem**	= to lose
[2] **Wu**	= what a…, such a…	[5] **u**	= to be open
[3] **yil**	= under	[6] **yodalhá**	= glutton

Free Translation

Once long ago a dog was going along a road. It saw some food on the ground; it said, "What good food! I want it!" And it took the food and began to carry it. The dog stopped at some water. It saw a dog and some food under the water. It said, "I want it!" And then it lost the food, because its mouth was open. And—as anyone can see—because it was a glutton.

Supplemental Section

1. | **Bíi lothel le** | **owa roshehé wa.** | the sun is warm |
   |---|---|---|
   | | **oth shenidalehé** | a network is important |
   | | **lalewida withehé** | the woman is (joyfully) pregnant |
   | | **elasháana withehé** | the woman is menstruating for the first time |
   | | **zháadin withehé** | the woman is menopausing |
   | | **eril lhedehé** | there was discord-in-the-home (**lhed** = discord-in-the-home) |
   | | **aril rashahé** | there will be discord |

   I know that (SENTENCE)_____.

NOTE: Remember that in the embedded sentences above the verb will be first in the sentence, or the auxiliary will if one is present. (This is the reverse of what appears in the English translations.) The word for "network" is "**shenidal**"; the others should be clear.

Lesson 13

Pattern
This is another lesson about embedding one sentence in another; this time we will be looking at what are called "relative clauses" in English. They will be in brackets in the examples.

Vocabulary
elahela	celebration
oth	to be important
Hathamesháal	Sunday
shóo	to happen, come to pass, take place
dom	to remember
-háa	relative clause embedding marker

Examples
1. **Bíi aril shóo elahela Hathamesháaleya wáa.**
   The celebration will happen on Sunday.

   Bíi oth [aril shóo elahela Hathamesháaleyaháa] wáa.
   The celebration that will happen on Sunday is important.

2. **Bíi dom le [hal withehé] wa.**
   I remember that the woman works.

   Bíi dom le [hal witheháa] wa.
   I remember the woman that works.

Rules and Explanation

1. To embed a sentence as a relative clause, add the ending "**háa**" to the last word of the embedded sentence. (NOTE: When this ending follows the case-marking ending of PLACE, "**-ha**," it has an alternate form "**sháa.**")

2. The primary purpose of the examples in (1) is to show you what is just about the longest and most complicated-appearing word (to an English speaker) that you are likely to have to deal with in Láadan. The complexity of the form is more in its appearaance than in reality, however; let's analyze "**Hathamesháaleyaháa**" to see what it's made of. You will see the root "**sháal**" in the middle of the long word and recognize it as the word for "day." "**Hathamesháal**" is equivalent to "Sunday." The TIME ending, "**-ya**," has been added, along with an "**e**" to separate the two consonants, and then the embedding marker "**-háa**" has been added to that.

3. The purpose of the two examples in (2) is to show you why just one embedding marker won't be sufficient.

4. It would be absurd to pretend that the grammar explanation in this lesson and Lesson 12 has been complete enough. Many more examples and explanations would be required before that claim could be made. But you will have a general overview of the embedding processes of Láadan, and would be able to understand complex sentences like these in reading and listening even if you could not comfortably construct them yourself. Their proper place in any more detailed discussion is in a more advanced grammar of the language—please do not be concerned if you are not at ease with them.

Supplemental Section

1. **Bíi néde le rahíya beyeháa   wa.**   big, large

	éthe	clean
	shane	downy, furry
	dazh	soft, pliant

I want something that is _____ .

Lesson 14

This is the final lesson in this simple grammar; like Lessons 12 and 13, it is intended only to present material briefly so that you will be able to deal with it in reading or listening. The subject of the lesson is WH-questions (a very English term that owes its form to the fact that most English question words start with WH), questions that cannot be answered with "yes" or "no." They are very simply formed in Láadan, but look so different from their English counterparts that they are likely to be awkward for English speakers at first. I will just provide an example of each kind, which means that the format of this lesson will be unlike any of the others.

These questions begin with "**báa**" like any other question, although in speech that word may not appear when it is not necessary for clarity. (Obviously, if you want to use any of the endings that show that you ask your question in anger, or in jest, etc., you cannot drop the "**Báa**" to which those endings are attached.) Then the item of information that is being requested appears as the pronoun "**be**," plus "**-báa**" to mark it as interrogative, followed by the proper case-marking ending. Here are the examples, for your information.

1. **Báa   eril   yod   bebáa   thilith?**
   Ø   past   eat   somebody   fish
   Who ate the fish?

NOTE: Since the SUBJECT CASE ENDING is Ø, "**bebáa**" has no other marker. The same thing will be true for an Identifier.

2. **Báa eril yod thili bebáath?**
   What did the fish eat?

3. **Báa eril sháad ne bebáadi?**
   Where did you go (to)?

4. **Báa eril sháad ne bebáade?**
   Where did you come from?

5. **Báa eril thod ne bebáanan?**
   What did you write with?
6. **Báa eril hal ne bebáaden?**
   Who did you work with?
7. **Báa eril hal ne bebúaya?**
   When did you work?
8. **Báa eril hal ne bebáaha?**
   Where did you work (at)?
9. **Báa eril hal ne bebáanal?**
   How (in what manner) did you work?
10. **Báa eril hal ne bebáawan?**
    What caused you to work?

    Báa eril hal ne bebáawáan?
    To what end did you work?
11. **Báa eril hal ne bebáada?**
    Who did you work for?
12. **Báa eril wéedan ne áabe bebáathoth?**
    Whose book did you read?
13. **Báa bebáa omá?**
    Who is a/the teacher?

Lesson Set Two: Going to the Con

Lesson 1

Athid, Sha, Thad and the Dragon Are Going to the Con

Vocabulary

Athid Person's name
Sha Person's name
Thad Person's name
óowamid dragon
hi this
sháad go; come
buzh convention; "con"
bil fun
bíi I say to you, as a statement
wa The reason I claim that what I'm saying is true is that I have perceived it myself

ril a word used to indicate present time
aril a word used to indicate future time
-hóo a MORPHEME that is used to indicate special importance, or to give a word or phrase extra emphasis
-di a MORPHEME that means "to," as in "I walked to the house."

Examples

1. **Bíi hi Athid wa.**
   This is Athid.

   NOTE: All we need in this sentence is the SPEECH ACT word at the beginning of the sentence, the evidential at the end, and this/**Athid** in between. We don't need a word for is and we don't need one for a.

2. **Bíi hi Sha wa.**
   This is Sha.

3. **Bíi hi Thad wa.**
   This is Thad.

4. **Bíi hi óowamid wa.**
   This is a dragon.

5. **Bíi ril sháad Athid buzhedi wa.**
   Athid is going to the con.

6. **Bíi ril sháad Sha buzhedi wa.**
   Sha is going to the con.

7. **Bíi ril sháad Thad buzhedi wa.**
   Thad is going to the con.

8. **Bíi ril sháad óowamid buzhedi wa.**
   The dragon is going to the con.

9. **Bíi aril bilehóo buzh wa!**
   The convention will be *fun*!

Láadan Grammar Facts

1. Láadan doesn't allow "consonant clusters." That is, it doesn't let any two consonant sounds follow one right after the other (except for a very few words in which "**b**" is followed by "**r**").

   To keep sequences of two consonant sounds from happening, you put an "**e**" between them.

   So, when you add "**-di**" (the ending meaning "to") to "**buzh**" (the word for "convention" or "con"), you have to put an "**e**" between those two pieces to separate the consonant sound "**zh**" from the consonant sound "**d**."

   That's why "to the con" is "**buzhedi**" instead of just "**buzhdi**." "**Buzhdi**" could not be a Láadan word.

   By contrast, the Láadan word for "desert" is "**shée**." Since "**shée**" ends in a vowel sound, "to the desert" is just "**shéedi**," without any need for an inserted "**e**."

2. In the same way, Láadan doesn't allow "vowel clusters"—two vowels in a row—and it inserts an "**h**" to keep that sequence from happening.

So, if you add the plural MORPHEME "**me-**" at the beginning of the word "**eb**" (which means to buy or sell) the result has to be "**meheb.**" The "**h**" is added to separate the first vowel "**e**" from the second one.

NOTE: Two vowels together are allowed if one of them has high tone. So "**áa**" and "**aá**" are both allowed, without any need for an inserted "**h.**"

Pattern Practice[1]

Complete the following sentences by adding the appropriate ending to the Láadan word that follows the sentence.

Example:

Bíi ril sháad óowamid buzhedi wa.
The dragon is going to the con.

1. **Bíi ril sháad óowamid** _____ **wa.**
   to the cave; cave = **bethud**

2. **Bíi ril sháad óowamid** _____ **wa.**
   to the forest; forest = **olin**

3. **Bíi ril sháad óowamid** _____ **wa.**
   to the town; town = **miwith**

4. **Bíi ril sháad óowamid** _____ **wa.**
   to the spaceship; spaceship = **yo**

---

[1] For Pattern Practice answers, go to Appendix 4.

Lesson 2

For the Con, You Need a Suitcase

Vocabulary
    imedim   suitcase
    thi   have
    boó   three
    be   he, she, it
    –th   a MORPHEME that means "This is the direct object in this sentence."

Examples
1. **Bíi ril thi Athid imedimeth wa.**
   Athid has a suitcase.
2. **Bíi ril thi Sha imedimeth wa.**
   Sha has a suitcase.
3. **Bíi ril thi óowamid imedimeth boó wa.**
   The dragon has three suitcases.
4. **Bíi ril thi be imedimeth wa.**
   She (or he, or it) has a suitcase.
5. **Bíi ril thi be imedimeth boó wa.**
   It (or she, or he) has three suitcases.

Láadan Grammar Facts

1. Direct objects are the items in a sentence that things happen to; they answer "what" and "who" and "which" questions. In "Thad bought a book in the dealer's room," for example, buying is what happened and it was a book that the buying happened to. And "a book" is the answer to the question "What did Thad buy in the dealer's room?"

    In Láadan, you have to put the MORPHEME "**-th**" at the end of direct objects.

    And—because "**-th**" is a consonant—if the last sound in the word or phrase for the direct object is a consonant, you have to put an "**e**" between the word and the "**-th**." So, when you mark "**imedim**" as a direct object by adding "**-th**," the result will be "**imedimeth**."

2. If you need to specify exactly how many there are of something, you can do that in Láadan by putting a number right after the word for that something.

    So "**imedim boó**" means "three suitcases." "**Óowamid boó**" would mean "three dragons."

Pattern Practice[1]

Complete the following sentences by adding the appropriate ending to the Láadan word that follows the sentence.

> Example:
>
> **Bíi ril thi Athid imedimeth wa.**
> Athid has a suitcase.

1. **Bíi ril thi Athid** _____ **wa.**
    a book; book = **áabe**
2. **Bíi ril thi Athid** _____ **wa.**
    a cup; cup = **ni**
3. **Bíi ril thi Athid** _____ **wa.**
    a bed; bed = **dahan**
4. **Bíi ril thi Athid** _____ **wa.**
    a beer; beer = **webe**

---

[1] For Pattern Practice answers, go to Appendix 4.

Lesson 3

Asking Questions

Vocabulary

em	yes
ra	no; not
ne	you
Báa	I say to you as a question; I ask you

Examples

1. Question: **Báa ril sháad Athid buzhedi?** Answer: **Em.**
   Is Athid going to the con? Yes.

2. **Báa ril sháad Sha buzhedi? Em.**
   Is Sha going to the con? Yes.

3. **Báa ril sháad óowamid buzhedi? Em.**
   Is the dragon going to the con? Yes.

4. **Báa ril thi Athid imedimeth? Em.**
   Does Athid have a suitcase? Yes.

5. **Báa ril thi Sha imedimeth? Em.**
   Does Sha have a suitcase? Yes.

6. **Báa ril thi óowamid imedimeth? Ra—imedimeth boó wa!**
   Does the dragon have a suitcase? No—three suitcases!

7. **Báa ril sháad ne buzhedi? Em.**
   Are you going to the con? Yes.

8. **Báa ril sháad ne buzhedi? Ra.**
   Are you going to the con? No.

9. **Báa ril thi ne imedimeth? Em. (or Ra.)**
   Do you have a suitcase? Yes. (or No.)

Láadan Grammar Facts

1. The reason there's no evidential at the end of the questions above is because questions don't offer information and claim that it's true; questions *ask for* information.
2. In an ordinary conversation you wouldn't have to keep constantly repeating your SPEECH ACT words and time words and evidentials; you'd only need to include them in your sentences if things changed and you needed a different one, or if it was important to you to include them. This is why it's okay to just say "**Em**" or "**Ra**" as the answer to a yes/no question.

   However, if for some reason you wanted to make it clear that you were saying "yes" or "no" based on your own perceptions, you would say "**Em wa**" or "**Ra wa**."

Pattern Practice[1]

Complete the following sentences by adding the appropriate ending to the Láadan word that follows the sentence.

> Example:
>
> **Báa ril sháad ne buzhedi?**
> Are you going to the con?

1. **Báa ril sháad ne _____?**
   to the hotel; hotel = **both**
2. **Báa ril sháad ne _____?**
   to the moon; moon = **óol**
3. **Báa ril sháad ne _____?**
   to the ocean; ocean = **mela**
4. **Báa ril sháad ne _____?**
   to the room; room = **shod**)

---

[1] For Pattern Practice answers, go to Appendix 4.

Lesson 4

Getting to the Con

Vocabulary

le	I
yuloma	wing
mazh	car; automobile
shin	two
-nan	a MORPHEME meaning "by means of"; it indicates what is used to do something
-wáan	a MORPHEME meaning "the reason (cause) based upon which something is done"
wi	an evidential meaning "The reason I claim that what I'm saying is true is because it's self-evident; everybody can see that it's true, or everybody is in agreement that it's true."

Examples

1. **Sha: Bíi ril sháad le buzhedi mazhenan wa.**
   I'm going to the con by car.

2. **Athid: Bíi ril sháad le buzhedi mazhenan wa.**
   I'm going to the con by car.

3. **Thad: Bíi ril sháad le buzhedi mazhenan wa.**
   I'm going to the con by car.

4. **Óowamid: Bíi ril sháad ra le buzhedi mazhenan wa. Ril sháad le buzhedi yulomanan wa.**
   I'm not going to the con by car. I'm going by wing.

   NOTE: When you have sentences like this one right after the other from the same speaker, the SPEECH ACT word doesn't have to be repeated in every sentence. It would always be correct to repeat the SPEECH ACT word, which means that if you're not sure what to do it's safe to include it; but it doesn't have to be there.

5. **Sha: Báa bebáawáan?**
   Why? That is: For what reason?

6. **Óowamid: Bíi ril thi ra Sha yulomath wi. Ril thi ra Thad yulomath wi. Ril thi ra Athid yulomath wi. Ril thi le yulomath shin wi!**
   Sha doesn't have a wing. Thad doesn't have a wing. Athid doesn't have a wing. I have two wings!

   NOTE: "Reason" is ambiguous between two distinct Láadan cases.

   > -**wan** = purpose for which
   >
   > -**wáan** = cause from which

Láadan Grammar Facts

1. To make a sentence negative, put "**ra**" right after the verb.

   For example: "**Bíi ril sháad le buzhedi wa**" means "I'm going to the con"; "**Bíi ril sháad ra le buzhedi wa**" means "I'm not going to the con."

2. The word for "why" — "**bebáawáan**" — has three parts.

   It starts with the pronoun "**be**" for "it," which refers to the reason why.

   Next comes "**-báa-**," which marks it as a question word.

   It ends with a MORPHEME (called a "CASE MARKER") that makes its role in the sentence clear. It ends with "**-wáan**," which means "the reason because of which something is done."

Pattern Practice[1]

Complete the following sentences by adding the appropriate ending to the Láadan word that follows the sentence.

> Example:
>
> **Bíi ril sháad be buzhedi mazhenan wa.**
> He's going to the con by car.
>
> Or She's going, or It's going.

1. **Bíi ril sháad be buzhedi** _____ **wa.**
   by boat; boat = **esh**

2. **Bíi ril sháad be buzhedi** _____ **wa.**
   by train; train = **memazh**

3. **Bíi ril sháad be buzhedi** _____ **wa.**
   by plane; plane = **zhazh**

---

[1] For Pattern Practice answers, go to Appendix 4.

Lesson 5

Talking About Going to the Con

Vocabulary
- **di** — say; speak; talk
- **eril** — a word used to indicate past time
- **i** — and

Examples
1. **Bíi eril di Athid wa, "Ril sháad le buzhedi wa!"**
   Athid said, "I'm going to the con!"
2. **Bíi eril di Sha wa, "Ril sháad le buzhedi wa!"**
   Sha said, "I'm going to the con!"
3. **Bíi eril di Thad wa, "Ril sháad le buzhedi wa!"**
   Thad said, "I'm going to the con!"
4. **Bíi eril di óowamid wa, "I ril sháad lehóo buzhedi wa!"**
   The dragon said, "And *I'm* going to the con!"

Láadan Grammar Facts

1. When you're quoting somebody else's words, you don't have to put a SPEECH ACT word at the beginning of the quoted words unless it's different from the one at the beginning of your own sentence.

    That is, when you start with "**Bíi**" and quote somebody else, you don't have to repeat "**Bíi**" at the beginning of their words.

    However, if you start with "**Bíi**" and then quote somebody else's words that start with some other SPEECH ACT word, it has to be there.

    For example: "**Bíi eril di Athid wa, 'Báa ril sháad Thad buzhedi?'**" is how you would say that Athid asked whether Thad is going to the con.

Pattern Practice[1]

Complete the following sentences by adding the appropriate ending to the Láadan word that follows the sentence.

>   Example:
>
>   **Bíi eril di Athid wa, "Báa ril sháad ne buzhedi?"**
>   Athid said, "Are you going to the con?"

1. **Bíi eril di Athid wa, "Báa ril sháad ne _____?"**
   to the beach; beach = **sheshihoth**

2. **Bíi eril di Athid wa, "Báa ril sháad ne _____?"**
   to the road; road = **weth**

3. **Bíi eril di Athid wa, "Báa ril sháad ne _____?"**
   to the dance; dance = **amedara**

4. **Bíi eril di Athid wa, "Báa ril sháad ne _____?"**
   to the forest, to the woods; forest, woods = **olin**

---

[1] For Pattern Practice answers, go to Appendix 4.

Lesson 6

At the Hotel

Vocabulary

wida	carry
yide	hungry
hihath	now; right now
both	hotel
me-	plural MORPHEME used at the beginning of verbs and words that correspond to English adjectives
-ha	MORPHEME used to indicate where something or someone is located

Examples

1. **Bíi ril Athid botheha wa.**
   Athid is at the hotel.
2. **Bíi ril Sha botheha wa.**
   Sha is at the hotel.
3. **Bíi ril Thad botheha wa.**
   Thad is at the hotel.
4. **Bíi ril óowamid botheha wa.**
   The dragon is at the hotel.
5. **Bíi eril mewida Athid i Sha i Thad imedimeth wa.**
   Athid and Sha and Thad carried a suitcase.
6. **Bíi eril wida óowamid imedimeth boó wa.**
   The dragon carried three suitcases.
7. **Bíi ril meyide hihath Athid, Sha, Thad i óowamid wa.**
   Now Athid, Sha, Thad, and the dragon are hungry.

Láadan Grammar Facts

1. To make a verb plural—that is, to indicate that more than one subject is involved—just put "**me-**" at the very beginning of the verb.

   The rule is the same if the word you're using would be an adjective in English. So, for example, the Láadan word for "blue" is "**leyi**"; and the way to say "The suitcases are blue" in Láadan is "**Bíi ril meleyi imedim wa.**"

   Notice that you don't have to make any change in the word "suitcase"—only in the word "blue."

2. When the evidential "**wa**" is used at the end of a sentence that is about someone's internal state—like being hungry or thirsty or sleepy or bored, for example—it means that the speaker has actually heard that person say something like "I'm hungry" or "I'm thirsty," or has seen the person do something that unambiguously carries that meaning.

Pattern Practice[1]

Complete the following sentences by adding the appropriate ending to the Láadan word that follows the sentence.

    Example:

Bíi ril wida Athid webeth wa.
Athid is carrying a beer.

1. **Bíi ril wida Athid** _____ **wa.**
   a book; book = **áabe**

2. **Bíi ril wida Athid** _____ **wa.**
   a camera: camera = **ridadem**

3. **Bíi ril wida Athid** _____ **wa.**
   a cat; cat = **rul**

4. **Bíi ril wida Athid** _____ **wa.**
   an apple; apple = **doyu**

---

[1] For Pattern Practice answers, go to Appendix 4.

Lesson 7

Athid, Sha, Thad and the Dragon Are in the Bar

Vocabulary

yod	eat	**wáa**	an evidential, meaning "The reason I claim that what I'm saying is true is because I trust the source for my information."
rilin	drink		
rilinehoth	bar		
ana	food		
lalom	sing		
lom	song		
bezh	they (2–5)		
webe	beer		

Examples

1. **Bíi ril Athid i Sha i Thad rilinehotheha wáa.**
   Athid and Sha and Thad are in the bar.
2. **Bíi ril óowamid rilinehotheha wáa.**
   The dragon is in the bar.
3. **Bíi ril merilin bezh webeth wáa.**
   They are drinking beer.
4. **Bíi ril meyod bezh anath wáa.**
   They are eating food.
5. **Bíi ril melalom bezh lometh wáa.**
   They are singing songs.

Láadan Grammar Facts

1. The pronoun "be" ("he, she, it") refers to just one individual or item. To make it plural, you add either "**-zh**," for two to five, or "**-n**," for more than five.

Pattern Practice[1]

Complete the following sentences by adding the appropriate ending to the Láadan word that follows the sentence.

    Example:

Bíi ril merilin bezh webeth wáa.
They are drinking beer.

1. **Bíi ril merilin bezh** _____ **wáa.**
   juice; juice = **éeb**

2. **Bíi ril merilin bezh** _____ **wáa.**
   milk = **lal**

3. **Bíi ril merilin bezh** _____ **wáa.**
   tea; tea = **zhu**

4. **Bíi ril merilin bezh** _____ **wáa.**
   water; water = **ili**

---

[1] For Pattern Practice answers, go to Appendix 4.

Lesson 8

Sha Has a Panel at the Con

Vocabulary

alehala	to make art
bama	angry (for a reason, but not something that can be blamed on anybody and not something that it's possible to do anything about)
dihomedal	panel
eth	to be about (as in "a book about birds")
Dóo	"Well…"
néde	to want
íi	also; too

Examples

1. **Bíi ril thi Sha dihomedaleth wa.**
   Sha has a panel.
2. **Bíi aril eth dihomedal alehala wa.**
   The panel will be about making art.
3. **Bíi ril thi ra óowamid dihomedaleth wa.**
   The dragon doesn't have a panel.
4. **Bíi ril bama óowamid wa.**
   The dragon is angry.
5. **Bíi ril di óowamid, "Dóo, ril néde lehóo dihomedaleth íi" wa!**
   The dragon says, Well, *I* want a panel too!

Láadan Grammar Facts

1. In Láadan, emotions (like joy and sadness and anger) have a number of different forms. We will be discussing the forms one at a time as we learn them.

Pattern Practice[1]

Complete the following sentences by adding the appropriate ending to the Láadan word that follows the sentence.

Example:

Bíi ril néde le dihomedaleth wa.
I want a panel.

1. **Bíi ril néde le** _____ **wa.**
   a cape; cape = **rimáayo**

2. **Bíi ril néde le** _____ **wa.**
   a comb; comb = **don**

3. **Bíi ril néde le** _____ **wa.**
   a guitar; guitar = **lalen**

4. **Bíi ril néde le** _____ **wa.**
   a rocking chair; rocking chair = **lolin**

---

[1] For Pattern Practice answers, go to Appendix 4.

Lesson 9

The Dragon Has a Sales Table at the Con

Vocabulary

áabe	book	**dalehebewan**	sales table
dínídin	toy	**lezh**	we (five or fewer)
eb	sell; buy		
losh	money	**id**	and then
menedebe	many, a lot		

Examples

1. **Bíi ril thi óowamid dalehebewaneth buzheha wa.**
   The dragon has a sales table at the con.
2. **Bíi aril eb óowamid áabeth menedebe wa.**
   The dragon will sell many books.
3. **Bíi aril eb be dínídineth menedebe wa.**
   It will sell many toys.
4. **Bíi id aril thi óowamid losheth menedebe wa!**
   And then the dragon will have a lot of money!

Láadan Grammar Facts

1. For the Pattern Practice section, remember that you only have to make the *verb* plural. You don't need to make any change in the form of the nouns that list the items "we" will be selling.

Pattern Practice[1]

Complete the following sentences by adding the appropriate ending to the Láadan word that follows the sentence.

Example:

Bíi aril meheb lezh doyuth menedebe wa.
We will sell a lot of apples.

1. **Bíi aril meheb lezh** _____ **menedebe wa.**
   boats; boat = **esh**

2. **Bíi aril meheb lezh** _____ **menedebe wa.**
   cradles; cradle = **lulin**

3. **Bíi aril meheb lezh** _____ **menedebe wa.**
   computers; computer = **shinehal**

4. **Bíi aril meheb lezh** _____ **menedebe wa.**
   games; game = **shida**

---

[1] For Pattern Practice answers, go to Appendix 4.

Dictionaries

English to Láadan

a

a, the-final-one nonede
to be **able** thad
abortion wírabanenath
to be **about** eth
above rayil
absence mar
absence-of-desire ramaha
absence-of-pain shol
accountant lamithá
to be **accursed**, unholy rahéeda
to **accuse** ibádi
acoustics (the science) ezho
across mesh
administration eyon
acronautics czhazh
after, beyond ihée
afternoon udathihée
against, next to ib
agar (a seaweed) analel
aggressor rashonelhá
agree zhelith

agreement (written) zhethob
agriculture eróo, also ehábid
air shum
airplane zhazh
airport hozhazh
alcoholic ranahálh
ale wéebe
algae lelith
to be **alien** née
an **alien** (NOUN) néehá
to be **alive** wíi
all, every woho
all-power hohathad (like "omnipotence," but without the feature male)
all things, all-that-is abesh
to be **alone** sholan
alone and glad of it elasholan
alone at last, after tiresome people doólelasholan
alone in a crowd of people sholalan
alone "in the bosom of your family" búsholan

alone with grief óosholan
alone with terror héeyasholan
along óobe
aloud zhonal
also íi
altar obeham
although íizha
always hadihad
to be **amazed** míi
amber dathimithede
ambulance duthamazh
Amen Othe
among (many) menedebil
among (few) nedebenil
analysis yan
anarchy ralod
anatomy (the science) ehoba
and i
and then id
anesthesia duthawish
angel noline
angel-science enoline
anger[1] bara; bala; bama; bana; bina
animal mid
animal, domestic shamid

animal, wild romid
animal husbandry ewomil
anorexia rayide
ant halezhub
anthropology ewith
anticipate litharil
any waha
anything dal waha
anytime hath waha
anywhere hoth waha
ape omamid
apiarist thuha
apology pardon me hoda; excuse me = hóoda
apple doyu
apricot thuyu
April Athil (poetic form)[2]
arc thamewud
architect emathá
argument, **quarrel** rashon (not used of an "argument" in a theory or an equation or proposition)
Arkansas Arahanesha (a loanword); "pet" name, short form = Aranesha
arm (the body part) oda
around o

---

[1] Many nouns of emotion have a number of forms in Láadan; see Appendix 1-P, NOUN DECLENSIONS, for an explanation.

[2] See Appendix 2-B, months of the year.

to **arrive** nosháad

to "**art**," to **make art** alehala

to **ask** mime

assistant, helper dená

asteroid thamehaledal

astronomer ehashá

astronomy ehash

at last, finally doól

attacker, **aggressor** rashonelhá

to **attend**, **be present at** ham

attend, **attention**, **pay attention to** il

audiology ehoyu

aunt berídan

autumn wemon

AUXILIARIES See Appendix 1-A

as, **like** zhe

to be **ashamed** loláad lhohoth (that is, "perceive shame")

auction loshehalid

b

baby áwith (to indicate a male infant, use the masculine suffix "id": áwithid)

baby animal ámid

baby-nurse háawithá

back (body part) wan

back of the hand raniloma

to be **bad** rathal

to be **bad + good**[1] yéshile

bag, sack, purse dimod

baker balá

baking dish yam

ball, spherical object bab

balm ub; irritant substance = rahub

bandage duthahod

bank (financial) loshebelid

banker loshá

bankruptcy ralosh

bar, tavern rilinehoth

bark (as, bark of tree) boshoya

barn róomath

barren-one rawóobaná

barter, trade beheb

basket boóbidim

beach sheshihoth

bean edeni

to **bear**, **give birth** wóoban

to be **beautiful** áya; of a place = hóya; of a time = háya

beaver eduthemid

because bróo[2]

to **become** nahin

---

[1] Láadan has a number of predicates that combine polar opposites in this way, for example, to describe someone who is both bad and good at the same time.

[2] An exception to the sound rules.

bed dalehanawan
bed (short form) dahan
bedding, bed covers miméne
bee zhomid or zhozhub
beekeeper thuhá
beetle yum
before, in front of ihé or eril (of time)
beer webe
to be **beholden** dinime
to **believe** edeláad
believer edeláadá
bell limlim[1] (onomatopoeic)
benison, spoken blessing ath
berry dalatham
to **betray** ulhad[2]
between shinenil
beyond, after ihée
to be **big**, large rahíya
to be **big + little**[3] nóowid
billion (1,000,000,000) merod
biology emid
birch tree meláanin
bird babí
birth (the noun) woban

birth-blood luwili
birthday thade
birthgiver wóobaná
birth (time) wobaneya
to **bite** dashobe
to be **bitter** (taste) rúsho
bittersweet rúshoméenan
to be **black** loyo
to be **black + white** lóothi[4]
blackberry loyodalatham
bland, spiceless ralaheb
blanket owahúuzh
to be **blessed**, holy othel
blessed place othelehoth
blessing nayadi
blood luhili
blood vessel iluli
blow (trauma, noun) olob
to be **blue** leyi
blueberry leyidalatham
boat esh
bodily secretion obahéda
body oba
body language = dáan i oyi (IDIOM)
to **body-remember** (like remembering how to ride a bicycle) obadom

---

[1] An exception to the sound rules.
[2] The word is **u** + **lh** + **a** + **d**... the first syllable is **u**. the second **lhad**.
[3] Deictic pair, same action, but different points of view.
[4] Deictic pair, same action, but different points of view.

bone thud
book áabe
bookstore áabewehe
boss, ruler hu
boss, ruler (masc.) huhid
botany edala
bowels hodáath
bowl bin
boychild háawithid
to **braid** boóbin
brain uth
bramble nab
branch odayáaninetha
bread bal
bread box baladim
to **break** then
breast thol
breath wíyuleth
to **breathe** wíyul
breeder of animals womilá
brewer webehá
brick, concrete donilihud
bridge oódóo[1]
to **bring to birth** wóbáan
to **bring**, to take bel[2]
broom wush

to be **brown** leyan
brush (for hair) idon
brush (not for hair) enid
Buddha Buda
Buddhism (the religion) óobuda; worships Buddha
Buddhist óobudahá; Buddhism + affix for doer
building math
bundle of sticks menedebosh
burden dosh
bureaucracy rashenidal
burnout iboshara
to **bury** rumadoni
bush, shrub hemen
business (the science) ehohel
to be **busy** shóod
but izh
butcher (of meat) dehenihá
butter hob
butterfly áalaá[3]
to **buy**, to sell eb[4]
buyer or seller ebá
buyer (professional) nathá

---

[1] This is a visual/aural analog form.
[2] Deictic pair, same action, but different points of view.
[3] Visual/aural analog form.
[4] Deictic pair, same action, but different points of view.

C

cake thuzh
calculator shinishin
callousness raména (See also: ramína, ramóna, ramuna)
camel hibomid
camera, video recorder ridadem
candy thuhal
cane, walking stick nedeboshob
cape, cloak rimáayo
car mazh
career hal (hal = work)
- **career, beginning** didehal
- **career, middle** ruhobehal
- **career, retired** shawithehal

to **caress**, stroke lámála
to **caress with the lips**, kiss odámála
to **caress with the tongue** odithámála
caregiver, caretaker (of people) nayahá
carpenter belidá
carrot medalayun
to **carry** wida
cartology, cartography eluben
to **carve, sculpt** lámáhel

CASE MARKERS See Appendix 1-B
cat rul
to **cause** nin;
one responsible = niná;
one to blame = ninálh
cause, reason obed
to **cause** to VERB dó-
cave bethud
cease to thrive nótháa
celebration elahela
celibacy rashim
a **celibate** rashimá
to be **celibate**, by choice lath
celibate, not by choice ralath
center hatham
ceramics ebod
ceramist, potter ebodá
ceremonial clothing budeshun
ceremonial objects daleshun
ceremony, ritual shun
chair dalewodewan
change sheb;
resistance to change = rasheb
charm, charisma thuhul
to **chatter** ishidi
cheese ódon
chef emahiná
chemistry eshishid
chest (body part) rawan

to feel **cherished** nuháam

to **chew** dashobin

chick álub

chicken lub or yath

child háawith

child-science eháawith

chocolate ahana

chronemics, chronography ehath

church áatham

circle tham

city miwith

city dweller miwithá

classroom bedishod

a **clean** body obahéthe

to be **clean** éthe

- "**boss-clean**," highest level of clean huhéthe
- "**child-clean**" level of cleanliness at which a child considers her room háawithéthe
- "**family-clean**" usual state of affairs onidahéthe
- "**guest-clean**" level of cleaning you do for guests thóohéthe
- "**pig-clean**" state of your teenager's room mudahéthe

to be **clear** wedeth

clergy wíitham

clitoris abathede

cloak, cape rimáayo

to be **closed** rahu

cloth od;
weaver = odá;
textile science = ehod; textile scientist = ehodá

cloth-of-gold odobeyal

clothing (general term) bud

cloud boshum

clover boómi

clown emethá

to **clown** emeth

coat habo

cocoa ahanamezh

coffee yob

to be **cold** rahowa

color science eliri

to be **colored**, have **color** liri

comb don

to **come** to pass, happen shóo

to **come**, go[1] sháad

to **comfort** she;
comforter = shehá

comical, funny dóhada

coming-of-age ritual shebehatheshun

---

[1] Deictic pair, same action, but different points of view.

command room, for war ráatham

common sense bash

feeling of **community**, oppressive, negative lólh

feeling of **community** lol

a **community place** lolehoth

compassion mína, ména, móna, múna, méhéna[1]

competition halid

computer shinehal

computer printer raneran

computer science eshinehal

comset óozh

comset technician óozhá

concrete donilihud

condom obom

confess ibáyóodi

conifer dathimi

connection shasho

consensus zheláad

container dim

contentment nina, nena, nona, nuna, nehena[2]

contract, to make deal bédim

convention, conference buzh

cook anadalá

---

[1] Multiple forms, see Appendix 1-P, NOUN DECLENSIONS

[2] Multiple forms, see Appendix 1-P, NOUN DECLENSIONS

cooking (the science) emahin

cooking-pot mahin

cooking-utensil thibeb

cooperation zheshub

copier (photocopier) rimel

copulation, to sexual act shim

copulator (not lover) shimá

cordial (beverage) yurana

to be **correct** dóon

costume dedidebud

to **count** lamith

couple (noun) shinishidi

cousin edin

coven óoletham

to **cover**, **hide** rumad

coverings (bedding) miméne

cow dithemid

cradle lulin

cream onelal

to **create**, enact dóhin

creative urge mahela

creator, **maker** elá

creature mid

credit, money losh; economics = elosh; economist = eloshá; banker = loshá

crime ib

criminal ibálh

criminology ehib

crowd méwith

to **cry** (of babies) wée

to **cuddle** lemadama

cup ni

cupboard, dresser dimidim

curl (noun) aále

curtain demeren

curve, to be **curved** boósh

to **cut** humesh

d

daffodil léeli

to **dance** amedara

dandruff adelith

danger rayom

to be **dark-colored** loyu

darkness rahith

dawn nasháal

day sháal

DAYS OF THE WEEK See Appendix 2-A

to be **dead** rawíi

death shebasheb

debt lud; with negative connotation = lhud

to **decrease** náheb

to be **deep** ruhob

deer lemamid (lema = be gentle + mid = creature)

deity (male) ebahóol

dentist edashá

dentistry edash

depression as a side effect of medication deshara, dutheshara

depression as result of major trauma olobeshara

depression as result of small event uhudeshara

desire (sexual) maha; absence of desire = ramaha

desk dalebediwan

despair rathena[1] (rathone, rathura, rathina, rathehena)

desert shée

dessert homana

diaper áwod

difficult radozh

digit (toe, finger) ishid

DIMINUTIVE SUFFIX, AFFECTIONATE -i

diner, one who eats yodá

direction wethene

to be **dirty** rahéthe

discord raoha (not of discord in the home)

discord-in-the-home lhed

disgust ílhi; also "ílhilh"[2]

---

[1] Multiple forms, see Appendix 1-P.

[2] **lh** is always pejorative.

dish bod;
ceramics = ebod

to **do** shub

to **do well**, thrive thaá

doctor, physician eduthahá

dog lanemid

to **dominate** dórado

to **dominate** with evil intent dólhórado

door áath

down heb

to be **downy**, furry shane

dowry heth

dragon óowamid

dream ozh

dress, gown owe;
man's garment = owehid

to **drink** rilin

drink, beverage rana;
drinker = ranahá;
alcoholic = ranahálh

to **drop**, spill, let fall héda

drought ralali

drug desh

to be **dry** ralili

duck yazh

dulcimer shelalen

DURATION MARKERS See Appendix 1-E

during obée

e

ear oyu;
audiology = ehoyu

to be **early** dide

earth, **soil**, **ground** doni

Earth Thera (loanword), or Doni

earthquake donithen

earthworm shéeba

east hene

easy dozh

to **eat** yod

eating-utensil min

echo zhorumi

economics elosh

economist eloshá

edge (sharp) hubod

edge (non-sharp) nodal

education ehom

egg máa

eight (8) nib

eighteen (18) nibethab

eighty (80) thabenib

either...or e...e

ejaculate aáláthon

elder, honored shawith

elephant domid

eleven (11) nedethab

EMBEDDING MARKERS See Appendix 1-F

embroidery dademadal

emotion wihi[1]

emotionlessness rawihi; not a complimentary term

empathically impaired ráahedethi

empathically impaired, intentionally ráahedethilh

empathy (total) wohosheni

to **enable** shóoba; or dothad

to **enable another in self destructive behavior** dóthadelh

enabler dóthadá or dóthadelhá

to **encourage** nayadithal

END-OF-PRAYER Othe (used like "Amen")

enemy leb; also lheb (strong pejorative)

engineer eduthá

engineering eduth

enigma, puzzle zhab

ephemeral hahí

et cetera minidibi

evening háanáal

every woho

---

[1] For Láadan, the sentence pattern for emotions is "X perceives-internally Emotion Y."

every time hath woho

evidence meloth

EVIDENCE MORPHEMES See Appendix 1-J

evil (theological sense) ramíili

excuse me, apology for leaving hóoda

to **exhaust** oneself ibo; ibolh (strong pejorative)

exhibitionistically damash

to **exile** rahabelhid; an exile, outcast = rahabelhidá

to **exist** in

eye oyi

f

face (body part) ona

fact nedeloth

to **fall** háda

family onida

famine rahana

to be **far** thed

farm ábed

farmfield, pasture ábedun

farmer ábedá

to be **fast** ralóolo

to **fast** dod

fat, grease zhebom

fawn háalemamid

to **fear** héeya

feather hosh; or yulish

to feel, as if directly, another's feelings lowitheláad

to feel with the skin (perceptive touch) láad oyanan

female (noun) ludihá

to be **female** ludi

to **female-sexual act** lila; lover, female = lilahá (not used to refer to males)

feminist-angel anahelilith

to be **fertile, creative** shinóoya

few or several nedebe

to fidget ishish

field of a farm, pasture ábedun

fifteen (15) shanethab

fifty (50) thabeshan

to **fill, fill up** lob

final one, last one nonede

finally doól

to **find** redeb

fire óowa

first nedeya

fish thili

fist (body part) thahoma

five (5) shan

fleecy-clouded (said of skies) bol

floor rabobosh

flour edemezh

flower mahina

fluid, thick behili

flute déethel

to **fly** shumáad

FOCUS MARKER -hóo

fog úushili

to **fold** dóhibeyóo

to **follow** doth

food ana; **nutrition** = ehana; **junk food** = rahana

"fool's gold" rahobeyal

foot (body part) óoma

for-sure (emphatic) hulehul

foremother wohothul

foremother wisdom wohothulewoth

forest olin

forever hathehath

forevermore ril i aril i rilrili

to **forgive** baneban

fork batha

formalism scientific notation eéden

forty (40) thabebin

four (4) bim

fourteen (14) bimethab

fourth bimeya

fowl, poultry lub

fox dumidal

fraction marker -yi-
to be fragrant aba
fret ihith
Friday Rayileshául
friend lan
friendliness dina, dena, dona, duna, dehena[1]
frog ríibib
frost nith
fruit yu
frustration dala, dama, dana, dara, dina
to be full, abundant ume
fun bil
furniture mo
future aril (TIME AUXILIARY)

g

gadget rahed
game shida
gap, hole maradal
garden déela
gas (oxygen, etc.) wish
gate urahu
to gather buth (not said of people)
to gather, assemble lolin (of people)
to be gentle lema
geography ehoth
geometry etham; geometrician = ethamá
gestalt wésha
genitalia (female, outer) wodama
genitalia (female, all) wohóol
to get, obtain thel
to get by thaáhel
gift bini
gift with strings attached rabinilh
to give ban
to give-and-take báanibel
glass (for drinking) hed
globe, sphere, planet thamehal
glory hohama
gloves, mittens, socks, stocking ishida
glutton yodalhá
goat éczh
to go, come shául[2]
goddess, deity Lushede
gold obeyal

---

[1] Many nouns of emotion have a number of forms in Láadan; see Appendix 2–c for an explanation.

[2] Deictic pair, same action, but different points of view.

to be **good** thal;
of time = hathal;
of place = hothal

goose yáazh

gospel thaledan

government yon

grain ede

grand-daughter hóowith;

grandmother hothul;

granary edemath

grape éelen

grapevine éelenethil

grass hesh

gratitude wéná, wóná, wúná, wíná, wéhená[1]

to be **gray**, **grey** líithin

great aunt hoberídan

great grand-daughter shinehóowith

great grandmother shinehothul

great niece hosherídan

grease zhebom

to be **green** liyen

greet dibithim

greeting Wil sha (literally, "Let there be harmony")

grief shara, shala, shama, shana, shina[2]

to **grind** mezhel

grocery store, market anawehe

group olowod

grow, **growth** náwí

growth through transcendence sháadehul

guardian lúul

guest thóo

- **door guest**, one who just shows up at your door áathethóo
- **invited guest** shineshidethóo
- **guest who calls ahead** widadethethóo
- **refrigerator guest**, a guest who shows up unannounced, comes on in and helps herself to whatever's in the fridge— and that's a good thing nithedimethóo

guilt ihitheril

guinea pig humazhomid

guitar lalen

---

[1] Many nouns of emotion have a number of forms in Láadan; see Appendix 1-P, NOUN DECLENSIONS, an explanation.

[2] Many nouns of emotion have a number of forms in Láadan; see Appendix 1-P, NOUN DECLENSIONS, an explanation.

h

hail (weather term) hishud
hair delith
hal work
ham radio hidel
hand oma
handicap won
happen shóo
harbor réele
to be **hard**, firm radazh
harmony sha
science of **harmony** esh
harvest róo;
harvester, gatherer = róohá
hat yen
to **have** thi;
owner, possessor = thihá
to **have to**, be obliged to dush
head on
to **heal** dutha;
medicine = edutha
healer duthahá
health lam
to **hear**, to perceive with the ears, perceptive hearing laad oyunan
heart óoya
heartbeat, pulse óoyaáláan
heaven olim

to be **heavy** sho
hedgehog or **porcupine** dathimid
to **help** den
helper dená
to **hem** nohadal
herb thesh
herbal remedy duthesh
herstory told by women dedideheril
here nu
hide (noun) shoya
to **hide** an emotion or aspect of self mad
to **hide**, cover, put away rumad
to be **high, tall** íthi
hill hibo
hip rum
historian erihá
history eri
his-story told by men dedideherilid
to **hoard** raheb
to **hold** widom
hole, gap maradal
holiday diídin
Holy-One, Deity Lahila
holy day shehéeda
home beth

honey thu;
beekeeper = thuhá

hope ul

hops (the plant) webesh

horn, antler onethud

horse omid

hose (for liquids) ilu

hospital duthahoth

hospitality ethóo

hot flash (menopause symptom) zháahóowadin

hotel both

hours between dawn and rising dideshá

hours between midnight and dawn honáal

house belid

house management science elob

housebound shodá

household lod

housewife/housekeeper/househusband elodá

how widaweth

to **hunger**, to be **hungry** yide

hurricane yulehul

to **hurt**, feel pain úuya

hypothesis lithewil

hypothetical rilrili

i

I le (See also la, li)

if...then bre...ébre[1]

ignorance raloth

to **ignore** rahil;
with evil intent = rahilh

illusion búláa

harmful **illusion** búláalh

to be **important** oth

inappropriate shulhe

to **increase** náraheb

indifference lash

to be **infinite** ranonede

information loth

information science eloth

to **inherit** thazh

insane, crazy búlith

insect zhub

noxious **insect** lhezhub

inside nil

insomnia raháana

intent nédeshub

interacting ladinime

interface dodel

to **interpret** déedan

interruption theni

intersection sheni

---

[1] Exception to Láadan sound rules.

to **itch** oyada
intuition loyan
investigation ezhab
investigator ezhabá
invited shineshid
to be **irresponsible** ráhesh
irritant substance rahub
island mari
ivy boóbil

j

Jesus of Nazareth Zheshu (loan word)
jewel thede
jonquil, daffodil léeli
joy thina, thena, thona, thuna, thehena[1]
juice, sap éeb
to **jump** oób
junk food rahana (ra = non + ana = food)

k

to **keep track** (of) riweth
kelp yáalin
kettle dizh
kidney yeb
king unáhid

king, boss or ruler, masc. huhid
knick knack, useless object mathom (Tolkien loanword)
knife hum
to **know** (of people) an (as in "I know Amy")
to **know** (not people) lothel
knowledge lesson bedeloth
kudzu huthil

l

labia owo
labia majora and minora liliháaláa
lake wilidun
lamp, light ithedal
to **land** (as a ship or plane), a landing adoni
language dan
to be **large** ramihí
to be **last**, to be final rush
last one, final one nonede
later aril
to **laugh** ada
lava udólo
lavish, luxurious dimel
layer bre[2]

---

[1] Multiple forms. See Appendix 1–P.

[2] exception to Láadan sound rules.

to **lead** un;
leader = uná

leaf mi

to **learn** bedi;
student, learner = bedihá

to **learn a skill**, to body-learn obedi

leavetaking, farewell aril

left hiwetha

leg óoda

lemon hezh

length rabohí

lesson bedina

- **knowledge-lesson** bediloth
- **Useless-knowledge-lesson** bedilhoth
- **wisdom-lesson** bediwoth

let there be, would that… Wil

lettuce ilimeda

lexical gap édáan

library wéehoth

to **lie down** rúu

life wí

light ith

to **lightning** lish

lightning bolt ezhahith

to be **like** (X like Y) zhe;
identical-sibling = zhehá

like, as zhe

lilac lehina

lime hizh

line (of a computer program, or a line drawn on a surface) bod

to **linger over** bolith

linguist edaná

linguistics edan

lip, lips odama

list (noun) wilibod

to **listen**, to **listen to** ma[1]

to **live in**, inhabit habelid

liver web

livestock womil

lizard éezha

long-ago eríli

long-ahead, far future aríli

long-lived rahahí

to **lose** wem

love; also, to **love** a (of inanimates only)

to **love**[2] am, azh, áazh, ad, ab, ashon, sham, éeme, áayáa, aye

love for evil ralhoham

---

[1] This verb takes SPEECH ACT affixes optionally. See Appendixes 1-L, N and O.

[2] Láadan has numerous words for "love" of various kinds; for translations, see Appendix 2-C.

love for that which is Holy oham

lover lilahá (not used of males)

lover azhur

lovingkindness donidan; donidaná (channel for lovingkindness)

lustfully, desiringly mahanal (not a negative term)

m

machine zhob

magic, enchantment yahanesh

Magic Granny Shósho (a character in stories)

magic-maker, witch, magician yahaneshá

to **make** el

male-identified withidetho

mall wehebuth

Mama Emath

man withid

to **manifest** dam (That is, to show signs of some state or emotion.)

manners, courtesy shal

man-time hatherilid

many (6 or more) menedebe

map luben

market, store wehe

marsh, swamp alu

mask onabel

masquerade budehalid

massage (noun and verb) lilathun

mathematics elamith

matrix (in geology) wodazhud

mattress hóo

mead thuwebe

meadow dun

meal (lunch, etc.) anadal; cook = anadalá

meat deheni

medicine edutha

meditate wodehahodo

meditation room láashod

to **meet, meet with** bithim

melody wethalehale (literally, "music path")

melon ozhi

memory elothel

to **menopause** zháadin;
- uneventfully = azháadin;
- when it's welcome = elazháadin

menstrual blood óolewil

menopause-induced insanity zháadinebúlith

to **menstruate** osháana;
- early = desháana

- for the first time = elasháana
- in sync with another woman = zesháana
- joyfully = asháana
- late = wesháana
- painfully = husháana

mercy yidan

meta lée-

metal badazh

metaphor, simile zhedal

middle shiniledal

milk (noun) lal; mother's milk = lalal

million (1,000,000) rod

mind óoyahonetha

mineral bad

mirror betheb

misogyny withelhebe

mist shili

to **mistranslate** rahéedan

to **mistranslate** deliberately and with evil intent: rahéelhedan

misunderstand rahen

mode nub

modem modem (loanword)

"momilies," mother-daughter knowledge hothulewoth

Monday Henesháal

money, credit losh

month hathóol

MONTHS OF YEAR See Appendix 2-B

moon óol

mop iliwush

morning háasháal

morning glory elathil

morpheme yudáan

moth óoloó

mother shathul (formal term = honored mother)

mother mathul (informal intimate term)

mother's milk lalal

motivation nédashubel

mountain bo

to **mourn** óom

mouse edemid

mouth óoyo

to **move** mina; transportation = emina

mud donili

mule wothemid

to be **murky**, obscure rawedeth

muscle thun

mushroom mud

to **"music"** alehale (that is, to sing or whistle or use a musical instrument)

musical instrument dalehale

mystery lush

myth dedidewoth (literally, "story-wisdom"; does not mean untruth)

n

nail, **claw** (body part) bath

name zha

narrow híyamesh

nation shishidebeth

native tongue wobanedan

near thoma

neck (body part) womedim

nectar hom

nectarine homeyu

need them

needle dathi

to do **needlework** dathim

negative, **no** ra

neighbor obeth

network shenidal

nerve bid

neurology ebid

never rahadihad; or rahath

nevertheless éde

news shóodal

news device (newspaper, magazine) dishóodale

nibble, caress with teeth dashelámála

niece sherídan;
great-niece = hosherídan

night náal

nine (9) bud

nineteen (19) budethab

ninety (90) thabebud

no, **not** ra (this form is also the word "no")

nobody rawith

no how, in **no way** ranal

non-crime rahib

non-cup, hollow accomplishment rani

none, not at all rawoho

non-game rashida

non-garden radéela

non-gestalt raweshalh

non-guest rathóo

non-heart sibling rahéena

non-holiday radiídin

non-interface radodelh

non-meta ralée

non-neighbor rahobeth

non-pearl ranem

non-perceive raláad

non-perceiver raláadá

non-perceiver, deliberate raláadalh

non-pillow rathom

non-synergy rarulh

non-teach rahom
non-think ralith
non-thunder, hot air, commotion ralorolo
non-touch radama
non-touch with evil intent radamalh
non-use, deliberate raduth
node rad
noise zholh
none, notatall rawoho
noon udath
north hun
nose oyo
to **not-fit**, to be wrong for shulhe
to **not-heal** radutha
not-healer raduthahá
not-healer, with evil intent raduthahálh
nothing radal
novelist dedidethodá
now, present time ril
now, right now hihath
nowhere rahoth
nuisance uhud
number lami
NUMBERS, NUMERALS See Appendix 2-D
nurse onin

nut yumal
nutrition, science of food ehana
nut-tree mal

o

oak doyáanin
to **obfuscate** ralhewedeth
object dale
ocean mela
ocean-dweller melahá
office, workplace hohal
often hath menedebe
oil (household) bom
to be **old** balin
on, upon nol
once hath nede
one (1) nede
one hundred (100) debe
one hundred and one (101) debe i nede
one thousand (1,000) thob
one thousand and one (1,001) thob i nede
onion bremeda[1]
only neda
to be **open** u
opera dedidelom

---

[1] Exception to Láadan rules.

or, either...or e...e
orange (the fruit) yun
to be **orange** layun
ornament dimilin
ore badazhud
orphan nuthul
otter elalimid
outcast rahabelhidá
outline, silhouette oyabod
outside, **out** ranil
ovary hib
oven óob
to **overflow** (as of water) shulin
owl húumid
owner thihá

p

page (of book) miháabe
pain heyi
absence of **pain** shol
pain or loss that comes as a relief doóledosh
palm (of hand) óoyaha oma, also niloma
panel discussion dihomedal
pansy onahina
paper mel
paradise olim
parent thul

park heshehoth
parsley aálesh
part (of machine, etc.) wud
past eril
pasta ededal
peace shon;
peace-science = eshon;
peace-scientist = eshona;
peace-maker = shoná;
aggressor = rashonelhá
pearl nem
peel, **peeling** (noun) yuhoya
penis bom
to **perceive**[1] láad
to **perceive**-internally[2] loláad
perceiver láadá
perception láa
perception teacher láahomá
to **perform**, act wilomina

---

[1] Láadan uses these two verbs for the concepts expressed by English "to see, to hear, to taste, etc." and for both senses of "to feel." To say in Láadan "I see X," requires "I perceive X with my eyes"; to say "I feel the wind" requires "I perceive the wind with my flesh"; to say "I feel anger" requires "I perceive-internally anger." A literal translation of English "I am angry," for example, is not possible. Appendix 1, Rules of Láadan Grammar, should clarify this somewhat.

[2] See Note 1, above.

person with; anthropology = ewith; anthropologist = ewithá; science of male persons = ewithid

persona zheledam

perverse, quirky, odd, hard to understand bú

pharmacy eduthawehe; edutha = medicine

philosopher ehená

philosophy ehen

physician eduthahá

piano zhuth

to **pick up**, lift up héedá

picture dadem

pie thizh

pig muda

pillow thom

pin (noun) dathidal

pine tree dathimi

pitcher raliha

place hoth

to be **placid**, **still** wam

plain, flat plain rabo

plain, simple radimil

planet thamehal

plant dala

to **plant** madoni

plate rin

to **play** elash

Please... Lu...

to **please** shi

pleasure méesh (not said of sexual pleasure)

pleasure (sexual) méeshim

plow donihum

poem dáanelom, or lalidáan

poet dáanashoná; or lalidáaná

poetics edáanashon

poetry edáanelom

point (of needle) dath

poison lhu

to **police** zhethalel

police officer zhethalelá

to be **poor** shud

portentous éeba

potato udemeda

potential é-

poultry, fowl lub

powder mezh

power (extraordinary, omnipotence) hohathad

to **practice** olanin

praise dithal

prayer ohamedi

predicate (noun) shoth

predict, foretell diharil

to be **pregnant** lawida

- for the first time = lewidan
- joyfully = lalewida
- late in term and eager for the end = widazhad
- wearily = lóda

presence ram
to be present ham
price nath
principle dolelith
prisoner zhilhad
prize bish
program (of computer) bodibod
to promise bédi
PRONOUNS See Appendix 2-E
proposition, argument halith
protect, shield dóyom
psalm sháam (a loan word)
psychologist elithá
psychology elith
pulse, heartbeat óoyaáláan
to be pure, perfect shad
to be purple lula
to purr thenazho; or rulelo
purse, sack, bag dimod
puzzle zhab

q

to **quest** for truth sháadoni
to **quest** internally nárilim
quilt (not patchwork) balish
patchwork **quilt** báalish

r

rabbit shanemid
radiance míili
radio del
rain, also, to **rain** lali
rake heshedon
rape (noun and verb) ralh
rapport, also, to experience **rapport** óothadama
to **read** wéedan
reason, cause obed
to **recognize** láadom
to **record**, keep **records** ri
rectum nohodáath
to be **red** laya
redwood óowáanin
to **refrain from asking** ramime
refrigerator nithedim
to **regret**[1] zhala, zhana, zhama, zhara , zhima

---

[1] Many nouns of emotion have a number of forms in Láadan; see Appendix 1-P, NOUN DECLENSIONS, an explanation.

to **rejoice** lo
relief doóleshol
religion ehéeda
to **relinquish** a cherished perception zhaláad
to **remember** dom
reminisce diheril or litheril
repeatedly, at random bada (See also: badan, brada, bradan, bradá)
REPETITION MORPHEMES See Appendix 1-K
to **rescue**, save bóodan
resemble zhedam
reservoir wilidunedal
respect[1] ohina, ohena, ohona, ohuna, ohehena
respiration rate wíyaáláan
to be **responsible** áhesh
to give **rest**, to **refresh**, to **rest** dul
rhetoric edi
rhetorician edihá
rhythm alehaáláan
rhythmic-water-flow-noises áalilomáa
rhythmic-wave-noises áalilomáan

---

[1] Many nouns of emotion have a number of forms in Láadan; see Appendix 1–P, NOUN DECLENSIONS, an explanation.

rice ilihede
right (direction) hiwetho
to be **rigorous** shel
rind yushoya
to **rise**, stand up thib
ritual bath shunobahéthe
river, creek wili
road weth
to **rock** (of babies) luth
rocking chair lolin
room shod
root dol
rope methid
rose shahina
rosemary domesh
rubber dazhéeb
rug, carpet ren
ruler, boss hu
to **run** yime

S

sack, purse dimod
to be **sacred** héeda
sacred drink héedarana
sage, the herb wothesh
sage, wise person wothá
to be **safe** yom
sailor eshá
saint lawith

sales table dalehebewan

salt máan

salt marsh malu

salty máanan

sand sheshi

sanitary napkin óolewod

Saturday Yilesháal

save bóodan

savory (the herb) edenesh

to **say**, tell, speak = di; rhetoric = edi; speaker = dihá

scene, view, experience of a place wohóoha

school ulin

school group, class bediholowod

school trip bedihim

scientist ehá

scientifically enal

scissors muhum

scratch (noun) iboth

to **scratch** ibath (not said of scratching an itch)

to **scratch** an itch ubath

seaweed lel

second shineya

to **see**, perceive with the eyes, perceptive seeing láad oyinan

seed thon

seldom hath nedebe

self, identity zheledal

to **sell**, buy eb[1]

self-time, regular óothasháal

to **send** nori

to **sense**, be aware of loláad óoyanan

sentence déeladáan

seven (7) um

seventeen (17) umethab

seventy (70) thabum

several nedebe

to **sew** adal

sewage plant, waste water plant waludal

to **"sexual act"** shim; one who performs a sexual act = shimá (cannot mean "lover")

shadow rum

shame lhoho

to **share** edethi

to be **sharp** huma

sheep éesh

sheet (bedding) úuzh

shelf dob

shell, carapace, hull udoya

shirt bon

shoe óomi

---

[1] Deictic pair, same action, but different points of view.

short in length bohí
shoulder rim
shovel (noun and verb) donim
shower obahéthethib
sibling-by-birth hena
sibling, identical zhehá
sibling-of-the-heart héena
sickness éeya
to **sift** shumezh
to **sign** (as in ASL) lishid
signer lishidá
silence rile
- **silence**, comfortable rilehana
- **silence**, denial that it's happening rilehum
- **silence**, malicious rilelh
- **silence**, painful on one side rileraham
- **silence**, refusal to discuss riledim

silver yeth
similar zhe
sin lha
to **sing** lalom
sink for washing bid
to **sit** wod
six (6) bath
sixteen (16) bathethab
sixty (60) thabebath

skill (noun) oloth
skin, flesh oya
skirt áayo
sky thosh
slave rahulh
sleep áana
to be **slow** lóolo
to be **small** híya
to be **small** (area) mihí
to **smell** attentive smelling shu
to **smell**, to perceive with the nose, perceptive smelling láad oyonan (See also: il oyonan)
smile áada
smith, metalsmith badazhelá
smith-craft badazhel
snake ezha
snow hish
soap éthedale
socks, stockings ishida
song lom
sorrel (the herb) thezh
soul óotha
sound zho; aloud = zhonal
sound of rain on roof lalilom
sound of rain on leaves lalimilom
sound of rhythmic waves áalilomáan

soup thulana

to be **sour** yem

south han

space (outer) delin

spaceliner yoda

spaceship yo

speaker dihá

spectator, audience member ilá

SPEECH ACT MORPHEMES See Appendixes 1-L, N and O.

sphere thamehal

spice laheb

spider dathimemid or dathimezhub

spine (body part) doluth

spiral bretham[1]

spoon bada

spouse eba

to **spray** (as water) aálá

spring (season of year) wemen

squander rahol

to **squeeze** thamehib

squirrel elashemid

stable, place for animals midemath

stag lemamidid

stage, in a theater wilominahoth

star ash

STATE-OF-CONSCIOUSNESS MORPHEMES See Appendix 1-M

statue udadem

to **stay** benem

to be **still**, placid, calm (as of water, wind) wam

to **stink**, reek rabalh

stomach hod

stone ud

to **store** ol

store, market wehe

storm rohoro

story dedide

stove dimóowa

straight raboósh

strip mall wehebuthebod

string thid

to be **strong** do

student, learner bedihá

to **study** ulanin

Such a... What a... Wu...

sudden bishib

suitcase imedin

sugar meén

summer wuman

sun rosh

Sunday Hathameshául

---

[1] Exception to Láadan sound rules.

sunrise nasháal

sunset nanáal

to **surpass** hesho (used in comparatives)

to be **sweet** (taste) meénan

to **swim** ilisháad

symbol (of a notation, or an alphabet or orthography) uzh

synergistics eru

synergy ru; **synergist** eruhá

t

table daleyodewan

tactile deprivation ralámálha

tail hoyo

to **take**, to bring bel[1]

to **take-away-from** raban

to **take care of** naya; care-giver = nayahá

tall íithi

tampon nilewod

tank for liquid háawilidunedal

tape recorder rizho

tarragon abash

to **taste** (attentive) il óoyonan

to **taste** (perceptive) láad óoyonan

tea zhu

---
[1] Deictic pair, same action, but different points of view.

to **teach** om

teacher omá

teenaged animal yáamid

teenager yáawith

telephone widadith

television thèle (loanword)

to **tell news** dishóo

temptation erabalh

ten (10) thab

terror eéle

testicle hibid

thank-you áala

that DEMONSTRATIVE PRONOUN hithed or núuhi (See chart, p. 133, or Appendix 2-E)

theater wilominabelid

then ébre

there núu

therefore owáano

these, few DEMONSTRATIVE PRONOUN hizhethoma or nuhizh (See chart, p. 133, or Appendix 2-E)

these, many DEMONSTRATIVE PRONOUN hinethoma or nuhin (See chart, p. 133, or Appendix 2-E)

these, those, few DEMONSTRATIVE PRONOUN hizh (See chart, p. 133, or Appendix 2-E)

these, those, **many** DEMONSTRATIVE PRONOUN hin (See chart, p. 133, or Appendix 2-E)

thing dal

to **think** lith; psychology = elith

third boóya

to **thirst** yada

thirteen (13) boóthab

thirty (30) thabeboó

this DEMONSTRATIVE PRONOUN hithoma or nuhi (See chart, p. 133, or Appendix 2-E)

this, that DEMONSTRATIVE PRONOUN hi (See chart, p. 133, or Appendix 2-E)

thorn bash

those, few DEMONSTRATIVE PRONOUN hizhethed or núuhizh (See chart, p. 133, or Appendix 2-E)

those, many DEMONSTRATIVE PRONOUN hinethed or núuin (See chart, p. 133, or Appendix 2-E)

threat éholob

threat, particularly malicious éholhob

three (3) boó

thrice hath boó

throat wom

through obe

thunder lorolo

Thursday Haneshául

thus hinal

thyme háami

tick (the insect) uhudemid; also uhudezhub

to **tickle** adama; also adadama

time hath

together shidi

toilet, W.C. al

tone-deaf, musically deprived ráalehale

tongue odith

tool ed

tooth dash; dentist = edashá

	SINGULAR	SEVERAL	MANY
DEMONSTRATIVES	hi	hizh	hin
nearer **(this, these)**	hithoma/ nuhi	hizhethoma/ nuhizh	hinethoma/ nuhin
farther **(that, those)**	hithed/ núuhi	hizhethed/ núuhizh	hineehed/ núuhin

to **torment** rashe

tornado thameyul

to **torture** rashelh

to **touch** dama[1]; science-of-touch = edama

towel dib

tower (noun) shumath

town, city miwith; city-dweller = miwithá

toy dínídin

tractor demáazh

train memazh

to **translate** héedan

transportation emina

to **travel** im

tray dobi

tree yáanin

tribe shonida

trunk (for storage) yomedim

truth, **honor** shadon

to **try** to X du- plus verb; try to speak = dudi

to **try** in vain to X dúu- plus verb; try in vain to speak = dúudi

trousers, pants inad

Tuesday Honesháal

tulip hodo

turn wetham

turtle, tortoise balinemid

twelve (12) shinethab

twenty (20) thabeshin

twice hath shin

twin, identical sibling zhehá

two (2) shin

typewriter ran

u

to be **ugly** modi

unable to feel, also to be empathically impaired lowitheláad or ráahedethil

under yil

underground than

to **understand** en; philosophy = ehen

underwear hem

unfriendliness radena, radona, raduna, radina, radehena[2]

to be **united** shishid

until hathobéeya

unwilling ranime

unwilling to feel, also, to be deliberately emphatically impaired lowitheláad or ráahedethilh

---

[1] This form takes SPEECH ACT affixes. See Appendixes 1-L, N and O for an explanation.

[2] See Appendixes 1-P, NOUN DECLENSIONS.

up raheb
urine iliyeb
to use duth

U

vacuum cleaner éthedal
vagina lul
valley yed
vegetable meda
vehicle razh
vine thil
vintner rushihá
violet oyimahina
violin dóolon
to visualize umeloláad
vividly lishenal
voice dith

W

wait neril
walk óomasháad
wall (noun and verb) thibá
to want néde
war rashonelh
wardrobe budim
warehouse, storehouse dalemath
to be warm owa
washcloth éthehod

wasp resh
to waste, squander rahol
to watch, pay attention il oyinan
to watch internally, to pay inward attention lohil
water ili
wave aáláan
wax (beeswax or candle wax) yibom
way, road, path, etc. weth
we len (See also lezh, lan, lazh, lin, lizh)
to be weak rado
to wear une
to be weary óoha
weather ro
weave osh
weaver odá
Wednesday Hunesháal
weed nish
week híyahath
to weep delishe (not said of infants)
Well… Dóo…
west hon
to be wet lili
wetness caused by sexual desire éebemaha
whale uthemid

when widahath

where widahoth

to **whistle** humazho

to be **white** líithi

why widahuth

wide rahíyamesh

widow sheba

wild ro-

will (theological) yoth

to be **willing** nime

wind yul

window dem;
someone you can see right through = demá

wine rushi

wing yuloma

winter weman

wire widáahith

wisdom woth;
sage, wise one = wothá

wisdom lesson bediwoth

without raden

with-regard-to shé

wolf holanemid

womantime hatheril

womb wóoya

wood bosh

word dáan

word angel dáanoline

work, also to work hal

work counter, surface behal

work identity zhelehal

work that is constantly being interrupted halehadihahal

worker halá

worry lhitharil

Would that, Let there be... Wil...

to **wrap** thamesho, also dóho

wreath oshetham

to **wring, wring out** thamerili

wrinkle (in skin) zháa

to **write** thod

writing implement dalethodewan, short form = thodi

y

to **yearn, yearn for** loyada

to be **yellow** léli

yes em

to be **yielding**, pliant dazh

you ne (See also na, nan, nazh, nen, ni, nin, nizh, lhena, lhenen, lhenezh)

to be **young** rabalin

young animal háamid

yourself neyóo

yourselves neyóon (See also neyóozh, nayóozh, nayóon, niyóozh, niyóon, lheneyóozh, lheneyóon)

You're welcome Oho

z

zoology emid (e = science of + mid = creature)

Láadan to English

As is true in the translation from any language into another, many words of Láadan cannot be translated into English except by lengthy explanation.

We wish to note that the pejorative element "**lh**" can always be added to a word to give it a negative connotation, so long as it precedes or follows a vowel and does not violate the rules of the Láadan sound system by creating a forbidden cluster. The addition of "**lh**" need not create an actual new word; for example, "**áwith**" means "baby"—to use instead "**lháwith**" (or "**áwithelh**") means only something like "the darned baby" and is ordinarily a temporary addition. But it is very handy indeed; we are indebted to the Navajo language for this device.

a

a love (for inanimates only; to love (inanimates only)

áabe book

áabewehe bookstore (**áabe** = book + **wehe** = store)

áada smile

aálá spray, to spray (as in water)

áala thank-you

áalaá butterfly

aáláan wave of water (on ocean or lake)

aáláthon ejaculate (**aálá** = spray + **thon** = seed)

aále curl, ruffle, to curl

aálesh parsley, the herb

áalilomáa sound of rhythmically flowing water

áalilomáan sound of rhythmic waves

áana sleep, to sleep (synonym: **ina**)

áath door

áatham church (**áath** = door + **tham** = circle)

áathethóo door guest, a guest who just shows up at your door (**áath** = door + **(e)thóo** = guest) (See also: **thóo, nithedimethóo, shineshidethóo, widadithethóo**)

áayáa mysterious love, not yet known to be welcome or unwelcome

áayo skirt

áazh love for one sexually desired at one time, but not now

ab love for one liked but not respected

aba fragrance, to be fragrant

abash tarragon, the herb

abathede clitoris (**aba** = fragrant + **thede** = jewel)

ábed farm, to farm

ábedá farmer (**ábed** = farm + **-á** = suffix for doer)

ábedun field of a farm (noun) (**ábed** = farm + **dun** = meadow)

abesh all things, all-that-is

ad love for one respected but not liked

ada laugh, to laugh

adadama tickle, to tickle (**ada** = laugh + **dama** = touch)

adal sew, to sew

adama tickle, to tickle (**ada** = laugh + **dama** = touch)

adelith dandruff

adoni to land (as a ship or plane); also a landing (**doni** = earth)

ahana chocolate (**a** = love + **(h)ana** = food)

ahanamezh cocoa (**ahana** = chocolate + **mezh** = powder)

áhesh responsibility, to be responsible

al toilet

alehaáláan rhythm (**alehale** = music + **áaláan** = wave)

alehala art, to "art," to make art

alehale music, to make music (sing, whistle, play a musical instrument)

alu marsh, swamp

álub chick (**á** = infant + **lub** = fowl). See **yath** = chicken, and **áyath** = chicken hatchling

am love for one related by blood

amedara dance, to dance

ámid baby animal, very young creature (**á-** = baby + **mid** = animal) (See also: **háamid, yáamid**)

an to know (of people)

ana food

anadal meal (general term) (breakfast, lunch, dinner, etc.) (**ana** = food + **dal** = thing)

anadalá cook (**anadal** = meal + **-á** = suffix for doer)

anahelilith feminist-angel (loanword: Greek/Akkadian)

analel agar (a seaweed) (**ana** = food + **lel** = seaweed)

anawehe grocery store, food store, to grocery shop (**ana** = food + **wehe** = store)

Arahanesha Arkansas (loanword), seldom used

Aranesha Arkansas ("pet" name, short form)

aril future (TIME AUXILIARY)

aril later, after (in time)

aril good-bye, leavetaking, farewell (**aril** = later)

aríli far future, long ahead (TIME AUXILIARY) (**aril** = later)

ash star

áshãana to menstruate joyfully (**osháana** – to menstruate)

ashon love for one not related by blood, but heart-kin

ath benison, spoken blessing, to give a spoken blessing

Athil April

áwith baby, infant, very young person (**â-** = baby + **with** = person) (See also: **háawith**, **yáawith**)

áwithid male baby, male infant (**áwith** = baby + **-id** = suffix for male)

áwod diaper

áya to be beautiful

aye love which is unwelcome and a burden

azh love for one sexually desired now

azháadin to menopause uneventfully (**zháadin** = to menopause)

azhur lover

b

báa I say to you as a question ...; I ask... (QUESTION SPEECH ACT, NEUTRAL)[1]

- **báad**: in anger, I ask...
- **báada**: in jest, I ask...
- **báade**: as a story, I ask...
- **báadi**: in teaching, I ask...
- **báadu**: as poetry, I ask...

---

[1] Sentences begun with this SPEECH ACT do not need an EVIDENCE MORPHEME, because the speaker is asking for information rather than offering any. There are no English equivalents for these speech acts.

- **báalan**: in celebration, I ask…
- **báali**: in love, I ask…
- **báath**: in pain, I ask…
- **báaya**: in fear, I ask…;

báanibel give and take, to give and take

báalish patchwork quilt (See also: **balish**)

báanil give and take

bab ball; a spherical object, any of various movable and round or oblong objects used in various athletic activities and games.

baneban to forgive (**ban** = to give)

babí bird

bad mineral

bada spoon

bada repeatedly, at random (REPETITION MORPHEME) (See also: **badan, brada, bradan, bradá**)

badan repeatedly, in a pattern over which humans have no control (REPETITION MORPHEME) (See also: **bada, brada, bradan, bradá**)

badazh metal

badazhel smith-craft (**badazh** = metal + **el** = make)

badazhelá smith, metal smith (**badazh** = metal + **el** = make + **á** = suffix for doer)

badazhud ore (**badazh** = metal + **ud** = stone)

bal bread

bala anger with reason, with someone to blame, which is not futile (See also: **bara, bana, bama, bina**)

balá baker (**bal** = bread + **á** = suffix for doer)

baledim breadbox (**bal** = bread + **(e)dim** = container)

balin to be old

balinemid turtle, tortoise (**balin** = old + **mid** = creature)

balish quilt, not patchwork (See also: **báalish**)

bama anger with reason, but with no one to blame, which is futile (See also: **bala, bana, bara, bina**)

ban to give, to make a present of, to place in the hands of, to pass from one to another

bana anger with reason, with no one to blame, which is not futile (See also: **bala, bama, bara, bina**)

baneban forgiveness, to forgive

bara anger with reason, with someone to blame, which is futile (See also: **bala, bama, bana, bina**)

bash thorn, a sharp pointed woody extension of a stem or leaf

bash common sense

bath six (6) number

bath nail, fingernail, toenail, claw (body part)

batha fork

bathethab sixteen (16) number (**bath** = 6 + **thab** = 10)

be[1] it/she/he (PRONOUN: 3RD PERSON: SINGULAR: NEUTRAL)

Below are the forms of "**be**":

- **ba**: beloved
- **bi**: honored
- **ihebe**: despised

Below are GENDER MARKERS for "**be**":

- **behid** he (**be** = it + **-id** = male
- **behizh** she (**be** = it + **-izh** = female)

---

[1] To be used in gender-neutral situations or when gender is obvious and doesn't need to be explicitly stated. To explicitly state a gender, add the appropriate suffix: **behid** or **behizh**. No English equivalent.

bé I say as a promise… (SPEECH ACT NEUTRAL, MORPHEME)

- **béd**: in anger, I say as a promise…
- **béda**: in jest, I say as a promise…
- **béde**: as a story, I say as a promise…
- **bédi**: in teaching, I say as a promise…
- **bédu**: as poetry, I say as a promise…
- **bélan**: in celebration, I say as a promise…
- **béli**: in love, I say as a promise…
- **béth**: in pain, I say as a promise…
- **béya**: in fear, I say as a promise…

bedi to learn, a learning

bédi to promise

bedihá student, learner (**bedi** = learning + **á** = suffix for doer)

bedihim school field trip, travel for purpose of learning (**bedi** = learn + (**h**)**im** = travel)

bediholowod class, group of students who are taught together (**bedi** = learn + (**h**) **olowod** = group)

bedilhoth useless knowledge lesson (**bedi** = learn + **-lh-** = pejorative + **loth** = information) (See also: **bedina**, **bediloth**, **bediwoth**)

bediloth knowledge lesson (**bedi** = learn + **loth** = information) (See also: **bedina**, **bedilhoth**, **bediwoth**)

bédim contract, deal

bedina lesson (See also: **bediloth**, **bedilhoth**, **bediwoth**)

bedishod classroom (**bedi** = learn + **shod** = room)

bediwoth wisdom lesson (**bedi** = learn + **woth** = wisdom) (See also: **bedina**, **bediloth**, **bedilhoth**)

bée[1] I say in warning (SPEECH ACT MORPHEME, NEUTRAL)

- **béed**: in anger, I say in warning...
- **béeda**: in jest, I say in warning...
- **béede**: as a story, I say in warning...
- **béedi**: in teaching, I say in warning...
- **béedu**: in poetry, I say in warning...
- **béelan**: in celebration, I say in warning...
- **béeli**: in love, I say in warning...
- **béeth**: in pain, I say in warning...
- **béeya**: in fear, I say in warning...

behal work counter, work surface; surface

beheb barter, trade, to barter, to trade; **eb** = buy/sell)

behili fluid (thick), such as corn syrup consistency

bel to transport, to bring

belid house (See also: **beth**)

belidá carpenter (**belid** = house + **-á** = suffix for doer)

ben (PRONOUN: 3RD PERSON: SIX OR MORE: NEUTRAL)

- **bin**: honored
- **ban**: beloved
- **iheben**: despised

benem to stay in a place or condition

beneth them (many) (PRONOUN, 3RD PERSON, MANY, NEUTRAL, OBJECT) (**ben** = they + **-th** = object marker)

berídan aunt

beth home, place where one lives (See also: **belid**)

betheb mirror, to mirror

---

[1] No Engish equivalent.

bethud cave (**beth** = home + **ud** = stone)

beye[1] one unidentified somebody/someone/something (INDEFINITE PRONOUN, SINGULAR, NEUTRAL). Look to verb to disambiguate between person (someone) and thing (something).

- **beyen**: many, six or more, unidentifed somebodies/somethings (INDEFINITE PRONOUN, MANY, NEUTRAL)
- **beyezh**: few/several, two to five, unidentifed somebodies/somethings (INDEFINITE PRONOUN, FEW, NEUTRAL)

beyóo[2] itself/herself/himself (**be** = it/she/he + **-yóo** = reflexive marker) To be used in gender-neutral situations or when gender is obvious and doesn't need to be explicitly stated. To explicitly state a gender, add the appropriate suffix:

- **beyóohid**: himself

- **beyóon**: themselves, many (**ben** = they, many + **-(e)yóo** = reflexive marker) (3RD PERSON, MANY, REFLEXIVE PRONOUN)
- **beyóozh**: themselves, several (**bezh** = they, several + **-(e)yóo** = reflexive marker): (3RD PERSON, SEVERAL, REFLEXIVE PRONOUN)

bezh they (several, 2 to 5 individuals) (PRONOUN, 3RD PERSON, NEUTRAL)

- **bazh**: beloved
- **bizh**: honored
- **lhebezh**: despised

bid nerve (body part)

bid sink, a basin used for washing

bíi I say…: "I say to you, as a statement" (DECLARATIVE, SPEECH ACT NEUTRAL, optional once established)

- **bíid**: in anger, I say…
- **bíida**: in jest, I say…
- **bíide**: as a story, I say…
- **bíidi**: in teaching, I say…
- **bíidu**: as a poem, I say…
- **bíilan**: in celebration, I say…
- **bíili**: in love, I say…

---

[1] The indefinite adjectives can also follow another noun to emphasize that it is unknown. English doesn't have specific words for these forms. See Appendix 2-E, REFLEXIVES for further information.

[2] See Appendix 2-E, REFLEXIVES for further information.

- **bíith**: in pain, I say…
- **bíiya**: in fear, I say…

bil fun, to be fun

bim four (4) number

bimethab fourteen (14) number (**bim** = 4 + **thab** = 10)

bimeya fourth (**bim** = four + **-(e)ya** = suffix for time)

bin bowl, a round container

bina anger with no reason, with no one to blame, which is not futile (See also: **bala, bama, bana, bara**)

bini a gift

bish prize

bishib to be sudden, suddenness

bithim to meet, to meet with, a meeting

bo mountain

bó I command… (COMMAND, SPEECH ACT MORPHEME) (very rare except to small children)

- **bód**: in anger, I command…
- **bóda**: in jest, I command…
- **bóde**: as a story, I command…
- **bódi**: in teaching, I command…
- **bódu**: as poetry, I command…
- **bólan**: in celebration, I command…
- **ból**: in love, I command…
- **bóth**: in pain, I command…
- **bóya**: in fear, I command…

bod line (on a surface or of a computer program)

bod dish, general kitchen term, a container

bodibod program for a computer, to program a computer (**bod** = line + **i** = and)

bohí to be short in length

bol fleecy-clouded (of skies)

bolith to linger over something that one has the skill to complete quickly

bom oil, household oil, to oil

bom penis

bon shirt, blouse

boó three (3)

bóo I request (REQUEST, SPEECH ACT, NEUTRAL) polite, usual "command" form

- **bóod**: in anger, I request…

- **bóoda**: in jest, I request...
- **bóode**: as a story, I request...
- **bóodi**: in teaching, I request...
- **bóodu**: as poetry, I request...
- **bóolan**: in celebration, I request...
- **bóoli**: in love, I request...
- **bóoth**: in pain, I request...
- **bóoya**: in fear, I request...

boóbidim basket (**boóbin** = to braid + **dim** = container)

boóbil ivy plant (**boóbin** = to braid + **thil** = vine)

boóbin braid, to braid (**boó** = 3)

bóodan rescue, save, to rescue, to save

boómi clover plant, oxalis (**boó** = 3 + **mi** = leaf)

boósh curve, to be curved

boóya third (**boó** = 3 + **-ya** = suffix for time)

bosh wood, general word for wood from a tree

boóthab thirteen (13) (**boó** = 3 + **thab** = 10)

boshoya bark of tree (**bosh** = wood + **oya** = skin)

boshum cloud (**bo** = mountain + **shum** = air)

both hotel, motel

brada[1] repeatedly, in a pattern fixed arbitrarily by human beings, repeatedly in an artificial pattern (REPETITION MORPHEME) (See also: **bada, badan, bradá, bradan**)

bradá repeatedly, in what appears to be a pattern but cannot be demonstrated or proved to be one (REPETITION MORPHEME) (See also: **bada, badan, brada, bradan**)

bradan repeatedly, in a pattern fixed by humans by analogy to some phenomenon, such as the seasons (REPETITION MORPHEME) (See also: **bada, badan, bradá, brada**)

bre layer, material laid on or spread over a surface

bre...ébre if...then

bremeda onion (**bre** = layer + **meda** = vegetable)

bretham spiral, to spiral (**bre** = layer + **tham** = circle)

bróo because

---

[1] Word sets that contain "**br**" (brada, bradá, bradan, bre, etc.) do not follow Láadan consonant rule.

bú to be perverse, quirky, odd, hard to understand

bud nine (9)

bud clothing (general term)

buda buddha (loan word); should have a capital B when it refers to "the" Buddha

budehalid masquerade (**bud** = clothing + (**e**)**halid** = competition)

budeshun ceremonial clothing, ritual clothing (**bud** = clothing + (**e**)**shun** = ceremony)

budethab nineteen (19) (**bud** = 9 + **thab** = 10)

budim wardrobe (**bud** = clothing + **dim** = container)

búláa illusion, erroneous perception of reality (**bú** = perverse + **láa** = perception)

búláalh perverse/harmful illusion (**bú** = perverse + **láa** = perception + **-lh** = pejorative)

búlith crazy, insane (**bú** = perverse/odd + **lith** = think)

búsholan alone "in the bosom of one's family"

buth to gather (not used with people) (See also: **lolin**)

buzh convention, "con," conference, a large formal assembly of a group with common interests

d

dáan word (**dan** = language)

dáan i oyi body language (**dáan** = word, **i** = and, **oyi** = eye)

dáanashoná poet

dáanelom poem (**dáan** = word + **lom** = song)

dáanoline word angel (**dáan** = word + **noline** = angel)

dadem picture

dademadal embroidery, to embroider (**dadem** = picture + **adal** = sew)

dahan bed (short form)

dal thing

dal waha anything (**dal** = thing + **waha** = any)

dala frustration with reason, with someone to blame, which is not futile (See also: **dama**, **dana**, **dara**, **dina** = frustration)

dala plant, any growing thing

dalatham berry (**dala** = plant + **tham** = circle)

dale object, any made thing

dalebediwan desk (**dale** = object + **bedi** = learning + **-wan** = suffix for purpose, in order to)

dalehale musical instrument

dalehanawan bed (**dale** = object + **áana** = sleep + **-wan** = suffix for purpose, in order to)

dalehebewan sales table (**dale** = object + (**h**)**eb** = buy, sell + (**e**)**wan** = in order to, purpose)

dalemath warehouse, storehouse (**dale** = object + **math** = building)

daleshun ceremonial object (**dale** = object + **shun** = ceremony)

dalethodewan writing implement (**dale** = object + **thod** = to write + -(**e**)**wan** = sufiix for purpose, in order to)

dalewodewan chair (**dale** = object + **wod** = to sit + **-wan** suffix for purpose, in order to)

daleyodewan table (**dale** = object + **yod** = to eat + **-wan** = suffix for purpose, in order to)

dam to manifest, to show signs of some state or emotion

dama to touch, to feel with the skin. (See also: **láad oyanan**, perceptive touch and **il oyanan**, attentive touch)

dama frustration with reason, without someone to blame, which is futile (See also: **dala**, **dana**, **dara**, **dina** = frustration)

damash exhibitionisticly demonstrate one's skill (not a pejorative) (**dam** = manifest + **ash** = star)

dan language (**dáan** = word)

dana frustration with reason, without someone to blame, which is not futile (See also: **dala**, **dama**, **dara**, **dina** = frustration)

dara frustration with reason, with someone to blame, which is futile (See also: **dala**, **dama**, **dana**, **dina** = frustration)

dash tooth

dashelámála nibble, caress with teeth (**dash** = tooth + **lámála** = caress)

dashobe bite, to bite (**dash** = tooth + **obe** = through)

dashobin to chew

dath point

dathi needle

dathidal pin (noun) (**dathi** = needle + **dal** = thing)

dathIm needlework, to needlework

dathimemid spider (**dathim** = needlework + **mid** = creature)

dathimezhub spider (**dathim** = needlework + **zhub** = insect)

dathimi conifer, pine tree (**dathi** = needle + **mi** = leaf)

dathimid hedgehog (American English, porcupine) (**dathi** = needle + **mid** = creature)

dathimithede amber (the gem) (**dathimi** – pine + **thede** = jewel)

dazh to be yielding, pliant, soft

dazhéeb rubber (**dazh** = yielding + **éeb** = juice)

debe one-hundred (100)

debe i nede one-hundred-and-one (101) (**debe** = 100 + **i** = and + **nede** = 1)

dedide story

dedidebud costume (**dedide** = story + **bud** = clothing)

dedideheril herstory, the stories women tell of their past, usually based on interpersonal relationships: births, deaths, relocations, marriages, etc.; "Mary was pregnant with her second when…," "Just about the time the tribe moved to…" Differentiated from "**eri** = history" in that "**eri**" strives for neutral record keeping, whereas both "**dedideheril**" and "**dedideherilid**" stress the story of the past. (**dedide** = story + (**h**)**eril** = past)

dedideherilid his-story; the stories men tell of their past, usually based on wars, conquests, major disasters; the way the past is told in most late 20th century "history" books. Differentiated from "**eri** = history" in that "**eri**" strives for neutral record keeping, whereas both "**dedideheril**" and "**dedideherilid**" stress the story of the past. (**dedide** = story + (**h**)**eril** = past + **-id** = male)

dedidelom opera (**dedide** = story + **lom** = song)

dedidethodá novelist, storywriter (**dedide** = story + **thod** = write + **á** = suffix for doer)

dedidewoth myth, does not mean untruth (**dedide** = story + **woth** = wisdom)

déedan to interpret (**dan** = language)

déela garden

déeladáan sentence (**déela** = garden + **dáan** = word)

déethel flute

dehena friendliness, despite negative circumstances (See also: **dena, dina, dona, duna** = friendliness)

deheni meat

dehenihá butcher (of meat) (**deheni** = meat + **-(h)á** = suffix for doer)

del radio

delin space (outer)

delishe to weep, cry (not said of babies)

delith hair

dem window

demá someone you can see right through (**dem** = window + **-á** = suffix for doer)

demáazh tractor

demeren curtain (**dem** = window + **ren** = rug, carpet)

den help, to help

dena friendliness for good reason, to be friendly (See also: **dehena, dina, dona, duna** = friendliness)

dená assistant, helper

desh drug

desháana to menstruate early, menstruation (**osháana** = to menstruate)

deshara depression as a side effect of medication

di to speak, say, tell, talk

dib towel

dibithim to greet (**di** = say + **bithim** = to meet)

dide to be early

didehal beginning career, early career, the first career you take after college (**dide** = early + **hal** = work) (See also: **ruhobehal, shawithehal**)

dideshá hours between dawn and rising time

dihá speaker (**di** = to say + **-á** = suffix for doer)

diharil predict; foretell (**di** = speak + **aril** = future)

diheril reminisce; recount past events (**di** = speak + **eril** = past)

dihomedal panel, convention panel discussion (**di** = talk + **(h)om** = teach + **(e)dal** = thing)

diídin holiday

dim container

dimidim cupboard, dresser (**dim** = container + **i** = and + **dim** = container)

dimil lavish, luxurious, sumptuous

dimilin ornament

dimod bag, sack, purse (**dim** = container + **od** = cloth)

dimóowa stove (**dim** = container + **óowa** = fire)

dina friendliness for no reason (See also: **dehena, dena, dona, duna** = friendliness)

dina frustration without reason, without someone to blame, which is not futile (See also: **dala, dama, dana, dara** = frustration)

dínídin toy

dinime to be beholden

dishóo to tell news (**di** = tell + **shóo** = happen; come to pass)

dishóodale newspaper, magazine, device to receive news. (**dishóo** = tell news + **dal** = made thing

dith voice

dithal praise, to praise (**di** = speak + **thal** = good)

dithemid cow (**dith** = voice + **mid** = creature)

dizh kettle

do to be strong

dó- to cause to

dob shelf

dobi tray, affectionate diminuative of dob

dod to fast (not eat), fast

dodel interface, to interface (It would be appropriate for the interface the linguists used in the *Native Tongue* trilogy to let their infants acquire alien languages natively; it would be appropriate for the interface that was used to allow human/dolphin interaction in that area of research. It would be appropriate for those diagrams that show two or more areas with overlapping bits— territory where both or all of the areas overlap.)

dóhada be funny; be comical (**dó** = cause to + **ada** = laugh)

dóhibeyóo to fold (**dó** = cause to + **ib** = against + **beyóo** = itself)

dóhin to create, enact (**dó-** = cause to + (**h**)**in** = exist)

dóho wrap, to wrap (**dó-** = cause to + (**h**)**o** = around)

dol root

dolelith principle (**dol** = root + **lith** = thought)

dólhórado to dominate with evil intent (**dólho** = force to + **ra** = non + **do** = be strong + **lh** = negative connotation; **rado** = be weak)

doluth spine (body part)

dom to remember

domesh rosemary

domid elephant (**dom** = remember + **mid** = creature)

don comb

dona friendliness for foolish reasons (See also: **dehena, dena, dina, duna** = friendliness)

doni ground, dirt, earth, soil

Doni Earth (the planet)

donidan lovingkindness

donidaná lovingkindnesser, one who channels lovingkindness (**donidan** = lovingkindness + **-á** = suffix for doer)

donihum plow, to plow (**doni** = ground + **hum** = knife)

donili mud

donilihud brick, thing you make walls out of, to brick (**donili** = mud + **ud** = stone)

donim shovel (**doni** = ground + **im** = travel)

donithen earthquake (**doni** = earth + **then** = to break)

dóo Well ... (phrase)

doól at last, finally

doóledosh pain or loss which comes as a relief by virtue of ending the anticipation of its coming (**doól** = at last + **dosh** = burden)

doóleshol relief (**doól** = at last + **shol** = absence-of-pain)

doólelasholan alone at last after tiresome experience or people (**doól** = at last + **elasholan** = to be alone, joyfully)

dóolon violin

dóon to be correct

dórado to dominate (**dó** = cause to + **ra** = non + **do** = be strong)

doroledim (sublimation with food accompanied by guilt about depriving others of the food) This word has no English equivalent whatsoever. Say you have an average woman. She has no control over her life. She has little or nothing in the way of a resource for being good to herself, even when it is necessary. She has family and animals and friends and associates that depend on her for sustenance of all kinds. She rarely has adequate sleep or rest; she has no time for herself, no space of her own, little or no money to buy things for herself, no opportunity to consider her own emotional needs. She is at the beck and call of others, because she has these responsibilities and obligations and does not choose to (or cannot) abandon them. For such a woman, the one and only thing she is likely to have a little control over for indulging her own self is *food*. When such a woman overeats, the verb for that is "**doroledim.**" (And then she feels guilty, because there are women whose children are starving and who do not have even *that* option for self-indulgence…)

dosh burden

doth to follow

dóthad to enable, to make possible (**dó** = cause-to + **thad** = to be able)

dóthadá enabler, one who enables, makes things possible (**dó** = cause-to + **thad** = to be able + **á** = suffix for doer)

dóthadelh to enable another to persist in self-destructive behavior (for instance substance abuse) by providing excuses or by helping that individual avoid the consequences of such behavior (**dó-** = cause-to + **thad** = to be able + **-(e)lh** = pejorative)

dóthadelhá enabler, one who enables another to persist in self-destructive behavior (for instance substance abuse) by providing excuses or by helping that individual avoid the consequences of such behavior (**dó-** = cause-to + **thad** = to be able + **-(e)lh-** = pejorative + **-á** = suffix for doer)

doyáanin oak (**do** = strong + **yáanin** = tree)

dóyom protect, shield, safeguard (**dó-** = cause to + **yom** = be safe)

doyu apple (**do** = strong + **yu** = fruit)

dozh easy

du- (plus verb) try to VERB

dudi try to speak

dul to give rest, to refresh

dumidal fox (**mid** = creature)[1]

dun meadow, field

duna friendliness for bad reasons (See also: **dehena, dena, dina, dona** = friendliness)

dush to have to, to be obliged to

duth to use

dutha to heal

---

[1] From the Core Vocabulary. Does not follow Láadan morphology rules

duthahá healer (**dutha** = to heal + **-á** = suffix for doer)

duthahod bandage, to bandage (**dutha** = to heal + **od** = cloth)

duthahoth hospital (**dutha** = to heal + **hoth** = place)

duthamazh ambulance (**dutha** = to heal + **mazh** = car)

duthawish anesthesia (**dutha** = to heal + **wish** = gas)

duthesh herbal remedy

dutheshara depression as a side effect of herbal remedy

dúu (plus verb) to try in vain to VERB (**dúu** = to try to VERB)

dúudi try in vain to speak

e

e...e or, either/or

é potential

eb[1] to buy, to sell

eba spouse, to marry ("**Beii eril meheba X i Y wa.**" [X and Y got married. (More literally, "X and Y spoused.") The verb gets the plural prefix and an epenthetic "**h**."] Láadan wouldn't allow "X married Y" or "Y married X," which presuppose that marrying is something one person can do to another. It has to be a joint action, done together.)

ebá buyer or seller

ebahóol deity (male) (spouse of the moon; **eba** = spouse + **óol** = moon)

ebalá baker (science of bread doer)

ebid neurology (**e-** = science of + **bid** = nerve)

ebod ceramics (**e-** = science of + **bod** = dish)

ebodá ceramist, potter

ébre[2] then

ed tool

édáan lexical gap (**é** = potential + **dáan** = word)

edáanashon poetics (the science of poetry)

edáanelom poetry

edala botany (science of plants)

---

[1] Deictic pair, same action, but different points of view.

[2] Does not follow Láadan consonant rules.

edama science of touch (**e-** = science of + **dama** = touch)

edan linguistics (**e-** = science of + **dan** = language)

edaná linguist (**edan** = linguistics + **á** = suffix for doer)

edash dentistry (**e-** = science of + **dash** = tooth)

edashá dentist (**e-** = science of + **dash** = tooth + **-á** = suffix for doer)

ede grain

éde nevertheless

ededal pasta (**ede** = grain + **dal** = thing)

edeláad to believe, believe in (**láad** = to perceive)

edeláadá believer

edemath granary (**ede** = grain + **math** = building)

edemezh flour (**ede** = grain + **mezh** = powder)

edemid mouse (**ede** = grain + **mid** = creature)

edenesh savory (the herb)

edeni bean

edethi to share (**thi** = to have)

edi rhetoric (**e-** = science of + **di** = speak)

edin cousin

eduth engineering (**e-** = science of + **duth** = to use)

edutha medicine (**e-** = science of + **dutha** = to heal)

eduthá engineer (**eduth** = engineering + **-á** = suffix for doer)

eduthahá doctor, physician, healer (**edutha** = medicine + **-á** = suffix for doer)

eduthawehe pharmacy (**edutha** = science of healing + **wehe** = store)

eduthemid beaver (**eduth** = engineering + **mid** = creature)

éeb juice, sap

éeba portentous

éebemaha wetness caused by sexual desire (**éeb** = juice + **(e)maha** = desire [sexual])

eéden formalism, scientific notation

eéle terror

éelen grape

éelenethil grapevine (**éelen** = grape + **(e)thil** = vine)

éeme love for one neither liked nor respected

éesh sheep

éeya sickness, disease, illness

éezh goat

éezha lizard

ehá scientist (**e-** = science of + **-á** -suffix for doer)

eháawith child-science

ehábed science of farming; agriculture (**e-** = science of + **(h)ábed** = farm)

ehana nutrition (**e-** = science of + **ana** = food)

ehash astronomy (**e-** = science of + **ash** = star)

ehashá astronomer

ehath chronography (**e-** = science of + **hath** = time)

ehéeda religion (**e-** = science of + **héeda** = sacred)

ehen philosophy (**e-** = science of + **en** = to understand)

ehib criminology (**e-** = science of + **(h)ib** = crime)

ehoba anatomy (**e-** = science of + **oba** = body)

ehod textile science (**e-** = science of + **od** = cloth)

ehodá textile scientist

ehohel business (the science) (**e** = science of + **o** = around + **el** = make)

éholob particularly malicious threat, to threaten very maliciously. (**é-** = potential + **(h)olob** = trauma, blow)

éholhob threat, to threaten (**é-** = potential + **(h)olob** = trauma, blow)

ehom education (**e-** = science of + **om** = to teach)

ehoth geography (**e-** = science of + **hoth** = place)

ehoyu audiology (**e-** = science of + **oyu** = ear)

ela- joyfully, gladly

el to make

elá creator, maker

elahela celebration (**alehale** = to make music)

elalimid otter (**ela** = joyful + **ili** = water + **mid** = creature)

elamith mathematics (**e-** = science of + **lamith** = to count)

elash to play

elasháana to menstruate for the first time (**ela** = joyful + **osháana** = to menstruate)

elashemid squirrel (**elash** = play + **(e)mid** = creature)

elasholan alone and glad of it

elathil morning glory (**ela** = joyful + **thil** = vine)

elazháadin to menopause when it's welcome (**ela** = joyful + **zháadin** = to menopause)

eliri color science (**e-** = science + **liri** = to be colored)

elith psychology (**e-** = science of + **lith** = think)

elithá psychologist (**elith** = psychology + **á** = suffix for doer)

elod housekeeping, science of house management (**o-** = science of + **lod** = household)

elodá housekeeper, (**e-** = science of + **lod** = household + **á** = suffix for doer)

elosh economics (**e-** = science of + **losh** = money, credit)

eloshá economist (**e-** = science of + **losh** = money, credit + **-á** = suffix for doer)

eloth information science (**e-** = science of + **loth** = information)

elothel computer memory (**eloth** = information science; **e** = science of + **lothel** = to know)

eluben cartography (science of maps)

em yes

emahin cooking (the science)

emahiná chef

Emath mother, mama, mommy (intimate, informal) (See also: **Mathul**, **Shathul**)

emath architecture (**e** = science of + **math** = building)

emathá architect (**emath** = architecture + **á** = suffix for doer)

emeth to clown (LOANWORD based on Emmett Kelly's name)

emethá clown (**emeth** = clown + **á** = suffix for doer)

emid zoology (**e-** = science of + **mid** = creature)

emina transportation (**e-** = science of + **mina** = to move)

en to understand

enal scientifically

enid brush (not for hair)

enoline angel-science (**e-** = science of + **noline** = angel)

erabalh temptation

eri history (**e-** = science of + **ri** = to keep records)

erihá historian (**eri** = history + **-(h)á** = suffix for doer)

eril (1) past (TIME AUXILIARY); a word used to indicate past time (**eri** = history); (2) earlier, before (in time)

eríli far past, long ago (TIME AUXILIARY) (**eri** = history)

eróo agriculture (**e-** = science of + **róo** = harvest)

eru synergistics, science of synergy (**e-** = science of + **ru** = synergy)

eruhá synergist (**e-** = science of + **ru** = synergy + **-á** = suffix for doer)

esh boat

esha science of harmony, equivalent to "peacemaking" or "mediation" or "conflict resolution." (**e-** = science + **sha** = harmony)

eshá sailor, boatman, boater (**esh** = boat + **á** = suffix for doer)

eshinehal computer science (**e-** = science of + **shinehal** = computer)

eshishid chemistry (**e** = science of + **shishid** = to unite)

eshon peace-science (**e-** = science of + **shon** = peace)

eshoná peace scientist (**eshon** = peace-science + **á** = suffix for doer)

eth to be about "**Bíl ril eth áabe hi babíth wa.**" "This book is about birds."

etham geometry (**e-** = science of + **tham** = circle)

éthe clean, to be clean, to make clean (See also: **háawithéthe, huhéthe, mudahéthe, onidahéthe, thóohéthe**)

éthedal vacuum cleaner (**éthe** = clean + **dal** = thing)

éthedale soap

éthehod washcloth (**éthe** = clean + **od** = cloth)

ethóo hospitality (**e-** = science of + **thóo** = guest)

ewith anthropology (**e-** = science of + **with** = person)

ewithá anthropologist (**e-** = science of + **with** = person + **-á** = suffix for doer)

ewithid science of males (**e-** = science of + **with** = person + **-id** = suffix for male)

ewomil animal husbandry (**e-** = science of + **womil** = livestock)

eyon administration (**e-** = science of + **yon** = government)

ezha snake

ezhab investigation (**e-** = science of + **zhab** = puzzles)

ezhabá investigator (**ezhab** = investigation + **-á** = suffix for doer)

ezhahith lightning bolt (**ezha** = snake + **ith** = light)

ezhazh aeronautics (**e-** = science of + **zhazh** = airplanes)

ezho acoustics (**e-** = science of + **zho** = sound)

h

háalemamid fawn (**háa-** = young + **lemamid** = deer)

háami thyme, the herb (**háa** = child + **mi** = leaf)

háamid young animal, child creature (**háa-** = child + **mid** = animal) (See also: **ámid, yáamid**)

háanáal evening (**háa** = young + **náal** = night)

háasháal morning (**háa** = young + **sháal** = day)

háawilidunedal tank (for liquid) (**háa** = child + **wili** = river + **dun** = field + **dal** = thing)

háawith child, youth, child person, general term for offspring (**háa-** = child + **with** = person) (See also: **áwith, yáawith**)

háawithá baby nurse (**áwith** = baby + **á-** = suffix for doer)

háawithéthe child-clean, the level of cleanliness at which a child considers her room "clean" (**háawith** = child + **éthe** = clean) (See also: **éthe, huhéthe, mudahéthe, onidahéthe, thóohéthe**)

háawithid boy child (**háawith** = child + **-id** = suffix for male)

habelid to live in, inhabit (**ha-** = suffix for place + **belid** = house)

habo coat

hada to fall

hadihad always

hahí to be ephemeral; to be brief (time)

hahod to be in a state of (STATE OF CONSCIOUSNESS MARKER)

- **hahod** being a neutral state of consciousness, serene)
- **hahodib** be deliberately shut off from all feelings, (**hahod** = state of + **-ib** = shut off)
- **hahodihed** be in shock, be numb (**hahod** = state of + **-ihed** = numb)
- **hahodimi** be in positive bewilderment/ astonishment (**hahod** = state of + **-imi** = bewilderment/ astonishment)
- **hahodimilh** be in negative bewilderment/ astonishment (**hahod** = state of + **-imilh** = bewilderment/ astonishment)

- **hahoditha** be linked empathically with another (**hahod** = state of + **-itha** = emphatically linked)
- **hahodiyon** be in ecstasy, be ecstatic (**hahod** = state of + **-iyon** = ecstasy)
- **hahodo** be in a meditative state (**hahod** = state of + **-o** = meditation)
- **hahodóo** be in hypnotic trance (**hahod** = state of + **-óo** = hypnotic trance)

hal work, to work

halá worker (**hal** = work + **-á** = suffix for doer)

halehadihahal work which is constantly being interrupted

halezhub ant (**hal** = work + (**e**)**zhub** = insect)

hali to work and identify as male

halid competition (**hali** = to work + **-id** = identify as male)

halith proposition, argument

ham to be present, attend, there is/there are (a) Mary Smith is present (or is here). (b) Mary Smith will attend the meeting tomorrow (or will be at the meeting tomorrow). (c) There is a tree beside the church or there are trees beside the church. A tree is (or trees are) present in this scene, beside the church.

han south

Haneshául Thursday (South Day) (**han** = south + (**e**)**sháal** = day)

hath time

hath boó thrice, on three occasions

hath menedebe often (**hath** = time + **menedebe** = many)

hath nede once, one occasion

hath nedebe seldom (**hath** = time + **nedebe** = few)

hath shin twice, two occasions

hath waha anytime (**hath** = time + **waha** = any)

hath woho every time, on every occasion

hathal to be good (said of time) (**hath** = time + **thal** = to be good)

hatham center (**tham** = circle)

Hathamesháal Sunday (Center Day) (**hatham** = center + (**e**)**sháal** = day)

hathehath forever, time everlasting (**hath** = time + (**e**)**hath** = time)

hatheril woman-time; marking the passage of time based on interpersonal relationships: births, deaths, relocations, marriages, etc.; "Mary was pregnant with her second when…," "Just about the time the tribe moved to…" (**hath** = time + **eril** = past) (See also: **hatherilid**)

hatherilid man-time; marking the passage of time based on important sporting events, wars, conquests, major disasters; the way time is marked in most late 20th century "history" books. (**hath** = time + **eril** = past + **-id** = male) (See also: **hatheril**)

hathobéeya until

hathóol month (**hath** = time + **óol** = moon)

hathóoletham year (**hathóol** = month + **tham** = circle) Literally, circle of months

háya to be beautiful (said of time) (**áya** = to be beautiful)

heb down, the direction

hed glass (for drinking)

héda to drop, spill, let fall (**héedá** = to pick up, lift up)

héeda to be sacred, holy

héedá to pick up, lift up (**héda** = to drop, let fall)

héedan to translate (**dan** = language)

héedarana sacred drink, to drink sacred drink (**héeda** = sacred + **rana** = drink)

héena sibling of the heart (**hena** = sibling by birth)

héeya fear, to fear, to be afraid

héeyasholan alone with terror (**héeya** = be afraid + **sholan** = be alone)

hem underwear

hemen bush

hena sibling by birth (**héena** = sibling of the heart)

hene east

Henesháal Monday (East Day) (**hene** = east + **sháal** = day)

hesh grass

heshedon rake, to rake (**hesh** = grass + (**e**)**don** = comb)

heshehoth park (**hesh** = grass + (**e**)**hoth** = place)

hesho to surpass (used in comparatives), exceed

heth dowry

heyi pain

hezh lemon (**hizh** = lime)

hi this, that (DEMONSTRATIVE PRONOUN: SINGULAR)

hib ovary

hibid testicle

hibo hill (**híya** = small + **bo** = mountain)

hibomid camel (**hibo** = hill; **mid** = creature)

hidel ham radio (**híya** = small + **del** = radio)

hihath now, right now, right this instant (**hi** = this + **hath** = time)

hin these, those (DEMONSTRATIVE PRONOUN: MANY)

hinal thus (**hi** = this, that + **-nal** = suffix for manner)

hinethed those (many, far) (DEMONSTRATIVE PRONOUN: MANY) (**hin** = these/those, many + **thed** = be far) (See also: **núuhin**)

hinethoma these (many, near) (DEMONSTRATIVE PRONOUN) (**hin** = these, those, many + **thoma** = be near) (See also: **nuhin**)

hish snow

hishud hail (**hish** = snow + **ud** = stone)

hithed that (PRONOUN: SINGULAR) (**hi** = this/that + **thed** = far) (See also: **nuhi**)

hithoma this (DEMONSTRATIVE PRONOUN: SINGULAR) (**hi** = this/that + **thoma** = near)

hiwetha left (direction) (**hi** = this + **weth** = way + **a** = leftward)

hiwetho right (direction) (**hi** = this + **weth** = way + **o** = rightward)

híya to be small

híyahath week (**híya** = small + **hath** = time)

híyamesh narrow (**híya** = small + **mesh** = across)

hizh these, those (DEMONSTRATIVE PRONOUN: SEVERAL)

hizh lime (**hezh** = lemon)

hizhethed those several (DEMONSTRATIVE PRONOUN: SEVERAL) (**hizh** = these/those + (**e**)**thed** = to be far) (See also: **núuhizn**)

hizhethoma these several (DEMONSTRATIVE PRONOUN: SEVERAL) (**hizh** = these/those, several + (**e**)**thoma** = to be near) (See also: **nuhizh**)

hob butter

hoberídan great-aunt (**ho** = grand, ancestor + **berídan** = aunt)

hod stomach

hoda apology, pardon me, phrase to indicate that you regret whatever it is that you find yourself obliged to do—like interrupting someone (See also: **hóoda**)

hodáath bowels (**hod** = stomach + **áath** = door), intestines

hodo tulip

hohal office, workplace (**hal** = to work)

hohama glory

hohathad all-power, omnipotence (without the feature "male")

holanemid wolf (noun) (**ho-** = grand-; ancestor + **lanemid** = dog)

hom nectar

homana dessert, nectar food (**hom** = nectar + **ana** = food)

homeyu nectarine (**hom** = nectar + **yu** = fruit)

hon west

honáal hours between midnight and dawn

Honesháal Tuesday (West Day); (**hon** = west + **sháal** = day)

hóo mattress

hóoda apology, excuse me, phrase to indicate that you need to leave a particular location (See also: **hoda**)

hóowith granddaughter (**ho** = ancestor + **háawith** = child)

hóowithid grandson (**hóowith** + **-id** = suffix for male)

hosh feather

hosherídan great-niece (**ho** = ancestor + **sherídan** = niece)

hoth place

hoth waha anywhere (**hoth** = place + **waha** = any)

hothal to be good (said of a place)

hothul grandmother (**ho** = ancestor + **thul** = parent)

hothulewoth "momilies," some piece of knowledge or lore that has been passed from mother to daughter for at least two generations (**hothul** = grandmother + **woth** = wisdom)

hóya to be beautiful (said of a place) (**hoth** = place + **áya** = to be beautiful)

hoyo tail

hozhazh airport (**hoth** = place + **zhazh** = airplane)

hu ruler, boss

hubod edge (sharp) (**hum** = knife + **bod** = line)

huhéthe boss-clean, probably the highest level of cleaning you would need (**hu** = boss + (**h**)**éthe**) (See also: **éthe**, **háawithéthe**, **mudahéthe**, **onidahéthe**, **thóohéthe**)

huhid king (**hu** = ruler + -(**h**)**id** = male)

hulehul for sure (an emphatic, strong positive) (-**hul** = suffix denoting to an extreme degree)

hum knife

huma to be sharp

humazho whistle, to whistle (**huma** = sharp + **zho** = sound)

humazhomid guinea pig (**humazho** = whistle + **mid** = creature)

humesh to cut (**hum** = knife + **mesh** = across)

hun north

Hunesháal Wednesday (North Day) (**hun** = north + **sháal** = day)

husháana to mensruate painfully (**osháana** = to menstruate)

huthil kudzu (**hu** = ruler + **thil** = vine)

húumid owl (**húu** (ONOMATOPOEIA) + **mid** = creature)

i

i and

ib crime

ib against

ibádi to accuse (**ib** = crime + **á** = suffix for doer + **di** = speak)

ibálh criminal (**ib** = crime + **á** = suffix for doer + **lh** = negative connotation)

ibath to scratch (not said of scratching an itch) (**ib** = against + **bath** = fingernail)

ibáyóodi to confess (literally: to accuse oneself) (**ib** = crime + **á** = suffix for doer + -**yóo**- = reflexive (-self) + **di** = speak)

ibo to exhaust oneself, exhaustion

ibolh to exhaust with negative connotation, exhaustion

iboshara burnout (**ibo** - exhaust + **shara** = grief with cause, blame, but futile)

iboth scratch (noun)

id and then

idon brush (for hair)

ihé before (in space), in front of (**ihée** = after)

ihée after (in space), behind, beyond (**ihé** = before)

íi also

íizha although

il to see, to pay attention to, to attend to. (See also: **láad** = to perceive; **lohil** = to pay attention internally; **lo** = internal; **(h)il** = pay attention)

ilá spectator, audience member (**il** = pay attention + **á** = suffix for doer)

ílhi disgust (**lh** = negative connotation)

ílhilh disgust with pejorative overtones, disgust and disapproval (**lh** = negative connotation)

ili water

ilihede rice (**ili** = water + **ede** = grain)

ilimeda lettuce (**ili** = water + **meda** = vegetable)

ilisháad swim, to swim (**ili** = water + **sháad** = to come, to go)

iliwush mop (**ili** = water + **wush** = broom)

iliyeb urine (**ili** = water + **yeb** = kidney)

il óoyonan pay attention using the mouth, attentive tasting. (See also: **lóoyo**)

il oyanan pay attention using the skin, attentive feeling

il oyinan pay attention using the eyes, watch, look at

il oyonan pay attention using the nose, sniff, attentive smelling. (See also: **shu**)

il oyunan pay attention using the ears, listen (See also: **ma lohil**[1] = pay attention internally)

ilu hose (for liquids)

iluli blood vessel

im to travel

imedim suitcase (**im** = travel + **(e)dim** = container)

in to exist

ina sleep, to sleep (synonym: **áana**)

inad trousers, pants

ishid digit (fingers, toes)

ishida gloves, mittens, socks, stockings (**ishid** = digit (finger, toe)

ishidi to chatter (**ishish** = fidget + **di** = speak)

---

[1] Note: organ of perception for internal attention is assumed and would not be presented in an INSTRUMENT CASE phrase.

ishish to fidget

ith light

ithedal lamp, light, light-making object (**ith** = light + **dal** = thing)

íthi to be high, tall

izh but

l

la I (PRONOUN: 1ST PERSON: SINGULAR) beloved

láa perception (**láad** = to perceive)

láad to perceive (**láa** = perception) (See also **il**, to pay attention to)

láad óoyonan to perceive using the mouth, to taste. Perceptive tasting. "The dinner tastes good to me." (See also: **lóoyo**, attentive tasting)

láad oyanan to perceive using the skin, to feel something on your skin, touch. Perceptive feeling. "The silk feels good to me." (See also: **dama**, attentive touching)

láad oyinan to perceive using the eyes, to see, to look. Perceptive seeing. "I see the flower." (See also: **il**, attentive seeing)

láad oyonan to perceive using the nose, to smell. Perceptive smelling. "The candle smells good to me." (See also: **shu**, attentive smelling)

láad oyunan to perceive using the ears, to hear. Perceptive hearing. "The band sounds good to me." (See also: **ma**, attentive listening)

láadá perceiver, the one who perceives (**láad** = perceive + **á** = suffix for doer)

Láadan (perception language)

láadom to recognize (**láa** = perception + **dom** = remember)

láahomá perception teacher (**láa** = perception + (**h**)**omá** = teacher)

láashod meditation room, perception room, room where one goes to meditate and attain new perceptions of the world and oneself (**láa** = perception + **shod** = room)

ladinime to interact, interacting

laheb spice

Lahila Holy-One, Deity

lal milk

lalal mother's milk

lalen guitar

lalewida to be pregnant joyfully (**lawida** = to be pregnant)

lali rain, to rain (**ili** = water)

lalidáan poem (**lali** = rain + **dáan** = word)

lalidáaná poet (**lalidáan** = poem + **á** = suffix for doer)

lalilom sound of rain on the roof (**lali** = rain + **lom** = song)

lalimilom sound of rain on leaves (**lali** = rain + **mi** = leaf + **lom** = song)

lalom to sing

lam health

lámáhel to sculpt, carve (**lámala** = to caress + **el** to make)

lámála to caress, stroke

lami number, numeral

lamith to count

lamithá accountant (**lamith** = to count + **á** = suffix for doer)

lan We (PRONOUN: 1ST PERSON: MANY) beloved (See also **la**)

lan friend

lanemid dog (**lan** = friend + **mid** = creature)

lash indifference

lath to be celibate by choice (See also **ralath** = celibate, not by choice)

lawida to be pregnant

lawith saint (**Lahila** = Holy-One + **with** = person)

laya to be red

layun to be orange

lazh we (PRONOUN: 1ST PERSON: SEVERAL) beloved

le I (PRONOUN: 1ST PERSON: SINGULAR) neutral

leb enemy

led harmony in the home (See also **lhed** = discord in the home)

lée- meta- (prefix)

léeli jonquil, daffodil, narcissus

lehina lilac (the flower, bush)

lel seaweed

léli to be yellow

lelith algae

lema to be gentle

lemadama to cuddle (**lema** = gentle + **dama** = touch)

lemamid deer (**lema** = gentle + **mid** = creature)

lemamidid stag, male deer (**lema** = gentle + **mid** = creature + **-id** = male)

len we (PRONOUN: 1ST PERSON: MANY) neutral

lenedi to us (**len** = 1ST PERSON, MANY NEUTRAL + **-(e)di** = GOAL CASE MARKER)

leneth us (many) (PRONOUN. 1ST PERSON, MANY, NEUTRAL, OBJECT) (**len** = 1ST PERSON, MANY NEUTRAL + **-(e)th** = OBJECT CASE MARKER)

lenetha our (by reason of birth) (**len** = we-many + **-(e)tha** = POSESSIVE SUFFIX, by reason of birth)

lenetho our (**len** = we-many + **-(e)tho** = POSESSIVE SUFFIX, other)

lenethoth our (other, object) (**len** = 1ST PERSON, MANY NEUTRAL + **-(e)tho** = POSSESSIVE (other) + **-th** = OBJECT CASE MARKER)

leth me (PRONOUN, 1ST PERSON, SINGULAR, NEUTRAL, OBJECT) (**le** = I + **-th** = OBJECT MARKER)

lewidan to be pregnant for the first time (**lawida** = to be pregnant)

leyan to be brown

leyi to be blue

leyidalatham blueberry (**leyi** = blue + **dala** = plant + **tham** = circle)

leyóo myself (1ST PERSON, SINGULAR, NEUTRAL, REFLEXIVE PRONOUN)

leyóon ourselves (1ST PERSON, MANY, NEUTRAL, REFLEXIVE PRONOUN)

leyóozh ourselves (1ST PERSON, SEVERAL, NEUTRAL, REFLEXIVE PRONOUN)

lezh we (PRONOUN, 1ST PERSON, SEVERAL, NEUTRAL)

> Words beginning with **lh** can be found listed under the Láadan letter **lh** which follows **l**.

li I (PRONOUN, 1ST PERSON, SINGULAR, HONORED)

líithi to be white

líithin to be gray

lila to female-sexual-act

lilahá lover (female only, not used to refer to males) (**lila** = to female-sexual-act + **-á** = suffix for doer)

lilathun massage (noun and verb)

lili to be wet (**ili** = water)

liliháaláa labia majora and minora (**lili** + **áalaá**) (See also: **owo** = labia)

limlim bell (ONOMATOPOEIA)

lin we (PRONOUN, 1ST PERSON, MANY, HONORED)

liri to be colored, to have color

lirini[1] an achievement that seems small to others, but means a lot to the achiever

---
[1] No English equivalent.

lish to lightning

lishenal vividly (**lish** = lightning + (**e**)**nal** = suffix for manner)

lishid to sign (as in ASL)

lishidá signer (as in ASL) (**lishid** = to sign + **-á** = suffix for doer)

lith to think

litharil anticipate, think about the future (**lith** = to think + **aril** = future)

litheril reminisce, think about the past (**lith** = to think + **eril** = past)

lithewil hypothesis (**lith** = to think + **Wil…** = Let there be)

liyen to be green

lizh we (PRONOUN, 1ST PERSON, SEVERAL, HONORED)

lo to rejoice

lob to fill, fill up

lod household

lodá householder, housewife, househusband

lóda to be pregnant wearily (**lawida** = to be pregnant)

lodáhid male householder

lohil to pay attention to, internally (**lo** = internal + (**h**)**il** = pay attention to

lol a feeling of: community, togetherness, sisterhood, fellowship, belonging, cohesiveness; a group of people gathered with the intention of creating togetherness, sisterhood, fellowship, belonging, community, cohesiveness; different from a city or a general gathering of people because "**lol**" implies an intention to create a feeling of cohesiveness within the group. (See also: **lolh**)

loláad to perceive internally, to feel a mental state or emotion, perceive with the heart (metaphorically).

loláad lhohoth to be ashamed, to perceive one's shame (**loláad** = to perceive internally + **lhoho** = shame + **-th** = suffix for object)

loláad óoyanan to sense, be aware of

lolehoth a community place, building and grounds of a place intended to nurture the needs of the people who belong (**lol** = community + (**e**)**hoth** = place)

lolh an oppressive "**lol**"; a negative sense of community, togetherness, sisterhood, fellowship, belonging, cohesiveness; you "belong" but to your severe detriment, for instance being forced to give up valued aspects of yourself to be accepted by the community. (See also: **lol**)

lolin to gather, assemble; gathering, assembly (said of people)

lolin rocking chair

lom song

lóolo to be slow

lóothi[1] to be black and white

lóoyo to taste. To pay attention, using the mouth. "I am tasting the batter." (See also: **láad óoyonan**, perceive using the mouth)

lorolo thunder

losh credit, money

loshá banker (**losh** = money + **-á** = suffix for doer)

loshebelid bank (financial) (**losh** = money + **belid** = house)

loshehalid auction (**losh** = money + **halid** = competition)

loth information

lothel to know (not of people) (**loth** = information)

lowitheláad to feel, as if directly, another's feelings (pain/joy/anger/grief/surprise/etc.); to be empathetic, without the separation implied in empathy (**loláad** = to perceive internally + **with** = person)

loyada to yearn, yearn for (**lo** = internal + **yada** = thirst)

loyan intuition (**lo** = internal + **yan** = analysis)

loyo to be black

loyodalatham blackberry (**loyo** = black + **dala** = plant + **tham** = circle)

loyu to be dark-colored

lu please, polite phrase

lub poultry, fowl (chicken, duck, goose)

luben map

lud debt

ludá debtor, person in debt

ludi to be female

ludihă female (noun)

luhili blood

lul vagina

lula to be purple

lulin cradle (**lul** = vagina)

lush mystery

---

[1] Polar opposites

Lushede deity, goddess (informal address)

luth to rock (of babies)

lúul guardian

luwili birth-blood

lh

lha sin (**lh** = negative connotation)

lháada to smirk (**lh-** = pejorative + **áada** = smile)

lhada to laugh at, to scorn, to ridicule; scorn, ridicule (**lh-** = pejorative + **ada** = laugh)

lheb enemy, with pejorative overtones (**leb** = enemy + **lh** = negative overtones)

lhebe hatred

lhebe she/it/he (PRONOUN, 3RD PERSON, SINGULAR, DESPISED)

lheben they (PRONOUN, 3RD PERSON, MANY, DESPISED)

lhebezh they (PRONOUN, 3RD PERSON, SEVERAL, DESPISED)

lhed discord in the home (**lh** = negative connotation + **lod** = household)

lhele I (PRONOUN, 1ST PERSON, SINGULAR, DESPISED)

lhelen we (PRONOUN, 1ST PERSON, MANY, DESPISED)

lhelezh we (PRONOUN, 1ST PERSON, SEVERAL, DESPISED)

lhene you (PRONOUN, 2ND PERSON, SINGULAR, DESPISED)

lhenen you (PRONOUN, 2ND PERSON, MANY, DESPISED)

lhenezh you (PRONOUN, 2ND PERSON, SEVERAL, DESPISED)

lhezhub noxious insect (**lh** = negative connotation + **zhub** = insect)

ihith fret, have bad thought and feelings about something in the present (**lith** = think + **lh-** perjorative)

ihitharil worry, dread; have bad thoughts and feelings about something that will or may happen in the future (**ihith** = fret + **aril** = future)

ihitheril guilt; have bad thoughts and feelings about something in the past (**ihith** = fret + **eril** = past)

lhobom to rape (**ihoho** = shame + **bom** = penis) (See also: **ralh**)

lhoho shame (**lh** = negative connotation)

lhu poison, to poison (**lh** = negative connotation)

lhud debt, with pejorative overtones (**lh** = negative connotation + **lud** = debt)

m

ma to hear, to listen, to listen to. Attentive hearing. "I am listening for the buzzer." Synonym: **il oyunan** = pay attention using ears. (See also: **láad oyunan** = to hear, perceive using ears, perceptive hearing)

máa egg

máan salt

máanan to be salty

mad to hide an emotion or aspect of self (mirror image of **dam**)

madoni to plant (**mad** = hide-aspect + **doni** = earth)

maha desire (sexual)

mahanal desiringly, lustfully (*not* a negative term) (**maha** = desire (sexual) + **-nal** = suffix for manner)

mahela creative urge (**maha** = sexual desire + **el** = to make)

mahin cooking pot

mahina flower

mal nut-tree

malu salt marsh

mar absence, to be absent

maradal hole, gap (**mar** = absence + **radal** = nothing)

mari island

math building

mathom knick-knack, useless object (Tolkien loanword)

Mathul Mother, Mom (intimate informal term, but not Mama) (**ma** = to listen + **thul** = parent) (See also: **Emath**, **Shathul**)

mazh car, automobile

meda vegetable

medalayun carrot (**meda** = vegetable + **layun** = orange)

meén sugar

meénan to be sweet

meéná sweetener (**meénan** = to be sweet + **-á** = suffix for doer)

méesh pleasure (not said of sexual pleasure)

méeshim pleasure (sexual)

méhéna compassion despite negative circumstances (**ména, mína, móna, múna** = compassion)

mel paper

mela ocean, sea (**me-** = implies greater weight or size or importance + **ili** = water)

meláanin birch tree (**mel** = paper + **yáanin** = tree)

melahá ocean-dweller (**mela** = ocean + **-á** = suffix for doer)

meloth evidence (**me-** = implies greater weight or size or importance + **loth** = information)

memazh train (**mazh** = car + **me-** = implies greater weight or size or importance)

ména compassion for good reasons (**méhéna, mína, móna, múna** = compassion)

menedebe to be many (**me-** = implies greater weight or size or importance (QUANTIFIER) + **nedebe** = to be few) Never change form or add CASE MARKER.

menedebenil among (many) (**menedebe** = many + **nil** = inside)

menedebosh bundle of sticks, faggot (noun) (**me-** = plural + **nedebosh** = stick)

merod billion (1,000,000,000) (**me-** = implies greater weight or size or importance + **rod** = million (1,000,000))

mesh across

methid rope (**me-** = plural marker + **thid** = string)

méwith crowd (**me-** = implies greater weight or size or importance + **with** = person)

mezh powder

mezhel to grind (**mezh** = powder + **el** = to create)

mi leaf, as in leaf of a tree, not a page in a book

mid creature, any animal

midemath stable (**mid** = creature + **math** = building)

miháabe page (of book) (**mi** = leaf + **(h)áabe** = book)

mihí to be small (area)

míi amazement, to be amazed

míili radiance (**míi** = to be amazed)

mime to ask

miméne coverings, bedding

min eating utensil

mina to move

mína compassion for no reason (**ména, méhéna, móna, múna** = compassion)

minidibi et cetera

miwith town, city (**with** = person)

miwithá city-dweller (**miwith** = city + **-á** = suffix for doer)

mo furniture

modem modem (loanword)

modi to be ugly

móna compassion for foolish reasons (**méhéna, ména, mína, múna** = compassion)

mud mushroom

muda pig

mudahéthe pig-clean, the state of your teenager's room, to be used when teenager says "It's clean, mom!," and mom responds "Well, yeah, pig-clean!" (with apologies to poor slandered pigs, who we know are very clean animals) (**muda** = pig + **(h)éthe** = clean) (See also: **éthe**, **háawithéthe**, **huhéthe**, **onidahéthe**, **thóohéthe**)

muhum scissors (**hum** = knife + mirror image)

múna compassion for bad reasons (**méhéna**, **ména**, **mína**, **móna** = compassion)

n

na you (PRONOUN, 2ND PERSON, SINGULAR, BELOVED)

náal night

nab bramble

náheb to decrease (**ná** = to continue + **heb** = go down)

nahin[1] to become (**na** = to start to + **in** = exist)

nan you (PRONOUN, 2ND PERSON, MANY, BELOVED)

---

[1] Usage note: The subject of **nahin** is the thing/person that bcomes something else, and the thing the subject becomes is given in the IDENTIFIER CASE, e.g., "**Bíi aril nahin le omá wumaneya wa.**" "I shall become a teacher in the summer."

nanáal sunset (**na** = to start to + **náal** = night)

náraheb to increase (**ná** + **raheb**)

nárilim to quest internally

nasháal dawn, sunrise (**na** = to start to + **sháal** = day)

nath price

natha your (PRONOUN, 2ND PERSON, SINGULAR, BELOVED, BY REASON OF BIRTH) (**na** = 2nd person, singular, beloved + **-tha** = possessive by reason of birth)

nathá buyer (professional)

náwí grow, growth (**ná-** = continue to + **wí** = life)

naya to take care of, nurture

nayadi blessing, general term (**naya** = take care of + **di** = to speak)

nayadithal encourage, to provide encouragement

nayahá care-giver, caretaker of people (**naya** = to take care of + **-á** = suffix for doer)

nazh you (PRONOUN, 2ND PERSON, SEVERAL, BELOVED)

ne you (PRONOUN, 2ND PERSON, SINGULAR, NEUTRAL)

neda only

nede one (1)

néde to want

nedebe (QUANTIFIER) to be few, to be several (but not many) (NEVER CHANGE FORM OR ADD CASE MARKER)

nedebenil among (few/several) (**nedebe** = few/several + **nil** = inside)

nedebosh walking stick, cane (noun) (**nede** = one + **bosh** = wood)

nedeloth fact (**nede** = one + **loth** = information)

nédeshub intent (**néde** = to want + **shub** = to do)

nédeshubel motivation (**nédeshub** = to want + **el** = to make)

nedethab eleven (11) (**nede** = one (1) + **thab** = 10)

nedeya first (**nede** = one + **-ya** = suffix for time)

née to be alien

néehá alien (**née** = to be alien + **-á** = suffix for doer)

nehena contentment despite negative circumstances (**nena, nina, nona, nuna** = contentment)

nem pearl

nemeháalish clitoris (**nem** = pearl + **háalish** = DEGREE MARKER, to an extraordinary degree)

nen you (PRONOUN, 2ND PERSON, MANY, NEUTRAL)

nena contentment for good reasons (**nehena, nina, nona, nuna** = contentment)

neneth you (many) (PRONOUN, 2ND PERSON, MANY, NEUTRAL, OBJECT) (**nen** = you + **-th** = OBJECT MARKER)

neril wait, to wait

neth you (PRONOUN, 2ND PERSON, SINGULAR, NEUTRAL, OBJECT) (**ne** = you + **-th** = OBJECT MARKER)

neyóo yourself (PRONOUN, 2ND PERSON, SINGULAR, NEUTRAL) (**ne** = you + **-yóo** = REFLEXIVE MARKER)

neyóon yourselves (many) (PRONOUN, 2ND PERSON, MANY, NEUTRAL) (**nen** = you, many + **-yóo** = REFLEXIVE MARKER)

neyóozh yourselves (several) (PRONOUN, 2ND PERSON, SEVERAL, NEUTRAL) (**nezh** = you, several + **-yóo** = REFLEXIVE MARKER)

nezh you (PRONOUN, 2ND PERSON, SEVERAL, NEUTRAL)

nezheth you (several) (PRONOUN. 2ND PERSON, SEVERAL, NEUTRAL, OBJECT) (**nezh** = you + **-th** = OBJECT MARKER)

ni you (PRONOUN, 2ND PERSON, SINGULAR, HONORED)

ni cup

nib eight (8)

nibethab eighteen (18) (**nib** = 8 + **thab** = 10)

nil inside

nilewod tampon (**nil** = inside + **wod** = cloth)

niloma palm of the hand (**nil** = inside + **loma** = hand)

nime be willing, will (NOT FUTURE TENSE)

nin you (PRONOUN, 2ND PERSON, MANY, HONORED)

nin to cause, causal

nina contentment for no reason (**nehena, nena, nona, nuna** = contentment)

niná the one responsible (**nin** = to cause + **-á** = suffix for doer)

ninálh the one to blame (**niná** = the one responsible + **lh** = negative connotation)

nish weed

nith frost

nithedim refrigerator (**nith** = frost + **dim** = container)

nithedimethóo refrigerator guest, a guest who shows up unannounced, comes on in and helps herself to whatever's in the fridge—and that's a good thing. (**nithedim** = refrigerator + (**e**)**thóo** = guest) (See also: **thóo, áathethóo, shineshidethóo, widadithethóo**)

nizh you (PRONOUN, 2ND PERSON, SEVERAL, HONORED)

nodal edge (non-sharp)

nohadal to hem (**no** = to finish, complete + (**h**)**adal** = sew)

nohodáath rectum (**no-** = to finish + **hodáath** = bowels)

nol on, upon

noline angel

nolob to become full (**no-** = prefix implies completion + **lob** = to fill up, to fill)

nona contentment for foolish reasons (**nehena, nena, nina, nuna** = contentment)

nonede a, the final one, the last one (**no-** = prefix implies completion + **nede** = one, 1)

nóowid[1] to be big and little

nori to send

---

[1] Polar opposites form.

nosháad arrival, to arrive (**no-** = prefix implies completion + **sháad** = to come, go)

notháa to cease to thrive (**no-** = prefix implies completion + **tháa** = to thrive, to do well)

nu here

nub mode

núháam to feel oneself cherished, cared for, nurtured by someone

nuhi this (**nu** = here + **hi** = this/that) (See also: **hithoma**)

nuhin these, many (**nu** = here + **hin** = these/those, many) (See also: **hinethoma**)

nuhizh these, several (**nu** = here + **hizh** = these/those, several) (See also **hizhethonma**)

nuthul orphan (**thul** = parent)

núu there (**nu** = here)

núuhi that (**núu** = there + **hi** = this/that) (See also: **hithed**)

núuhin those, many (**núu** = there + **hin** = these/those, many) (See also: **hinethed**)

núuhizh those, several (**núu** = there + **hizh** = these/those, several) (See also: hizhethed)

nuna contentment for bad reasons (**nehena, nena, nina, nona** = contentment)

O

o around

oba body

obadom to body-remember (like remembering how to ride a bicycle) (**oba** = body + **dom** = remember)

obahéda bodily secretion (**oba** = body + **héda** = to drop or fall)

obahéthe a clean body, to clean one's body (**oba** = body + **(h)éthe** = clean) (See also: **obahéthewod, obahéthethib**)

obahéthethib shower, to take a shower (**oba** = body + **(h)éthe** = clean + **thib** = stand) (See also: **obahéthe, obahéthewod**)

obahéthewod bath, to take a bath, bathe (**oba** = body + **(h)éthe** = clean + **wod** = sit) (See also: **obahéthe, obahéthethib**)

obe through

obed cause, reason

obedi to learn a skill, to body-learn (**oba** = body + **bedi** = learn)

obée during (I work during the night. = **Bíi hal le náaleya obée wa.**)

obeham altar

obeth neighbor

obeyal gold

obom condom (**o** = around + **bom** = penis)

obuda study of Budah (without worship)

obudahá student of **obuda**

od cloth

oda arm (the body part)

odá weaver

odama lip, lips (of the mouth)

odámála to caress with the lips, kiss (**odama** = lips + **lámála** = caress)

odayáaninetha branch (**oda** = arm + **yáanin** = tree + **-tha** = suffix for possession by reason of birth)

odith tongue (**o** = around + **dith** = voice)

odithámála to caress with the tongue (**odith** = tongue + **lámála** = caress)

odobeyal cloth-of-gold (**od** = cloth + **obeyal** = gold)

ódon cheese

oham love for that which is holy

ohamedi prayer (**oham** = love for that which is holy + **di** = to say, speak)

ohehena respect despite negative circumstances (**ohena**, **ohina**, **ohona**, **ohuna** = respect)

ohena respect for good reasons (**ohehena, ohina, ohona, ohuna** = respect)

ohina respect for no reason (See also: ohena, ohehena, ohona, ohuna = respect)

Oho You're welcome (polite phrase)

ohona respect for foolish reasons (**ohena, ohena, ohina, ohuna** = respect)

ohuna respect for bad reasons (**ohehena, ohena, ohina, ohona** = respect)

ol to store

olanin to practice (**oba** = body + **ulanin** = study)

olim paradise, heaven

olimeha in heaven (**olim** = heaven + **-(e)ha** = PLACE CASE MARKER)

olin forest, woods

olob blow, trauma; to harm, to injure, to strike, to hit

olobeshara depression as result of major trauma (**olob** = trauma + **(e)shara** = grief)

oloth skill

olowod group

om to teach

oma hand

omá teacher (**om** = to teach + **-á** = suffix for doer)

omamid ape (**oma** = hand + **mid** = creature)

omid horse (**mid** = creature)

on head

ona face (the body part)

onabel mask, to mask (**ona** = face + **bel** = bring/take)

onahina pansy (**ona** = face + **mahina** = flower)

onelal cream (**on** = head + **lal** = milk)

onethud horn; antler (noun) (**on** = head + (**e**)**thud** = bone)

onida family

onidahéthe family-clean, the usual state of affairs (**onida** = family + (**h**)**éthe** = clean) (See also: **éthe, háawithéthe, huhéthe, mudahéthe, thóohéthe**)

onin nurse

oób to jump

óob oven

óobe along

óobuda Buddism, the religion

óobudahá Buddist

oódóo bridge

óoda leg

óoha to be tired, weary

óol moon

óoletham coven, worship circle (**óol** = moon + **tham** = circle)

óolewil menstrual blood (**óol** = moon + **luwili** = birth blood)

óolewod sanitary napkin (**óolewil** = menstrual blood + **od** = cloth)

óoloó moth (butterfly = **áalaá** pattern using moon = **óol**)

óom to mourn

óoma foot (the body part)

óomasháad walk; go on/by foot (**óoma** = foot + **sháad** = go/come)

óomi shoe (**óoma** = foot)

óosholan alone with grief (**óom** = grief + **sholan** = be alone)

óotha soul

óothadama rapport; also, to experience rapport (**óotha** + **dama**)

óothanuthul spiritual orphanhood, being utterly bereft of a spiritual community (**óotha** = soul + **nuthul** = orphan)

óothasháal regular self-time (daily, weekly, or monthly)

óowa fire

óowáanin redwood (**óowa** = fire + **yáanin** = tree)

óowabo volcano (**óowa** = fire + **bo** = mountain)

óowabobin volcanic crater (**óowabo** = volcano + **bin** = bowl)

óowamid dragon (**óowa** = fire + **mid** = creature)

óoya heart

óoyaáláan pulse, heartbeat (**óoya** = heart + **aáláan** = wave)

óoyaha oma palm of the hand (see also: **niloma**)

óoyahonetha mind (**óoya** = heart + **on** = head + **-tha** = suffix for possession by reason of birth)

óoyashául time of greatest energy each day (**óoya** = heart + **shául** = day)

óoyo mouth

óozh comset

óozhá comset technician (**óozh** = comset + **-á** = suffix for doer)

osh to weave

osháana to menstruate, menstrual, menstruation

oshetham wreath (**osh** = weave + (**e**)**tham** = circle)

oth to be important

Othe Amen, Selah, end of prayer phrase

othel to be blessed, holy

othelehoth blessed place (**othel** = blessed + (**e**)**hoth** = place)

owa to be warm, hot

owáano therefore

owahúuzh blanket (**owa** = to be warm + **úuzh** = bedding, covering)

owe dress, gown

owehid men's garment (**owe** = dress + **-id** = suffix for male)

owo labia

oya skin, flesh

oyabod outline, silhouette (**oya** = skin + **bod** = line)

oyada to itch (**oya** = skin + **yada** = be thirsty)

oyi eye

oyimahina violet

oyo nose

oyu ear

ozh dream, to dream

ozhi melon

R

ra no, not (INTERJECTION); to make a sentence negative, put "ra" right after the verb.

ra- anti-, as in forming opposites of words. (prefix)

ra- PREFIX non-

ráahedethi to be unable to feel **lowitheláad**, to be empathically impaired (**ra** = non- + **edethi** = to share)

ráahedethilh to be unwilling to feel **lowitheláad**; to be deliberately empathically impaired (**ráahedethi** = to be unable to feel **lowitheláad** + **lh** = negative connotation)

ráalehale to be musically or euphonically deprived, tone deaf (**ra** = non + **alehale** = music)

ráatham command room, for war; (**ra-** = non + **áatham** = church) literally, anti-church

rabalh to stink, reek (**ra** = non- + **aba** = fragrant + **lh** = negative connotation)

rabalin to be young (**ra** = non- + **balin** = to be old)

raban to take away from (**ra** = non- + **ban** = to give)

rabinilh gift with strings attached (**ra** = non- + **bini** = gift + **lh** = negative connotation)

rabo plain, ground foundation (**ra** = non- + **bo** = mountain)

rabobosh floor (**ra** = non- + **bo** = mountain + **bosh** = wood)

rabohí to be long (length)

raboósh straight, to be straight (**ra** = not + **bóosh** = curved)

rad node

radal nothing (**ra** = non- + **dal** = thing)

radama to non-touch, avoiding touch, to actively refrain from touching (**ra** = non- + **dama** = to touch)

radamalh to non-touch with evil intent (**radama** = to non-touch + **lh** = negative connotation)

radazh to be hard, firm (**ra** = non + **dazh** = soft, pliant)

radéela non-garden, a place that has much flash and glitter and ornament, but no beauty (**ra** = non- + **déela** = garden)

raden without, accompanied by/with no one/nothing (when following a noun), without X (**ra** = non + **den** = ASSOCIATE CASE)

radena unfriendliness for good reasons (**ra** = non- + **dena** = friendliness for good reasons) (See also: **radehena, radina, radona, raduna** = unfriendliness)

radozh difficult (**ra** = non + **dozh** = be easy)

radiídin non-holiday, holiday more work than it's worth, a time allegedly a holiday but actually so much a burden because of work and preparations that it is a dreaded occasion; especially when there are too many guests and none of them help. (**ra** = non + **diídin** = holiday)

radimil plain, simple, unadorned (**ra** = not + **dimil** = lavish)

radina unfriendliness for no reason (**ra** = non- + **dina** = friendliness for no reason) (See also: **radehena, radena, radona, raduna** = unfriendliness)

rado to be weak (**ra** = non- + **do** = to be strong)

radodelh non-interface, a situation which has not one single point in common on which to base interaction, often used of personal relationships (**ra** = non- + **dodel** = interface + **lh** = negative connotation)

radona unfriendliness for foolish reasons (**ra** = non- + **dona** = friendliness for foolish reasons) (See also: **radehena, radena, radina, raduna** = unfriendliness)

raduna unfriendliness for bad reasons (**ra** = non- + **duna** = friendliness for bad reasons) (See also: **radehena, radena, radina, radona** = unfriendliness)

raduth to non-use, to deliberately deprive someone of any useful function in the world, as in enforced retirement or when a human being is kept as a plaything or a pet (**ra** = non- + **duth** = to use)

radutha to not-heal, medicine or treatment which does not heal (**ra** = non + **dutha** = heal)

raduthahá not-healer

raduthahálh non-healer with evil intent

raháana insomnia (**ra** = non- + **áana** = sleep)

rahabelhid to exile (**ra** = non- + **habelid** = to dwell + **ih** = negative connotation)

rahabelhidá an exile, outcast (**rahabelhid** – to exile + **-á** – suffix for doer)

rahdiha never (**ra** = non- + **hadihad** = always)

rahahí to be temporally extensive; to be long-lived (time)

rahana 1) famine (**ra** = non- + **ana** = food); 2) junk food

rahath never (**ra** = non + **hath** = time)

raheb up (**ra** = non- + **heb** = down)

raheb to hoard; a hoard (**ra** = non- + **(h)eb** = to buy, sell)

rahed gadget, useless non-tool (**ra** = non- + **(h)ed** = tool)

rahéeda accursed, unholy, to be accursed, to be unholy (**ra** = non- + **héeda** = to be sacred)

rahéedan to mistranslate (**ra** = non- + **héedan** = to translate)

rahéelhedan to deliberately mistranslate with evil intent (**rahéedan** = to mistranslate + **lh** = negative connotation)

rahéena non-heart-sibling, one so entirely incompatible with another that there is no hope of ever achieving any kind of understanding or anything more than a truce, and no hope of ever making such a one understand why (does not mean "enemy") (**ra** = non- + **héena** = sibling of the heart)

rahen to misunderstand, misunderstanding (**ra** = not + **(h)en** = understand)

rahesh to be irresponsible (**ra** = non- + **áhesh** = to be responsible)

rahéthe to be dirty (**ra** = non- + **éthe** = to be clean)

rahib non-crime, a terrible thing done because it's necessary but for which there is no blame because there is no choice (never an accident) (**ra** = non- + **ib** = crime)

rahil to non-attend, ignore, withhold attention (**ra** = non- + **il** = pay attention to)

rahilh to non-attend, ignore, withhold attention with evil intent (**rahil** = to withhold attention + **lh** = negative connotation)

rahith darkness (**ra** = non- + **ith** = light)

rahíya to be big, large (**ra** = non- + **híya** = to be small)

rahíyamesh wide (**ra** = not + **híyamesh** = narrow)

rahobeth non-neighbor, one who lives nearby but does not fulfill a neighbor's role (not necessarily pejorative) (**ra** = non + **obeth** = neighbor)

rahobeyal fool's gold (**ra** = non- + **obeyal** = gold)

rahol to waste, squander (**ra** = non- + **ol** = to store)

rahom to non-teach, to deliberately fill students' minds with empty data or false information; (can be used only of persons in a teacher/student relationship); (**ra** = non- + **om** = to teach)

rahoth nowhere (**ra** = non- + **hoth** = place)

rahowa to be cold (**ra** = non- + **owa** = to be warm)

rahu to be closed (**ra** = non- + **u** = to be open)

rahub irritant substance (**ra** = non- + **ub** = balm)

rahulh slave (**ra** = non- + **hu** = ruler + **lh** = negative connotation)

raláad to non-perceive (**ra** = non- + **láad** = to perceive)

raláadá non-perceiver; one who fails to perceive (**raláad** = to non-perceive + **-á** = suffix for doer)

raláadálh non-perceiver, one who fails to perceive deliberately and with evil intent (**raláadá** = non-perceiver + **lh** = negative connotation)

ralaheb something utterly spiceless, bland, "like warm spit," repulsively bland and blah (**ra** = non- + **laheb** = spice)

ralali drought (**ra** = non- + **lali** = rain)

ralámálha tactile deprivation (**ra** = non- + **lámála** = to caress + **lh** = negative connotation)

ralath to be celibate not by choice

ralée- non-meta (prefix), something absurdly or dangerously narrow in scope or range

ralh rape; to rape

ralhewedeth to obfuscate (**ra** = non- + **lh** = negative connotation+ **wedeth** = to be clear)

ralhoham love for evil (**ra** = non- + **lh** = negative connotation + **oham** = love for that which is holy)

raliha pitcher

ralili to be dry (**ra** = not + **lili** = wet)

ralith to deliberately refrain from thinking about something, to wall it off in one's mind by deliberate act (**ra** = non- + **lith** = to think)

ralod anarchy (**ra** = non- + **lod** = household)

ralóolo to be fast (**ra** = non- + **lóolo** = to be slow)

ralorolo non-thunder, much talk and commotion from one (or more) with no real knowledge of what they're talking about or trying to do, something like "hot air" but more so (**ra** = non + **lorolo** = thunder)

ralosh bankruptcy (**ra** = non- + **losh** = money)

raloth ignorance (**ra** = non- + **loth** = information)

ram presence

ramaha absence of desire (**ra** = non- + **maha** = sexual desire)

raména callousness for good reasons, disregard, to be callous (**ra** = non- + **ména** = compassion for good reasons) (See also: **raméhéna, ramina, ramona, ramuna** = callousness)

ramihí to be large (area) (**ra** = non + **mihí** = small)

ramíili evil (theological) (**ra** = non- + **míili** = radiance)

ramíilide from evil (theological) (**ra** = non- + **míili** = radiance + **-de** = SOURCE CASE MARKER)

ramime to refrain from asking, out of courtesy or kindness (**ra** = non- + **mime** = to ask)

ramimelh to refrain from asking, with evil intent; especially when it is clear that someone badly wants the other to ask (**ramime** = to refrain from asking + **lh** = negative connotation)

ramína callousness for no reason, disregard, to be callous (**ra** = non- + **mína** = compassion for no reason) (See also: **raméhéna, raména, ramóna, ramúna** = callousness)

ramóna callousness for foolish reasons, disregard, to be callous (**ra** = non- + **móna** = compassion for foolish reasons) (See also: **raméhéna, raména, ramína, ramúna** = callousness)

ramúna callousness for bad reasons, disregard, to be callous (**ra** = non- + **múna** = compassion for bad reasons) (See also: **raméhéna, raména, ramína, ramóna** = callousness)

ran typewriter

rana drink, beverage (**rilin** = to drink)

ranahá drinker (**rana** = drink + **-á** = suffix for doer)

ranahálh alcoholic (**ranahá** = drinker + **lh** = negative connotation)

ranal no how, in no way (**ra** = non- + **-nal** = suffix for manner)

ranem non-pearl, an ugly thing one builds layer by layer as an oyster does a pearl (**ra** = non + **nem** = pearl)

raneran printer, computer printer (**ran** = typewriter)

rani non-cup, a hollow accomplishment, something one acquires or receives or accomplishes but is empty of all satisfaction (**ra** = non- + **ni** = cup)

ranil outside, out (**ra** = non- + **nil** = inside)

raniloma back of the hand

ranime be unwilling (**ra** = not + **nime** = willing)

ranonede to be infinite (**ra** = non + **nonede** = last one/final one)

rarilh to deliberately refrain from recording; for example, the failure throughout history to record the accomplishments of women (**ra** = non- + **ri** = to record, keep records + **lh** = negative connotation)

rarulh non-synergy, that which when combined only makes things worse, less efficient, etc. (**ra** = non- + **ru** = synergy + **lh** = negative connotation)

rasha discord (not discord in the home) (**ra** = non- + **sha** = harmony)

rashe to torment (**ra** = non- + **she** = comfort)

rasheb resistance to change (**ra** = non- + **sheb** = change)

rashelh to torture (**rashe** = to torment + **lh** = negative connotation)

rashelith worry (**ra** = not + **she** = to comfort + **lith** = think) (See also: **lhitharil**)

rashenidal bureaucracy (**ra** = non- + **shenidal** = network)

rashida non-game, a cruel "playing" that is a game only for the dominant "player" with the power to force others to participate (**ra** = non- + **shida** = game)

rashim celibacy (**ra** = non- + **shim** = to sexual act) (See also: **lath** = celibate by choice; **ralath** = celibate not by choice)

rashimá a celibate, one who does not have sex (**rashIm** = celibacy + **-á** = suffix for doer)

rashon argument, quarrel, not used of an "argument" in a theory or an equation or a proposition (**ra** = non- + **shon** = peace)

rashonelh war (**rashon** = quarrel + **lh** = negative connotation)

rashonelhá attacker, aggressor (**rashonelh** = war + **-á** = suffix for doer)

rathal to be bad (**ra** = non- + **thal** = to be good)

rathena despair for good reasons (**ra** = non- + **thena** = joy for good reasons) (See also: **rathehena, rathina, rathona, rathuna** = despair)

rathina despair for no reason (**ra** = non- + **thina** = joy for no reason) (See also: **rathahena, rathena, rathona, rathuna** = despair)

rathom non-pillow, one who lures another to trust and rely on them but has no intention of following through, a "lean on me so I can step aside and let you fall" person (**ra** = non- + **thom** = pillow)

rathona despair for foolish reasons (**ra** = non- + **thona** = joy for foolish reasons) (See also: **rathehena, rathena, rathina, rathuna** = despair)

rathóo non-guest, someone who comes to visit knowing perfectly well that they are intruding and causing difficulty (**ra** = non- + **thóo** = guest)

rathuna despair for bad reasons (**ra** = non- + **thuna** = joy for bad reasons) (See also: **rathehena, rathena, rathina, rathona** = despair)

rawan chest (body part)

rawedeth to be murky, obscure (**ra** = non- + **wedeth** = to be clear)

raweshalh non-gestalt, a collection of parts with no relationship other than coincidence, a perverse choice of items to call a set; especially when used as "evidence" (**ra** = non- + **wésha** = gestalt + **lh** = negative connotation)

rawihi emotionlessness (*not a complimentary term*) (**ra** = non- + **wihi** = emotion)

rawíi to be dead (**ra** = non- + **wíi** = to be alive)

rawith nobody (**ra** = non- + **with** = person)

rawoho none, not at all (**ra** = non- + **woho** = all)

rawóobaná barren one (**ra** = non- + **wóobaná** = birth giver)

rayide anorexia, to be anorexic (**ra** = non- + **yide** = hunger)

rayil above, to be above (**ra** = non- + **yil** = under)

Rayilesháal Friday (Above Day) (**rayil** = above + **sháal** = day)

rayom danger (**ra** = non- + **yom** = safe)

razh vehicle

redeb to find

réele harbor

ren rug, carpet

resh wasp

ri to record, keep records

ridadem camera, VCR, camcorder (**ri** = to record + **dadem** = picture)

ríibib frog

ril present time, now (TIME AUXILIARY)

ril i aril irilrili forevermore

rile silence

- **rilédáan** silence due to a lexical gap (**rile** = silence + **édáan** = lexical gap)
- **riledim** silent refusal to discuss (**rile** = silence + **dim** = container)
- **rilehana** silence that is comfortable and natural (**rile** = silence + **ana** = food)
- **rilehum** silence that is a purposeful refusal to communicate, with a denial that it's even happening (See also: **rilhehum**) (**rile** = silence + **hum** = knife)
- **rilelh** malicious silence (**rile** = silence + **lh** = pejorative)
- **rilerahum** silence acutely painful to you, but the other person seems totally unaware (**rile** = silence + **plus** = absence)
- **rilerashum** silence imposed by internal force of will because all words are wrong words and silence is the sole defense against disintegration (**rile** = silence + **ra** = non + **shum** = air)
- **rilhedim** malicious silent refusal to discuss (**rilhe** = malicious silence + **dim** = container)
- **rilheham** malicious silence that is a purposeful refusal to communicate, with a denial that it's even happening (See also: rilehum) (**rilhe** = malicious silence + **hum** = knife)
- **rilherahum** malicious silence acutely painful to you, but the other person seems totally unaware. (**rile** = silence + **lh** = pejorative + **raham** = absence)

rilin to drink (**rana** = drink, noun)

rilinehoth bar (**rilin** = drink + (**e**)**hoth** = place)

rilrili hypothetical, would, might, let's suppose (TIME AUXILIARY)

rim shoulder

rimáayo cloak, cape (**rim** = shoulder + **áayo** = skirt)

rimel copier (like Xerox) (**ri** = to record + **mel** = paper)

rin plate (dish)

riweth to keep track of (**re** = to record + **weth** = road, path)

rizho tape recorder (**ri** = to record + **zho** = sound)

ro weather

rod million (1,000,000)

rohoro storm (**ro** = weather)

romid wild animal (**ro** = wild + **mid** = creature)

róo harvest

róohá harvester, gatherer (**róo** = harvest + **-á** = suffix for doer)

róomath barn (**róo** = harvest + **math** = building)

rosh sun

rothil wild vine (**ro-** = wild + **thil** = vine)

ru synergy

ruhob to be deep

ruhobehal middle career, deep career, the career you take after your mid-life crisis (**ruhob** = deep + **hal** = work) (See also: **didehal, shawithehal**)

rul cat

rulelo to purr (**rul** = cat + **lo** = rejoice) (See also: **thenazho**)

rum hip (body part)

rumad to hide, cover, put away

rumadoni to bury (**rumad** = to hide + **doni** = dirt)

rumi shadow

rush to be last, final

rushi wine

rushihá vintner (**rushi** = wine + **-(h)á** = suffix for doer)

rúsho to be bitter (to taste)

rúshomeénan bittersweet (**rúsho** = bitter + **meénan** = sweet)

rúu to lie down

sh

sha harmony

sháad[1] to come, to go (differentiated by the "source" or "goal" marker on the following noun)

---

[1] Deictic pair; same action but different point of view.

sháadehul growth through transcendence, either of a person, a non-human, or thing (for example, an organization, or a city, or a sect) (**sháad** = to come, go + **-hul** = suffix denoting to an extreme degree)

sháadoni to quest for truth

sháal day

sháam psalm (loanword)

sháana to menstruate joyfully (**ásháana** = to menstruate)

shad to be perfect, pure

shadon truth, honor, conforming to the harmony of the universe (**shad** = to be perfect, pure + **on** = head)

shahina rose

shal manners, courtesy

shala grief with reason, with blame, and not futile (See also: **shama, shana, shara, shina**)

sham love for the child of one's body, presupposing neither love nor respect nor their absence

shama grief with reason, but with no blame and futile (See also: **shala, shana, shara, shina**)

shamid domestic animal (**sha** = harmony + **mid** = creature)

shan five (5)

shana grief with reason, but with no blame and not futile (See also: **shala, shama, shara, shina**)

shane to be downy, furry

shanemid rabbit (**shane** = furry + **mid** = creature)

shanethab fifteen (15) (**shan** = 5 + **thab** = 10)

shara grief with reason, with blame, and futile (See also: **shala, shama, shana, shina**)

shasho connection

Shathul Mother (formal term, honored mother) (**sha** = harmony + **thul** = parent) (See also: **Mathul, Ethul**)

shawith elder, honored adult (**sha** = harmony + **with** = person)

shawithehal retired career, elder career, the work you do after you've officially retired (**shawith** = elder + (**e**)**hal** = work) (See also: **didehal, ruhobehal**)

she to comfort

shé with regard to (loanword)

sheb change, to change

sheba widow (**sheb** = change + **eba** = spouse)

shebasheb death (**sheb** = change)

shebehatheshun all coming-of-age rituals and change-of-life rituals, rite of passage (**sheb** = change + (**e**)**hath** = time + (**e**)**shun** = ritual)

shée desert

shéeba earthworm

shehá comforter (**she** = to comfort + **-á** = suffix for doer)

shehéeda holy day (**she** = to comfort + **héeda** = to be sacred)

shel to be rigorous

shelalen dulcimer

sheni intersection

shenidal network (**sheni** = intersection + **dal** = thing)

sherídan niece

sherídanid nephew

sheshi sand

sheshihoth beach (**sheshi** = sand + **hoth** = place)

shi to please

shida game (**shi** = to please)

shidi to be together

shili mist

shim to "sexual act," engage in sex, copulation (abstract and completely neutral term)

shimá one who performs a sexual act, copulater (cannot mean lover) (**shim** = to "sexual act" + **-á** = suffix for doer)

shin to be two, two (2)

shina grief without reason or blame, not futile (See also: **shala, shama, shana, shara**)

shinehal computer (**shin** = two + **hal** = to work)

shinehóowith great-granddaughter (**shin** = two + **hóowith** = granddaughter)

shinehothul great-grandmother (**shin** = two + **hothul** = grandmother)

shinenil between (**shin** = two + **nil** = inside)

shineshid to be invited

shineshidethóo invited guest (**shineshid** = invited + (**e**)**thóo** = guest) (See also: **thóo, áathethóo, nithedimethóo, widadithethóo**)

shinethab twelve (12) (**shin** = 2 + **thab** = 10)

shineya second (**shin** = two + **-(e)ya** = SUFFIX FOR TIME)

shiniledal middle (**shinenil** = between + **dal** = thing)

shinishidi couple (**shin** = two + **i** = and + **shidi** = together)

shinishin calculator (**shin** = 2 + **i** = and + **shin** = 2)

shinóoya to be fertile, creative (**shin** = two + **óoya** = heart)

shishid united

shishidebeth nation

sho to be heavy

shod room

shóda to feel housebound, cut off due to family responsibilities

shol absence-of-pain

sholalan alone in a crowd of people

sholan to be alone

shon peace

shoná peacemaker (**shon** = peace + **-á** = suffix for doer)

shonida tribe

shóo to come to pass, to happen

shóoban to enable, to help make happen, remove barriers and provide encouragement (**shóo** = to happen + **ban** = to give)

shóod busy, to be busy

shóodal news (**shóo** = happen, come to pass + **dal** = thing)

Shósho Magic Granny (character in stories)

shoth predicate

shoya hide, animal skin (NOUN)

shu to smell, to sniff, attentive smelling. "Here, smell this." (See also: **láad oyonan** perceptive smelling)

shub to do

shud to be poor

shulhe to be inappropriate, to not fit, to be wrong for

shulin to overflow, as water does

shum air

shumáad to fly (**shum** = air + **sháad** = to go/come)

shumath tower (**shum** = air + **math** = building)

shumezh to sift (**shum** = air + **mezh** = powder)

shun ceremony, ritual

shunobahéthe ritual bath, to ritually bathe (**shun** = ceremony, ritual + **obahéthe** = bath)

th

tháa to do well, to thrive

tháahel to get by (**tháa** = to thrive + **hel** = to a trivial degree)

thab ten (10)

thabebath sixty (60) (**thab** = ten + (**e**)**bath** = six)

thabebath i nede sixty-one (61) (**thabebath** = sixty + **i** = and + **nede** = one)

thabebim forty (40) (**thab** = ten + (**e**)**bim** = four)

thabeboó thirty (30) (**thab** = ten + **boó** = three)

thabebud ninety (90) (**thab** = ten + (**e**)**bud** = nine)

thabenib eighty (80) (**thab** = ten + (**e**)**nib** = eight)

thabeshan fifty (50) (**thab** = ten + (**e**)**shan** = five)

thabeshin twenty (20) (**thab** = ten + (**e**)**shin** = two)

thabeya tenth (**thab** = ten + -(**e**)**ya** = suffix for time)

thabum seventy (70) (**thab** = ten + **um** = seven)

thad to be able

thade birthday

thahoma fist (body part)

thal to be good, fine, satisfactory

thaledan gospel (**thal** = good + (**e**)**dan** = language)

tham circle

thamehal globe, sphere, planet (**tham** = circle + -(**e**)**hal** = unusual degree)

thamehaledal asteroid (**thamehal** = globe + **dal** = thing)

thamehib to squeeze

thamerili to wring, wring out (**tham** = circle + (**e**)**ra** = not + **ili** = water)

thamesho to wrap (**tham** = circle + **mesh** = across + **o** = around)

thamewud arc (**tham** = circle + (**e**)**wud** = part)

thameyul tornado (**tham** = circle + **yul** = wind)

than underground

thazh to inherit

thed far, to be far

thede jewel

théewóoban soon to give birth (**thée-** = about to + **wóoban** = to give birth)

thehena joy, despite negative circumstances (**thena, thina, thona, thuna** = joy)

thel to get, obtain

thėle television (loanword)

them to need

then to break

thenazho to purr (**thena** = joy for good reason + **zho** = sound) (See also: **rulelo**)

thena joy for good reasons (**thehena, thina, thona, thuna** = joy)

theni interruption (**then** = to break)

Thera Earth, Terra (loanword)

thesh herb

théwóoban on the point of giving birth (**thé-** = about to any minute + **wóoban** = to give birth)

thezh sorrel (the herb)

thi to have

thib to rise up, stand up

thibá wall (**thib** = stand up + **-á** = suffix for doer)

thibeb cooking utensil

thid thread, string, to thread, to string

thihá owner, possessor (**thi** = to have + **-á** = suffix for doer)

thil vine

thili fish

thina joy, for no reason, joyful (**thehena, thena, thona, thuna** = joy)

thizh pie

thob one thousand (1,000)

thob i nede one thousand and one (1,001)

thod to write

thodi writing instrument; short form of **dalethodewan**

thol breast

thom pillow

thoma near

thon seed

thona joy, for foolish reasons, to be joyful (**thehena, thena, thina, thuna** = joy)

thóo guest (See also: **áathethóo, nithedimethóo, shineshidethóo, widadithethóo**)

thóohéthe guest-clean, the level of cleaning you need to do for guests (**thóo** = guest + **(h)éthe** = clean) (See also: **éthe, háawithéthe, huhéthe, mudahéthe, onidahéthe**)

thosh sky

thówóoban to have just given birth (**thó-** = to have just + **wóoban** = to give birth)

thu honey

thud bone

thuhá beekeeper, apiarist (**thu** = honey + **-(h)á** = suffix for doer)

thuhal candy

thuhul charm, charisma

thul parent

thulana soup (**thul** = parent + **ana** = food)

thun muscle

thuna joy, for bad reasons (**thehena, thena, thina, thona** = joy)

thuwebe mead (**thu** = honey + **webe** – beer)

thuyu apricot (**thu** = honey + **yu** = fruit)

thuzh cake

u

u to be open

ub balm, soothing substance

ubath to scratch an itch (**ub** = balm + **bath** = fingernail)

ud stone

udadem statue (**ud** = stone + **dadem** = picture/image)

udath noon

udathihée afternoon (**udath** = noon + **ihée** = after)

udemeda potato (**ud** = stone + **(e)meda** = vegetable)

udólo lava

udoya shell, carapace (**ud** = stone + **oya** = skin)

uhud nuisance

uhudemid tick (insect; literally, nuisance creature)

uhudeshara depression as result of small event

uhudezhub tick, the insect (**uhud** = nuisance + **zhub** = insect)

ul hope, to hope

ulanin to study (**ulin** = school)

ulhad to betray (**lh** gives negative connotation)

ulin school

um seven (7)

ume to be full, abundant

umeloláad visualization, to visualize

umethab seventeen (17) (**um** = seven + **thab** = ten)

un to lead

uná leader (**un** = to lead + **á** = suffix for doer)

unáhid king (**uná** = leader + **-(h)id** = male)

une to wear

urahu gate (**u** = to be open + **rahu** = to be closed)

uth brain

uthemid whale (**uth** = brain + **mid** = creature)

úushili fog (**úuzh** = bedsheet + **shili** = mist)

úuya to hurt, feel pain

úuzh sheets, sheet bedding

uzh symbol (of notation or alphabet), character

w

wa known to X because perceived by X (externally or internally) (EVIDENCE MORPHEME): "The reason I claim that what I'm saying is true is that I have perceived it myself."

wáa assumed true by X because X trusts source (EVIDENCE MORPHEME)

waá assumed false by X because X distrusts source (EVIDENCE MORPHEME)

waálh assumed false by X because X distrusts source and X suspects source of acting with evil intent (EVIDENCE MORPHEME)

waha any

waludal sewage plant, waste water plant

wam to be placid, still, calm (as of water, wind)

wan back (body part)

we perceived by speaker in a dream, perceived by X in a dream (EVIDENCE MORPHEME)

web liver

webe beer (**wéebe** = ale)

webehá brewer (**webe** = beer + **-á** = suffix for doer)

webesh hops (the plant)

wedeth to be clear

wée cry (of babies) (onomatopoeia)

wéebe ale (**webe** = beer)

wéedan to read (**dan** = language)

wéehoth library (**wéedan** = to read + **hoth** = place)

wehe store, market

wehebuth mall, a gathering of stores (**wehe** = store + **buth** = gather)

wehebuthebod strip-mall (**wehebuth** = mall + **bod** = line)

wéhená gratitude despite negative circumstances (See also: **wéná, wíná, wóná, wúná**)

wem to lose

weman winter

wemen spring (season)

wemon autumn

wéná gratitude for good reasons (See also: **wéhená, wíná, wóná, wúná**)

wesha gestalt

wesháana to menstruate late, menstruation (**osháana** = to menstruate)

weth road, way, path, track

wethalehale melody (literally, music path)

wetham turn, make a turn

wethene direction

wi an evidential meaning "The reason I claim that what I'm saying is true is because it's self-evident; everybody can see that it's true, or everybody is in agreement that it's true"; known to X because self-evident (EVIDENCE MORPHEME)

wí life

wida to carry

widáahith wire (**wida** = carry + **ith** = light)

widadith telephone (**wida** = to carry + **dith** = voice)

widadithethóo phone guest, a guest who calls before they come (**widadith** = telephone + (**e**)**thóo** = guest) (See also: **thóo**, **áathethóo**, **nithedimethóo**, **shineshidethóo**.)

widahath when (**wida** = carry + **hath** = time) 1) **Bíi lalom le widahath hal le wa**. "I sing when I work."

widahoth where (**wida** = carry + **hoth** = place) Example: "**Bíi eril widahoth benem rale hal be wa**." "I didn't stay where she was working."

widahuth why (**wida** = carry + **huth** = root by analogy) **Bíi widahuth eril náhal with, rith ril lothel ra le wa**. "Why the woman kept working, I don't know."

widaweth how (**wida** = carry + **weth** = path) **Bíi widaweth aril mebedi háawith, ril lothel ra le wa**. "How the children will learn, I don't know."

widazhad to be pregnant late in term and eager for the end (**wida** = to carry + **lawida** = to be pregnant)

widom to hold

wihi emotion

wíi to be alive, living (**wí** = life)

wíitham clergy (**with** = person + **tham** = circle)

wil optative mode, indicating an option or wish (TIME AUXILIARY); let there be…, would that…, let it be

Wil sha greeting (hello), "Let there be harmony" (**wil** = optative mode + **sha** = harmony)

wili river, creek (**ili** = water)

wilibod list (**wili** = river + **bod** = line)

wilidun lake (**wili** = river + **dun** = field)

wilidunedal reservoir for fluids (**wilidun** = lake + (**e**)**dal** = thing)

wilomina to perform, act (**wil** = let/may + **oba** = body + **mina** = move)

wilominabelid theater (**wilomina** = act/perform + **belid** = house)

wilominahoth stage (**wilomina** = act/perform + **hoth** = place)

wíná gratitude, for no reason (See also: **wéhená, wéná, wóná, wúná**)

wírabanenath abortion, to have an abortion (**wí** = life + **raban** = to take away + **nath** = price)

wish gas (oxygen, nitrogen, etc.)

with person, woman, adult; to specify a male person, add the masculine suffix "**-id**"

withelhebe misogyny, hatred of women

withid man, male person (**with** = person + **-id** = suffix for male)

withidetho male identified (**withid** = male + **etho** = identify, about)

wíyaáláan respiration rate (**wíyul** = to breathe + **aáláan** = wave)

wíyul to breathe (**wí** = life + **yul** = wind)

wíyuleth breath

wo imagined or invented by hypothetical (EVIDENCE MORPHEME)

wóbáan to bring to birth (the activity of a midwife or other person helping with the delivery of an infant)

woban birth (NOUN) (origin, beginning)

wobanedan native tongue, birth language (**woban** = birth + (**e**)**dan** = language)

wobaneya birth (time) "at birth" (at the time she was born) (**woban** = birth + **-(e)ya** = CASE MARKER suffix for time)

wod to sit

wodama genitalia (female, outer) (**wo** = changes verb to object + **dama** = to touch)

wodazhud matrix (in geology)

wodehahodo meditate, to meditate, sit in a meditative state (**wod** = sit + **hahodo** = medatative state of consciousness)

woho all, every (don't change form or add CASE MARKER)

wohóoha scene, view, experience of a place (**woho** = all/every + **hóo** = emphasis + **ha** = place) (root = hoth)

wohóol genitalia (female, all), all female genitalia and reproductive organs (**wo** = all/every + **óol** = moon)

wohosheni total empathy, the opposite of alienation; to feel joined to, part of someone or something without reservations or barriers (**woho** = all + **sheni** = intersection)

wohothul foremother, ancestor (**woho** = all + **thul** = parent)

wohothulewoth foremother wisdom (**wohothul** = foremother + (**e**)**woth** = wisdom)

wom throat

womedim neck (body part) (**wom** = throat + **dim** = container)

womil livestock

womilá breeder of animals (**womil** = livestock + **-á** = suffix for doer)

won handicap

wóná gratitude for foolish reasons (See also: **wéhená, wéná, wíná, wúná**)

wonewith to be socially dyslexic; uncomprehending of the social signals of others (**won** = handicap + **with** = person)

wóo indicates speaker who has total lack of knowledge as to the validity of the matter (EVIDENCE MORPHEME)

wóoban to give birth, to bear

wóobaná birth-giver (**wóoban** = to give birth + **-á** = suffix for doer)

wóoya womb

woth wisdom

wothá sage, wise person (**woth** = wisdom + **á** = suffix for doer)

wothemid mule (**woth** = wisdom + **mid** = creature)

wothesh sage (the herb) (**woth** = wisdom + **thesh** = herb)

wu such a…, what a…

wud part (of a machine, etc.)

wuman summer

wúná gratitude for bad reasons (See also: **wúná, wéhená, wéná, wíná, wóná**)

wush broom

y

yáalin kelp (**yáanin** = tree + **ili** = water)

yáamid teenage animal, older but not full-grown creature (**yáa-** = teenage + **mid** = animal) (See also: **ámid**, **háamid**)

yáanin tree

yáawith teenager, older but not full-grown person (**yáa-** = teenage + **with** = person) (See also: **áwith**, **háawith**)

yáazh goose

yada thirst, to thirst, to be thirsty, thirsting

yahanesh magic enchantment

yahaneshá witch, magic-maker (**yahanesh** = magic + **á** = suffix for doer)

yam baking dish

yan analysis, to analyze

yath chicken

yazh duck

yeb kidney

yed valley

yem sour (to taste)

yen hat

yéshile[1] to be bad and good

yeth silver

---

[1] Polar opposites.

-yi- fraction marker

yib solid (as opposed to gas or liquid)

yibom wax (**yib** = solid + **bom** = oil)

yidan mercy

yide to hunger, to be hungry

yil to be under, below

Yileshául Saturday (**yil** + **sháal** Below Day)

yime to run

yo spaceship

yob coffee

yod to eat

yoda spaceliner (**yo** = spaceship)

yodá diner, one who eats (**yod** = to eat + **á** = suffix for doer)

yodálh glutton (**yodá** = diner + **lh** = negative connotation)

yóhud brick (**yó** = artificial + **ud** = stone) (See also: **donilihud**)

yom safe, secure

yomedim trunk (for storage) (**yom** = safe + **dim** = container)

yon government

yoth will (theological)

yu fruit

yudáan morpheme (**yu** = fruit + **dáan** = word)

yuhoya peel, peeling (noun) (**yu** = fruit + (**h**)**oya** = skin)

yul wind

yulehul hurricane (**yul** = wind + **-hul** = suffix denoting to an extreme degree)

yulish feather (**yul** = wind + **ishid** = finger)

yuloma wing (**yul** = wind + **oma** = hand)

yum beetle

yumal nut

yun orange (the fruit)

yurana cordial (the beverage) (**yu** = fruit + **rana** = drink)

yushoya rind (**yu** = fruit + **shoya** = hide)

zh

zha name

zháa wrinkle (in skin)

zháadin to menopause (**zháa** = wrinkle)

zháadinebúlith menopause-induced insanity (**zháadin** = menopause + (**e**)**búlith** = insanity)

zháahóowadin hot flash (menopause symptom) (**zháadin** = menopause + **óowa** = fire)

zhab enigma, puzzle

zhala regret with reason, with blame, and not futile (See also: **zhama, zhana, zhara, zhina**)

zhaláad the act of relinquishing a cherished/comforting/familiar illusion or frame of perception (**zhala** = regret + **láad** = to perceive)

zhama regret with reason, but with no blame, and futile (See also: **zhala, zhana, zhara, zhina**)

zhana regret with reason, but with no blame and not futile (See also: **zhala, zhama, zhara, zhina**)

zhara regret with reason, with blame, and futile (See also: **zhala, zhama, zhana, zhina**)

zhazh airplane

zhe to be like, similar

zhebom fat, grease (**zhe** = like + **bom** = oil)

zhedal metaphor, simile (**zhe** = like + **dal** = thing)

zhedam resemble; be reminiscent of (**zhe** = similar + **dam** = show signs of state or emotion)

zhedi agree, to agree verbally (**zhe** = alike + **di** = speak) (See also: **zhelith, zheshub, zheláad, zhethob**)

zhehá identical sibling (**zhe** = like + **-á** = suffix for doer)

zheláad consensus, to come to consensus (**zhe** = alike + **láad** = perceive) (See also: **zhelith, zhedi, zheshub, zhethob**)

zheledal self, identity (**zhe** = like + **le** = me + **dal** = thing)

zheledam persona (**zhe** = like + **le** = me + **dam** = manifest)

zhelehal work identity (**zhe** = like + **le** = me + **hal** = work)

zhelith agree, to think the same (**zhe** = alike + **lith** = think) (See also: **zhedi, zheshub, zheláad, zhethob**)

zhesháana to menstruate in sync with another woman, menstruation (**zhe** = like + **sháana**)

Zheshu Jesus of Nazareth (loan word)

zheshub cooperation, to cooperate (**zhe** = alike + **shub** = do) (See also: **zhelith, zhedi, zheláad, zhethob**)

zhethal to be just, fair, equitable (**zhe** = alike + **thal** = be good)

zhethalel to police; to act as police (**zhethal** = just(ice) + **el** = make)

zhethalelá police officer (**zhethal** = just(ice) + **á** = suffix for doer)

zhethob agreement, written agreement (**zhe** = alike + **thob** = write) (See also: **zhelith, zhedi, zheshub, zheláad**)

zhilhad prisoner

zhina regret without reason or blame, not futile (See also: **zhala, zhama, zhana, zhara**)

zho sound (audible)

zhob machine

zholh noise (**zho** = sound + **lh** = negative connotation)

zhomid bee (**zhu** = sound + **mid** = creature)

zhonal aloud (**zho** = sound + **-nal** = suffix for manner)

zhorumi echo (**zho** = sound + **rumi** = shadow)

zhozhub bee (**zho** = sound + **zhub** = insect)

zhu tea

zhub insect

zhuth piano

Affixes

AFFIXES ARE ADDITIONAL ELEMENTS placed at the beginning or end of a root, stem, or word, or in the body of a word, to modify its meaning.

a

-á suffix for doer, agent; MORPHEME used to mark someone as the "do-er" of an action; like English "-er" in "baker" or "dancer" or "ist" in "scientist" or "artist."

á- prefix to signify infant, baby, very young creature (See also: **háa-**, **yáa-**)

b

-báa- Interrogatives (who, which, what): use the base form, plus "**-báa-**", plus CASE MARKER

d

-d SPEECH ACT suffix; "said in anger"

-da CASE MARKER: used to identify the beneficiary of an action—the person (or other entity) for whom or for which an action is done; suffix for beneficiary—voluntarily. (See also: **-dá**, **-daá**, **-dáa**)

-da SPEECH ACT suffix: "said in jest"

-dá CASE MARKER: suffix for beneficiary-by-force, under coersion. (See also: **-da**, **-daá**, **-dáa**)

-daá CASE MARKER: suffix for beneficiary—accidentally (See also: **-da**, **-dá**, **-dáa**)

-dáa CASE MARKER: suffix for beneficiary—obligatorily, as by duty (See also: **-da**, **-dá**, **-daá**)

-dan CASE MARKER: suffix for associate—with pleasure (See also: also **-den**)

-de SPEECH ACT suffix: "said in narrative"

-de CASE MARKER: suffix for source from which/from whom an action is performed.

-den CASE MARKER: suffix for associate—neutral form (See also: **-dan**)

-di SPEECH ACT suffix: "said in teaching"

-di CASE MARKER suffix: for goal (the person, place or thing to/at/toward which an action is performed), as in "**Bíi ril sháad Athid buhedi wa**" (Athid is going to the con). (See also: **-dim**, an alternate sufix for use when/by speakers for whom **-di** is difficult to distinguish from **-de**, the source case suffix)

-dim CASE MARKER alternate suffix: for goal, as in "**Bíi ril sháad Athid buzhedim wa**" (Athid is going to the con). (See also: **-di**) For use when/by speakers for whom **-di** is difficult to distinguish from **-de**, the source case suffix.

dó- cause-to-VERB prefix

-du SPEECH ACT suffix: "said as poetry"

du- (plus verb) try-to-VERB, attempt-to-VERB prefix (try to speak = **dudi**); a MORPHEME that can be added to verbs (including those that would be classified as adjectives in English), meaning "try-to-VERB"

dúu- (plus verb) to-try-and-fail-to-VERB (**du-** = to-try-to-VERB) (try in vain to speak = **dúudi**); a MORPHEME that can be added to verbs (including those that would be classified as adjectives in English), meaning "try in vain to (VERB)," "try (but fail) to (VERB)"

e

e- prefix for science of

é- prefix for potential

ela- joyfully

h

-ha CASE MARKER: suffix for place that locates the action in space, not time, as in "**Bíi ril Athid botheha wa**" (Athid is at the hotel). (See also: **-sha**, an alternate for use when this suffix follows a word or a suffix ending in "…**ha**.")

-háa EMBEDDING MARKER: to embed a relative clause (like English "I know the woman who is tired") attached to the last element in the embedded clause (See also: **-hé**, **-hée**, **-sháa**, an alternate for use when this suffix follows a word or a suffix ending in "…**ha**")

háa- life-form prefix to signify child, youth, young creature (See also: **á** = infant, **yáa** = teenager)

-háalish DEGREE MARKER: to an extraordinary degree (See also: "**-hil**," "**-hal**," "**-hul**," "**-hel**")

-hal DEGREE MARKER: to an unusual degree, very (See also: "**-hil**," "**-hel**," "**-hul**," "**-háalish**")

-hé EMBEDDING MARKER: to embed a sentential complement (like English "I know that she left") attached to the last element in the embedded clause (See also: "**-háa**," "**-hée**")

When we want to put one English statement inside another one—a process called "embedding"—we can use the word "that" to mark the statement that is embedded. For example, "I know that science fiction conventions are fun" embeds the statement "science fiction conventions are fun" inside "I know (some other statement)," by putting "that" at the beginning of the embedded statement. Láadan embeds one statement in another by putting the MORPHEME "**-hé**" on the last word of the embedded statement. So, the statement "**radezhehul thod áabeth**"—"writing a book is very hard"—is marked as an embedded statement by adding "**-hé**" to "**áabeth**." (NOTE: An EMBEDDING MORPHEME is the *only* MORPHEME that can follow a CASE-MARKING MORPHEME.)

-hée EMBEDDING MARKER INTERROGATIVE: to embed a question (like English "I wonder whether/if she left") attached to the last element in the embedded clause (See also: "**-hé**," "**-háa**")

-hel DEGREE MARKER: to a trivial degree, slightly (See also: "**-hil**," "**-hal**," "**-hele**," "**-hul**," "**-háalish**")

-hele to a troublesome degree: DEGREE MARKER: specifically negative in meaning—never used in a positive sense (See also: **-shéle**)

hi- GENERAL PREFIX: diminutive, smaller, but not an affectionate diminutive like -**i**. Examples: **hibo** = hill (**hi-** = diminutive + **bo** = mountain; **hidel** = ham radio (**hi-** = diminutive + **del** = radio); **hiháak** = second, moment (**hi-** = diminutive + **áal** = minute)

-hil DEGREE MARKER: to a minor degree, rather (See also: "-**hel**," "-**hal**," "-**hul**," "-**háalish**")

-hile to a severe degree: DEGREE MARKER: specifically negative in meaning—never used in a positive sense (See also -**shíle**)

-hóo a MORPHEME: used to indicate special importance, or to give a word or phrase extra emphasis: **Bíi aril bilehóo buzh wa!** ("The convention will be *fun*!"): FOCUS MARKER

-hul DEGREE MARKER: to an extreme degree, extremely (See also: "-**hel**," "-**hal**," "-**hil**," "-**háalish**")

-hule to an intolerable degree: DEGREE MARKER: specifically negative in meaning—never used in a positive sense (See also: -**shúle**)

i

-i diminutive suffix, small, affectionate

-id suffix for male

l

-lan SPEECH ACT suffix: "said in celebration"

lée- meta- (prefix on any word)

lh- or **-lh** or **-lh-** Prefix, Suffix, Infix on any word, pejorative. The pejorative element "**lh**" can always be added to a word to give it a negative connotation, so long as it precedes and/or follows a vowel and does not violate the rules of the Láadan sound system by creating a forbidden cluster. The addition of "**lh**" need not create an actual new word; for example, "**áwith**" means "baby"; to use instead "**lháwith**" (or "**áwithelh**") means only something like "the darned baby" and is ordinarily a temporary addition. But it is very handy indeed. We are indebted to the Navajo language for this device.

-li SPEECH ACT SUFFIX; "said in love"

m

me- PLURAL MARKER, PLURAL MORPHEME: used at the beginning of verbs and words that correspond to English adjectives; always the first prefix in the word (beautiful women = **mewoháya wowith**)

me- GENERAL PREFIX: aggrandizer, higher-order. Examples: **mela** = ocean (**me-** = aggrandizer + **ili** = water); **meloth** = evidence (**me-** = aggrandizer + **loth** = information); **memazh** = train (**me-** = agrandizer + **mazh** = car); **menedebe** = many (**me-** = aggrandizer + **nedebe** = few/several); **merod** = one billion (**me-** = aggrandizer + **rod** = one million)

-mé LIFE-FORM PREFIX, COLLECTIVE NOUN FORM. Examples: **méwith** = crowd (**mé-** = COLLV + **with** = person); **mébabi** = flock of birds (**mé-** = COLLV + **babi** = bird); **méthili** = school of fish (**mé-** = COLLV + **thili** = fish)

n

-n pronoun suffix: many (six or more)

na- DURATION MARKER: prefix for "to begin to" VERB, to start VERBING. (See also: "**no-**," "**ná-**," "**ne-**," "**nó-**")

ná- DURATION MARKER: prefix for "to continue to" VERB, to keep VERBING. (See also: "**na-**," "**no-**," "**ne-**," "**nó-**")

-nal CASE MARKER: suffix for manner, the way an action is performed

-nan CASE MARKER: instrument, what is used to perform an action, as in "**Bíi aril sháad Athid buzhedi mazhenan wa**" (I'll go to the con by using a car). Care must be taken to choose the correct case, as both the instrument and associate cases are translated into English by the preposition, "with."

ne- DURATION MARKER: prefix for "to repeat," VERB again, repeat VERBING. (See also: "**na-**," "**ná-**," "**no-**," "**nó-**")

no- DURATION MARKER: prefix for "to finish," completion, complete VERBING, finish VERBING. (See also: "**na-**," "**ná-**," "**no-**," "**nó-**")

nó- DURATION MARKER: prefix for cease to VERB, stop VERBing (See also: "**na-**," "**ná-**," "**no-**," "**nó-**")

r

ra- non- (prefix on any word) **ra** is ambiguous, between simply "not" and "anti," that is, between negation and opposition.

ralée- non-meta (prefix on any word), something absurdly or dangerously narrow in scope or range. (**ra** = non + **lée** = meta)

ro- wild (**rothil** = wild vine, **romid** = wild animal)

sh

-sha CASE MARKER: alternate suffix for place, location at which action is performed, when applied to a word or to a suffix ending in "…**ha**" or "…**háa**."

-shéle DEGREE MARKER: to a troublesome degree (See also: -**hele**)

-shíle DEGREE MARKER: to a severe degree (See also: -**hile**)

-shúul DEGREE MARKER: to an intolerable degree (See also: -**hule**)

-shúle DEGREE MARKER: special emergency form; unbearable to a degree that would cause catastrophic events such as suicide; a signal for immediate help.

th

-th a MORPHEME: object, the person or thing that receives the action of the verb, as in "**Bíi thi Athid imedimeth wa**" (Athid has a suitcase).

-th SPEECH ACT SUFFIX: "said in pain"

-tha CASE MARKER: suffix for possession, by reason of birth (See also: "**-thi**," "**-the**," "**-thu**," "**-tho**")

-the CASE MARKER: suffix for possession, for unknown or unacknowledged reasons (See also: "**-tha**," "**-thi**," "**-thu**," "**-tho**")

thé- DURATION MARKER: about-to-VERB any minute prefix

thée- DURATION MARKER: about-to-VERB, potentially, but not "any minute"

-thi CASE MARKER: suffix for possession, by reason of chance (See also: "**-tha**," "**-the**," "**-thu**," "**-tho**")

-thíle DEGREE MARKER: to a more-than-pleasing degree; excellent

-tho CASE MARKER: suffix for possession, by purchase, gift, law, custom, etc. If the speaker/writer doesn't know the reason for possession but is sure there is a valid reason, use **-tho**. (See also: "**-tha**," "**-the**," "**-thi**," "**-thu**")

thó- DURATION MARKER: prefix, to-have-just-VERBed.

-thúul DEGREE MARKER: to an extraordinarily pleasing degree; magnificent

-thúle DEGREE MARKER: to the furthest degree of pleasingness possible; perfect

-thu CASE MARKER: suffix for possession, partitive (false possessive situations in which no actual ownership exists, e.g.: "a box of books," or "a wall of stone.") (See also: "**-thi**," "**-the**," "**-thu**," "**-tha**")

w

-wáan CASE MARKER: cause, the reason for which an action is performed, as in "**Bíi aril sháad le bethedi anadaleya yidewáan wa**" (I shall go home at mealtime because of hunger). Care must be taken to choose the right case because both the cause case (**-wáan**) and the purpose case (**-wan**) answer the English question, "Why?"

-wan CASE MARKER: purpose case, the purpose toward which, or in order to accomplish what, an action is performed, as in "**Bíi aril sháad le bethedi anadaleya yodewan wa**" (I shall go home at mealtime in order to eat). Care must be taken to choose the right case because both the purpose case (**-wan**) and the cause case (**-wáan**) answer the English question, "Why?"

wo- prefix on a paired set of one verb and one noun: relativizer. To "relativize" means to employ the verb to modify the noun. It is important to remember that what in English would be adjectives are simply verbs in Láadan. For example, **liyen** = to be green; **áya** = be beautiful, with the meaning of "to be" intrinsic to the verb, so no "cupola" (stand-alone verb "to be") is needed in Láadan. To form this construction in Láadan, simply add the prefix **wo** to both the verb and the noun, so "beautiful woman" would be **wohaya wowith**. Since only verbs in Láadan receive the plural **me**, "beautiful women" would have to be **mewohaya wowith**. Note: only one verb and one noun may be used in this consruction. English phrases such as, "little red brick wall" will require a different grammatical feature to translate.

y

-ya CASE MARKER: suffix for time; locates the action of the verb temporally.

-ya SPEECH ACT suffix; "said in fear"

yáa- LIFE-FORM PREFIX: adolescent, somewhat shy of maturity (See also: **á-**, **háa-**)

-ye- Indefinites: use the basic pronoun form, plus "**-ye-**," plus the CASE MARKER.

-yi- fraction marker (NUMBER INFIX) To form a fraction in Láadan, give the number for the numerator (top number), apply **-yi-**, then add the denominator (the bottom number). For example, **nedeyishin** = one-half (½); **shineyiboó** = two-thirds (⅔).

-yóo- REFLEXIVE PRONOUN (myself): use the base form, plus "**-yóo-**," plus CASE MARKER

z

-zh pronoun suffix: several

Exercises

Exercise 1

Birth Song
(to the tune of *House of the Rising Sun*)

Láadan	English
Thi with lometh nede neda	A woman has only one song,
Bedi be lom wobaneya—	the song she learns at birth.
Woshama wolom,	A sorrowing song,
Woshama wolom,	a sorrowing song—
Meshulhe dáan lom bethath.	Words don't *fit* her birthsong.

Morpheme-by-Morpheme Translation

Thi	with	lometh	nede	neda
HAVE	WOMAN	SONG-OBJ	ONE	ONLY—

Bedi	be	lom	wobaneya—
LEARN	SHE	SONG	BIRTH-AT (TIME)

Woshama	wolom,	woshama	wolom
[REL-GRIEF	REL-SONG	REL-GRIEF	REL-SONG]

Meshulhe	dáan	lom	bethath.
(PL-[NOT-FIT]	WORD	SONG	SHE+OF-BY-BIRTH

Exercise 2

The Lord's Prayer

Láadan	English
Bíili,	Our Parent
Thul lenetha Na[1] olimeha.	You are in heaven.
Wil héeda zha Natha.	May Your Name be holy.
Wil nosháad sha Natha lenedi.	May Your Harmony come upon us.
Wil shóo yoth Natha,	May Your will come to pass
Doniha zhe olimeha;	on Earth as in heaven.
Wil ban Na bal lenethoth lenedi	May You give us our bread.
I wil baneban Na lud lenethoth lenedi	May You forgive us our debts
Zhe mebaneban[2] len ludá lenethodi	as we forgive our debtors.
I wil un ra Na leneth erabalhedi	And lead us not into temptation
Izh wil bóodan Na leneth ramíilade	but deliver us from evil.
Bróo sha, sha Natha	For Harmony, it is Yours,
I hohathad, hohathad Natha	Power, it is Yours,
I hohama, hohama Natha	Glory, it is Yours.
Ril i aril i rilrili.	Forevermore.
Othe.	Amen

---

[1] The form "**na**" is a second person pronoun meaning "beloved you/thou"; the capital "N" indicates reverence for the deity.

[2] the endpoint of "arrive" is appropriately rendered in the GOAL CASE.

Morpheme-by-Morpheme Translation

Bíili,
I SAY TO YOU, IN LOVE,

| **Thul** | **lenetha** |
| PARENT | WE(MANY)-OF, BY BIRTH |

| **(Ø)** | **Na** | **olimeha.** |
| BE | YOU | HEAVEN-AT |

| **Wil** | **héeda** | **zha** | **Natha.** |
| LET-IT-BE | HOLY | NAME | YOU-OF |

| **Wil** | **nosháad** | **sha** | **Natha** | **lenedi.** |
| LET-IT-BE | ARRIVE | HARMONY | YOU-OF | US(MANY)-TO |

| **Wil** | **shóo** | **yoth** | **Natha,** |
| LET-IT-BE | COME-TO-PASS | WILL | YOU-OF |

| **Doniha** | **zhe** | **olimeha;** |
| EARTH-AT | AS | HEAVEN-AT |

| **Wil** | **ban** | **Na** | **bal** | **lenethoth** | **lenedi** |
| LET-IT-BE | GIVE | YOU | BREAD | WE(MANY) OF-OBJ | WE(WANT)-TO |

| **I** | **wil** | **baneban** | **Na** | **lud** | **lenethoth** | **lenedi** |
| AND | LET-IT-BE | FORGIVE | YOU | DEBT | WE(MANY)-OF-OBJ | WE(MANY)-TO |

| **Zhe** | **mebaneban** | **len** | **ludá** | **lenethodi** |
| AS | PL-FORGIVE | WE(MANY) | DEBTOR | WE(MANY)-OF-TO |

| **I** | **wil** | **un** | **ra** | **Na** | **leneth** | **erabalhedi** |
| AND | LET-IT-BE | LEAD | NEG | YOU | WE(MANY)-OBJ | TEMPTATION-TO |

| **Izh** | **wil** | **bóodan** | **Na** | **leneth** | **ramíilade** |
| BUT | LET-IT-BE | RESCUE | YOU | WE(MANY)-OBJ | EVIL-FROM |

| **Bróo** | **sha,** | **sha** | **Natha** |
| BECAUSE | HARMONY | HARMONY | YOU-OF |

I	hohathad,	hohathad	Natha
AND	POWER	POWER	YOU-OF

I	hohama,	hohama	Natha
AND	GLORY	GLORY	YOU-OF

ril i aril i rilrili.
FOREVERMORE

Othe.
AMEN.

Exercise 3

Sháam 100

Láadan

Bíidi, shishidibeth woho: bóo mehel nen wothena wozhoth Lahila Badim. Bóo nen donidaná Lahila Bada thenanan; Bóo mesháad nen Hamehamedim lomedan; Bóo melothel nen: Ba Lahila; Ba Elá len onida Lahila Batha i len mid menedebe naya Ba benetho háa. Bóo mesháad nen urahudim Batha áaladan i mesháad nen déeladim dithaledan melolaád nen áalath Badim i medi nen othel zha Batha. Bróo thal Lahila; hathehath yidan Batha; i hathehath shadon Batha. (Wáa.)

English

Make a joyful noise unto the Lord, All ye lands. Serve the Lord with gladness; come before His presence with singing. Know ye that the Lord He is God: It is He that has made us and not we ourselves; we are His people and the sheep of His pastures. Enter into His gates with Thanksgiving and into His courts with praise; be thankful unto Him and bless His name. For the Lord is good; His mercy is everlasting, and His truth endureth unto all generations.

Morpheme-by-Morpheme Translation

Bíidi,	shishidibeth	woho:
I SAY TO YOU, IN TEACHING,	NATIONS	ALL.

bóo	mehel	nen	wothena	wozhoth	Lahila	Badim.
IMP	PI-MAKE	PI-YOU	REL-JOY	REL-SOUND	HOLY-ONE	X-GOAL

Bóo	nen	donidaná	Lahila	Bada	thenanan;
IMP	PI-YOU	LK-ERS[1]	HOLY-ONE	X-FOR	JOY-INSTR

---

[1] LK-ERS = lovingkindnessers

Bóo meshóad	nen	Hamehamedim	lomedan;
IMP PL-GO	PL-YOU	HOLY-PRESENCE-GOAL	SONG-ASSOC-PLEASURE

Bóo melothel	nen:	Ba Lahila;	Ba Elá
IMP PL-KNOW	PL-YOU:	HOLY-ONE	MAKER

len	onida	Lahila	Batha
WE-PL	FAMILY	HOLY-ONE	POSS.

i	len	mid	menedebe
AND	WE-PL	CREATURE	MANY

naya	Ba	benetho	háa.
TAKE CARE Of	|X|	THEY-MANY	OBJ-REL

Bóo meshóad	nen	urahudim	Batha	áaladan
IMP	GO-PL	YOU-PL	GATE-GOAL	POSS	THANKS-ASSOC

i	meshóad	nen	déeladim	dithaledan
AND	GO-PL	YOU-PL	GARDEN-GOAL	PRAISE-ASSOC

melolóad	nen	áalath	Badim
PL-PERCEIVE	YOU-PL	THANKS-OBJ	X-GOAL

i	medi	nen	othel	zha	Batha.
AND	PL-SAY	YOU-PL	BLESSED	NAME	X-POSS

Bróo	thal	Lahila;	hathehath	yidan	Batha;
FOR	GOOD	HOLY-ONE	FOREVER	MERCY	X-OF

i	hathehath	shadon	Batha.
AND	FOREVER	TRUTH	X-OF

(Wáa.)
EVIDENCE MORPHEME: TRUSTED SOURCE

Exercise 4

Sháam 23

Sháam Thabeshin i Boó

Bíidi Lahila nayahá letha wa; them le rahóodaleth. Dórúu Ba leth mewoliyen woduneha. Dódoth Ba leth mewowam wohiliha ib; dónetháa Ba óotha lethath. Dódoth Ba leth weth shadethuha óobe zha Bathada. Íizha óomasháad le Yed Rawíthuha obe, héeya ra le ramíilith bróo Na leden; meshe dáan Natha i oyi Natha leth. Dóham Na anath i ranath leda ham lebethu letho rawáan. Boóbin Na delith lethath oma Nathanan; ume ni letho hadihad. Aril mesháad thal i yidan leden, hulehul, sháal wíthu lethaya woho; i habelid le lod Lahila Bathaha ril i aril i rilrili. Othe.

Psalm Twenty-Three

The Lord is my shepherd, I shall not want. He makes me lie down in green pastures. He leads me beside still waters; He restores my soul. He leads me in paths of righteousness for His name's sake. Even though I walk through the valley of the shadow of death, I fear no evil, for thou art with me; thy rod and thy staff, they comfort me. Thou preparest a table before me in the presence of my enemies. Thou anointest my head with oil, my cup overflows. Surely goodness and mercy shall follow me, all the days of my life; and I shall dwell in the house of the Lord forever. Amen.

Morpheme-by-Morpheme Translation
First Line: Láadan

Second Line: MORPHEME-BY-MORPHEME

Third Line: Free Translation

Sháam	Thabeshin	I	Boó
PSALM	TENxTWO = TWENTY	AND	THREE

Psalm Twenty-Three

Bíidi	Lahila	nayahá	letha
DECL+DIDACT	HOLY-ONE	CARE+DOER	I+POSSBIRTH+IDENT

wa;	them	le	rahóodaleth.
MYPERC	NEED	I	NON+THING = NOTHING+FOCUS+OBJ

The Holy One is my carer; I need nothing.

Dórúu	Ba	leth	mewoliyen	woduneha
CAUSETO+LIE DOWN	XLOVE1	I+OBJ	PL+REL+BE GREEN	REL+FIELD+PLC

S/He causes me to lie down in green fields.

Dódoth	Ba	leth	mewowam
CAUSETO+FOLLOW	XLOVE1	I+OBJ	PL+REL+BE -STILL

wohiliha	ib;
REL+WATER+PLC	AGAINST

S/He causes me to follow next to calm waters;

dónetháa	Ba	óotha	lethath.
CAUSETO+AGAIN+THRIVE	XLOVE1	SOUL	I+POSSBIRTH+OBJ

S/He causes my soul to thrive again.

Dódoth	Ba	leth	weth
CAUSE-TO+FOLLOW	XLOVE1	I+OBJ	PATH

shadethuha	óobe	zha	Bathada.
BE PERFECT+PARTV+PLC	ALONG	NAME	XLOVE1+POSSBIRTH+BENEF

S/He causes me to follow along path(s) of purity/perfection for Her/His name's sake.

Íizha	óomasháad	le	Yed
ALTHOUGH	FOOT+COME/GO = WALK	I	VALLEY

Rawíthuha		obe,	
NON+LIFE = DEATH+PARTV+PLC		THROUGH	

Although I walk through the Valley of Non-Life,

héeya	ra	le	ramíilith	bróo	Na	leden
TO-FEAR	NEG	I	NON+RADIANCE = EVIL+OBJ	BECAUSE	YOULOVE1	I+ASSOC

I do not fear evil because Thou art with me;

meshe	dáan	Natha	i	oyi
PL+COMFORT	WORD	YOULOVE1+POSSBIRTH	AND	EYE

Natha	leth.
YOULOVE1+POSSBIRTH	I+OBJ

Thy word and Thine eye comfort me.

Dóham	Na	anath	i
CAUSETO+BE-PRESENT	YOULOVE1	FOOD+OBJ	AND

ranath	leda	ham	lebethu
BEVERAGE+OBJ	I+BENEF	BE PRESENT	ENEMY+PARTV

letho	rawáan.
I+POSS	NON+COZ = DESPITE

Thou causest food and drink to be present for me despite the presence of my enemy(ies).

Boóbin	Na	delith	lethath
BRAID	YOULOVE1	HAIR	I+POSSBIRTH+OBJ

oma	Nathanan;	ume	ni
HAND	YOU-LOVE1+POSSBIRTH+INSTR	BE FULL/ABUNDANT	CUP

letho	hadihad
I+POSS	ALWAYS

Thou braidest my hair with Thine Own Hand; my cup is always full.

Aril	mesháad	thal	i	yidan	leden,
FUT	PL+COME/GO	BE GOOD	AND	MERCY	I+ASSOC

hulehul,	sháal	wíthu	lethaya	woho;
FOR-SURE	DAY	LIFE+PARTV	I+POSSBIRTH+TIME	ALL/EVERY

Goodness and mercy will go with me, for-sure, every day of my life,

i	habelid	le	lod	Lahila
AND	DWELL	I	HOUSEHOLD	HOLY-ONE

Bathaha	ril	i	aril	i	rilrili
XLOVE1+POSSBIRTH+PLC	PRES	AND	FUT	AND	HYPOTH

and I shall dwell in the Holy One's household eternally.

Othe
AMEN

–Amen

Exercise 5

Wohíya Wodedide Shósho Bethu[1]

(A Little Story About Magic Granny)

Bíide eril wod i alehale Shósho wo. Eril aba i owa sháal; eril tháa déela betho; loláad Shósho thena wo. "Bíi ril thi le shath wa," eril di be. "Wu sháal!" eril di Shósho. "Radiídin ra; hathalehal sháal hi wa!"

Linguist's Translation

First Line: Láadan

Second Line: MORPHEME-BY-MORPHEME

Third Line: Free Translation

Bíide	eril	wod	i	alehale
DECLARATIVE NARRATIVE	PAST	SIT	AND	MUSIC

Shósho	wo.
MAGIC GRANNY	PERCEIVED-HYPOTHETICALLY

This is a story I'm telling you, that I made up myself, about once when Magic Granny was sitting and music-ing.

Eril	aba	i	owa	sháal;	eril	tháa	déela	betho;
PAST	FRAGRANT	AND	WARM	DAY	PAST	THRIVE	GARDEN	HER-OF

The day was fragrant and warm; her garden was thriving.

---

[1] Reprinted from *Hot Wire*

loláad			Shósho	
PERCEIVE INTERNALLY			MAGIC GRANNY	
thena			wo.	
JOY-FOR-GOOD-REASONS			PERCEIVED-HYPOTHETICALLY	

Magic Granny was very happy, and with good reason.

"Bíi	ril	thi	le	shath
DECLARATIVE	PRESENT	HAVE	I	HARMONY + OBJECT
wa,"		eril	di	be.
MY-OWN-PERCEPTIONS		PAST	SAY	SHE.

"To my way of perceiving things, all's right with my world," she said.

"Wu	shaal!"	eril	di	Shósho.
SUCH-A	DAY!	PAST	SAY	MAGIC GRANNY

"Such a day!" said Magic Granny.

"Radiídin	ra;	hathalehal	sháal	hi	wa!"
NON-HOLIDAY	NO:	TIME-GOOD-VERY	DAY	THIS	MY-OWN-PERCEPTIONS.

"This is no non-holiday—this is a fandangous day!"

Notes on the Translation

English has no verb "to music," but Láadan does. That word "non-holiday" has no English equivalent, but means an alleged holiday when you have to work so hard that it's worse than a working day. "Fandangous" is a better word for "superb."

What I want to do here is change keys. I'm going to give you almost the same story, but with a slightly different vocabulary. You do the translation.

Wohíya Wodedide Shósho Bethu

Bíi eril wod i delishe Shósho wo. Eril líithin i modi sháal; eril nótháa déela betho; loláad Shósho shama wo. "Bíi ril thi ra le shath wa," eril di be. "Wu sháal!" eril di Shósho. "Radiídinelh hulehul; harathalehal sháal hi wa!"

Vocabulary:

delishe	to weep
líithin	gray
modi	ugly
nótháa	cease to thrive
shama	grief for good reasons, with no one to blame, and nothing to be done about it
ra	negative, no
radiídinelh	non-holiday + pejorative
hulehul	for-sure
harathalehal	very bad, said of time

Exercise 6

Aranesha Bethu[1]

Bíi nahóya Aranesha Athileya—nahóyaháalish wa. Memahina abesh; yáanin zhe mewolíithi woboshum, i mehel oyimahina reneth óoma netha yil wa. Melirihal babí zhe melirihul mahina. Hotheha woho, láad ne hodoth i lehinath i léelith, woliyeneth wohesheth i woyetheth wohilith. Wu hohama wa! Uhudehóo raden, aril hal ra rawith wa. Thalehal, owáano— thi Aranesha, Athileya, uhudemid. Wil mehothel uhudemid wa.

Vocabulary:

hóya	be beautiful (of a place)
líithi	be white
uhud	nuisance
uhudemid	tick (nuisance-creature)
Athil[2]	April
liri	be colored
thal	be good
othel	be blessed

---

[1] Reprinted from *Hot Wire*

[2] **Athil** is one of the original, "poetic" month names, which were replaced by numbered months. Both sets are listed in Appendix 2-B.

Linguist's Translation

First Line: Láadan

Second Line: MORPHEME-BY-MORPHEME

Third Line: Free Translation

Bíi nahóya Aranesha Athileya—
DECLARATIVE START-TO-BE BEAUTIFUL ARKANSAS APRIL-IN

nahóyaháalish
START-TO-BE BEAUTIFUL TO EXTRAORDINARY DEGREE

wa.
ACCORDING TO MY PERCEPTION

Arkansas begins to be incredibly beautiful, to my mind, in April.

Memahina abesh; yáanin
PLURAL-BLOOM ALL-THAT-IS TREES

zhe mewolíithi woboshum,
BE-LIKE REL-PL-CLOUD REL-PLURAL-BE-WHITE

Everything is in bloom; the trees are like white clouds,

i mehel oyimahina
AND PLURAL-MAKE VIOLET

and the violets

reneth óoma nethaha yil wa.
CARPET-OBJECT FOOT YOU-OF UNDER MY PERCEPTIONS.

make a carpet under your feet.

Melirihal babí zhe melirihul mahina.
PL-BE COLORED-VERY BIRD LIKE PL-BE COLORED-VERY FLOWER.

The birds are brightly colored like the flowers.

Hotheha woho, láad ne hodoth i lehinath
PLACE-AT EVERY PERCEIVE YOU TULIP-OBJECT AND LILAC-OBJECT

Everywhere, you see tulips and lilacs

i	léelith	woliyeneth	wohesheth
AND	JONQUIL-OBJ	REL-BE GREEN	REL-GRASS-OBJ

i	woyetheth	wohilith.	
AND	REL-BE SILVER	REL-WATER-OBJ	

and jonquils, green grass, and silver water.

Wu	hohama	wa!
WHAT-A	GLORY	MY PERCEPTIONS

What a glory!

Uhudehóo	raden,	aril	hal	ra	rawith
NUISANCE-FOCUS	WITHOUT	FUTURE	WORK	NOT	NOBODY

wa.					
MY PERCEPTIONS					

Without some specific nuisance, nobody would get any work done.

Thalehal,	owáano—	thi	Aranesha,	Athileya,
BE GOOD-VERY	THEREFORE	HAVE	ARKANSAS	APRIL-IN

uhudemid.
TICK

It's a very good thing, therefore, that Arkansas, in April, has ticks.

Wil	mehothel	uhudemid	wa.
LET-THERE-BE	PLURAL-BE BLESSED	TICK	MY PERCEPTIONS

Bless the ticks…

Notes on the Translation

1. The title means, literally. "Arkansas It-Of"; "About Arkansas," The word "**Aranesha**" is a loan word, a "Láadanization" from English.

2. Láadan has a set of degree markers, including "**-hal**" (neutral "very") and "**-hul**" ("very, to an extreme degree") and "**-háalish**" ("very, to extraordinary degree"); that lets you use the contrast between "**melirihal**" and "**melirihul**" to indicate that both the birds and the flowers are very colorful, but the flowers are more so.

3. In the sentence about seeing tulips and green grass and silver water, and so on, all the grammatical objects carry the object marker "**-th**" at the end; this is formally correct. However, whether you *must* use the object marker or not depends on your worldview. If you want to say that you speak Láadan (**di le Láadan**, SPEAK I LÁADAN), you absolutely don't have to add the marker (**Láadaneth**), because "the language speaks me" is entirely impossible. Similarly, if you were perceiving a book or a chair, you would need no object marker. But can the tulips and lilacs and so on "perceive you" back? If so, the object marker is required to indicate who or what is doing the perceiving. I've put them in to demonstrate; if you don't hold with sentient flowers and grass and water, you can take them back off; thus "you see lilacs" becomes just "**láad ne lehina**" instead of "**láad ne lehinath**."

4. Some of you may find that "RELATIVE" morpheme mystifying.... I suspect it looks like linguist jargon. English derives "the green grass" from "the grass which is green," with "which is green" the relative clause; when a language does that with a morpheme instead of by grammatical processes like moving things around and deleting and inserting stuff, the morpheme is called a "relativizer." So, "**liyen**," is "be green" and "**hesh**" is "grass"; "**woliyen wohesh**" is "green grass" because of the relativizing prefix.

5. The focus marker "**hóo**" was left out of the beginning dictionary (along with many other things, due to space constraints). It is added to a word to mean "this particular specific one" or for emphatic stress—the context will indicate which.

6. You might be interested in knowing a little more about the words for "bridge" and "butterfly." One of the things that women do in their language behavior, in all of the languages I know, is a whole lot of *body* language work. I wanted that work to be less in Láadan, and the language is therefore constructed to *lexicalize* body language.

   (That is, to give it a pronounced form, instead of leaving it all to be done by tone of voice and gesture and facial expression and so on.) That's why you have the set of words that tell whether the sentence coming up is a statement or question or something else; and that's why you have the endings that tell whether the sentence is meant as a joke or a lesson or a narrative or something else—to reduce the communications labor for the women speaking. The word for bridge, when its tone markers are in the right place, has a sound pattern like this: ⎯⎯⎤⎯⎡⎯⎯ The word for butterfly is like this: ⎯⎤⎯⎡⎯ Since intonation (the melody that carries the spoken words) is part of body language, this is another way of lexicalizing it. For both of these words, the voice makes the shape of the thing named, in the ear's space and the ear's time. Shapes "in the air," you perceive, but for the ear rather than for the eye.

Exercise 7

Wolaya Wohilub[1]
(The Little Red Hen)

Bíide:

Rilrili wolaya wohilub wo. Eril náhalehal be i naya álub bethath i thaáhel be wo. Wemeneya eril di lub, "Bíi aril dala le edeth wa." I mime be, "Báa aril den bebáa leth?" "Bíi ra le hulehul wa!" eril di muda bedim wo. "Bíi ra le hulehul wa!" eril di éesh bedim wo. I "Bíi ra le hulehul wa!" eril di dithemid bedim wo. I "Bíi aril hal le sholanenal wi," eril di lub. I eril shub be haleth wo.

Wumaneya eril di be, "Bíi aril róo le edeth i el le baleth wa. Báa aril den bebáa leth?" "Bíi ra le hulehul wa!" eril di muda. "Bíi ra le hulehul wa!" eril di éesh. I "Bíi ra le hulehul wa!" eril di dithemid. "Bíi aril hal le sholanenal wi," eril di lub. I eril shub be haleth wo.

Ihée di be, "Bíi aril nayod le baleth wa. Báada aril den bebáa leth?" "Bíi aril meden lezh neth hulehul wa!" medi muda i éesh i dithemid. "Bó mewam nezh!" eril di lub. "Bíidi aril meyod le i álub letha baleth—hulehul—wi!" Bíidi eril hinal wo.

---

[1] Reprinted from *Hot Wire*

Linguist's Translation

First Line: Láadan

Second Line: MORPHEME-BY-MORPHEME

Third Line: Free Translation

Bíide:	Rilrili (Ø)	wolaya	wohíya	lub
DEC-NAR	HYP	REL-RED	REL-LITTLE	HEN

wo.
HYPOTHETICAL

Once upon a time, there was a little red hen.

Eril	náhalehal	be	i	naya
PAST	CONTINUE-WORK-VERY	SHE	AND	LOOK-AFTER

álub	bethath
CHICK POSS-BY-BIRTH	OBJECT

She worked very hard, and looked after her chick.

i	thaáhel	be	wo.
AND	GET-BY	SHE	HYPOTHETICAL

and she got by.

Wemeneya	eril	di	lub,	"Bíi	aril	dala	le
SPRING-IN	PAST	SAY	HEN	DEC	FUTURE	PLANT	I

edeth	wa."
GRAIN-OBJ	MY PERCEPTIONS.

In the spring, the hen said, "I will plant the grain."

I	mime	be,	"Báa	aril	den	bebáa	leth?"
AND	ASK	SHE	Ø	FUTURE	HELP	3RD PERSON	1-OBJ

And she asked, "Who will help me?"

"Bíi	ra	le	hulehul	wa!"	eril	di
DEC	NEG	I	FOR-SURE	MY PERCEPTIONS	PAST	SAY

muda	bedim	wo.
PIG	SHE-TO	HYPOTHETICAL

"Not *me*!" said the pig to her.

[Repeat for "**éesh**" (the sheep) and "**dithemid**" (the cow).]

"Bíi	aril	hal	le	sholanenal	wi,"	eril	di	lub.
DEC	FUTURE	WORK	I	ALONE-MANNER	SELF-EVIDENT	PAST	SAY	HEN

"I will do it all by myself," said the hen.

I	eril	shub	be	haleth	wo.
AND	PAST	DO	SHE	WORK/OBJ	HYPOTHETICAL.

And she did the work.

Wumaneya	eril	di	be,
SUMMER-IN	PAST	SAY	SHE

In the summer, she said,

"Bíi	aril	róo	le	edeth	i	el	le	baleth
DEC	FUTURE	HARVEST	I	GRAIN-OBJ	AND	MAKE	I	BREAD-OBJ

wa.
HYPOTHETICAL

"I will harvest the grain and make the bread."
(Add "Who will help me?" and as before, they all say "Not me!" and she says she will do it alone, and she does.)

Ihée di be,	"Bíi	aril	nayod	le	baleth	wa
LATER SAY SHE	DEC	FUTURE	START-EAT	I	BREAD-OBJ	MY-PERCEPTIONS

Later she said, "I'm going to eat the bread."

Báada	aril	den	bebáa	leth?"
Q-JOKE	FUTURE	HELP	3RD-PERSON-Q	I-OBJ

"Who will help me?"

"Bíi	aril	meden	lezh neth	hulehul	wa!"
DEC	FUTURE	PLURAL-HELP	WE YOU-OBJ	FOR-SURE	MY PERCEPTIONS

"*We* will help you!"

medi	muda	i	éeah	i	dithemid.
PLURAL-SAY	PIG	AND	SHEEP	AND	COW

said the pig and the sheep and the cow.

"Bó	mewam	nezh!"	eril	di	lub.
COMMAND	PLURAL-BE STILL	YOU	PAST	SAY	HEN

"You just stay where you are!" said the hen.

"Bíidi	aril	meyod	le	i	álub	letha
DEC-TEACHING	FUTURE	PL-EAT	I-OBJ	AND	CHICK	ME-OBJ

baleth—	hulehul—	wi!"
BREAD-OBJ	FOR SURE	SELF-EVIDENT

"We will eat the bread, me and my chick!"

Bíidi	eril	hinal	wo.
DEC NAR	PAST	THUS	HYPOTHETICAL

And that's the way it was.

Notes on the Translation

1. The very first line of the Linguist's Translation has a null symbol (Ø) in it, as a courtesy to speakers of English. Láadan has no "copula"—that is, no obligatory form of "be" that has to appear; for "she is tired," Láadan, like many other languages, would have just "she tired." The null is where the "be" form would go if Láadan had one.

2. When the hen asks, "Who will help me?" for the last time, she puts the affix "-**da**" on the question word, "Báa." This "-**da**" is the marker that means "I say this to you only as a joke."

3. Finally, when she tells the do-nothings she doesn't need their help to eat the bread, the hen adds the *teaching* affix "-**di**" to the declarative, to let them know that she's hoping they will understand this and learn from it. And the command form "**Bó**" that starts her speech is one used very rarely, and usually for speaking to small children.

Exercise 8

A Nativity Story Written from Mary's Point of View

Vocabulary
- **éde** nevertheless
- **rathóo** non-guest, someone who comes to visit knowing perfectly well that they are intruding and causing difficulty. **ra-** = non + **thóo** = guest
- **wée** cry (of babies)
- **womil** livestock
- **womilá** shepherd. **womil** = livestock + **-á** = doer
- **Zheshu** Jesus of Nazareth (loanword)

Wóoban Méri Batha Láadan[1]:

Bíide eríli wóoban with wemaneya wáa. Wóoban bi áwithid i ban bi zhath "Zheshu" áwithidedi wáa. Shi áwithid bith, i di bi eba bithodi, "Bíili, bre aril tháa ra áwithehóo, ébre aril míi le!"

Id—bishibenal—menosháad womilá menedebe i noline menedebe i wothidá nedebe wáa. Medi, "Bóo aril meláad len áwithideth oyinan lu."

Bíide di with biyóodi, "Wulh hath áwitheláadewan! Methi ra bash i methi ra shal!"—i loláad bi ilhith. Izh di bi "Wil sha" zhonal: "Bóo mesháad nen i meláad."

Yide áwithid Zheshu i lili be wi. Nawée be i náwée be. Éde benem mélhewith. Lith with "Raláadá menedebe!"

---

[1] "In the fall of 1982 the journal *Women and Language News* published the first writing in the language, a Nativity story written from Mary's point of view." —Suzette Haden Elgin

I lámála with áwithideth i náluth beth. Bíid mesháad hath i mesháad hath. Doól di with biyóodi, "Bóo melith nen woho! Bíi ril nen rathóo wi! Báa melothel nen radaleth? Bíi rilrili meloláad thul nenetha lhohoth." I thib with i bel bi áwitheth i naya bi beth.

Bíide thi with zhath Méri wáa.

The Birth-Giving of Mary the Beloved
English:

Long ago, a woman gave birth in the wintertime. She had a baby boy, and she named him "Jesus." The baby pleased her, and she said to her spouse, "If this baby doesn't do well, I'll be very surprised."

And then—suddenly—there arrived many sheperds, many angels, and several wise men. They said, "May we please see the baby?"

"What a horrible time for a baby-viewing!" the woman said to herself. "They have no common sense and no manners!—and she was disgusted. But aloud she said, "Please come and see."

As would be obvious to any thinking person, the Baby Jesus was hungry and wet. He started crying, and he kept on crying. Nevertheless, the crowd stayed on. "What a lot of blind, deaf, dumb, thick-headed creatures!" the woman thought.

And she held the baby close and rocked him. Time went by… and more time went by. At last the woman said to herself, "All of you, please think! You're not guests any longer, you're nothing but trouble! Don't you know anything? Your parents would be ashamed." And she stood up and took the baby and took care of him.

That woman's name was Mary.

Linguist's Translation

First Line: Láadan
Second Line: MORPHEME-BY-MORPHEME[1]
Third Line: Free Translation

Wóoban	Méri	Batha
GIVE-BIRTH	MARY	X1(3RD-PERSON,SINGULAR; LOVE)+POSS-BIRTH

The Birth-Giving of Mary the Beloved

Bíide	eríli	wóoban	with
DECL+NARR	FARPAST	GIVE BIRTH	PERSON

wemaneya	wáa.	Wóoban	Bi
WINTER+TIME	TRUSTED	GIVE BIRTH	XHON1

Long ago, a woman gave birth in the wintertime.

áwithid	i	ban	bi
INFANT+PERSON=BABY+MALE	AND	GIVE	XHON1

zhath	"Zheshu"	áwithidedi	wáa.
NAME+OBJ	JESUS	BABY+MALE+GOAL	TRUSTED

She had a baby boy, and she named him "Jesus."

Shi	áwithid	bith,	i	di
PLEASE	BABY+MALE	XHON1+OBJ	AND	SAY

bi	eba	bithodi,
XHONE1	SPOUSE	XHON1+POSS+GOAL

The baby pleased her, and she said to her spouse,

"Bíili,	bre	aril	tháa	ra	áwithehóo,
DECL+LOVE	IF...	FUT	THRIVE	NEG	BABY+FOCUS

ébre	aril	míi	le!"
...THEN	FUT	BE-AMAZED	I

"If this baby doesn't do well, I'll be very surprised."

---

[1] This morpheme-by-morpheme translation (or in linguist terms, "gloss") includes some honorific forms which we have not encountered yet. Láadan honorifics are discussed in Lesson 59 of the Láadan Lessons, Láadanlanguage.com

Id	—bishibenal	—menosháad
AND-THEN	BE-SUDDEN+MANN	PL+FINISH+COME/GO=ARRIVE

womilá	menedebe
LIVESTOCK+DOER=SHEPHERD	MANY

And then—suddenly—there arrived many sheperds,

i	noline	menedebe	i	wothidá
AND	ANGEL	MANY	AND	WISDOM+MALE+DOER

nedebe	wáa.
SEVERAL	TRUSTED

many angels, and several wise men.

Medi, "Bóo aril meláad len áwithideth oyinan lu."
PL+SAY REQ FUT PL+PERCEIVE WE6^ BABY+MALE+OBJ
EYE+INSTR   PLEASE

They said, "May we please see the baby?"

Bíide	di	with	biyóodi,
DECL+NARR	SAY	PERSON	XHON1+REFLX+GOAL

"Wulh	hath	áwitheláadewan!
SUCH-A+PEJ	TIME	BABY+PERCEIVE+PURP

"What a horrible time for a baby-viewing!" the woman said to herself.

Methi ra	bash	i	methi	ra
PL+NEG	COMMON SENSE	AND	PL+HAVE	NEG

shal!"	—i	loláad	bi	ílhith.
MANNERS	AND	PERCEIVE-INTERNAL	XHON1	DISGUST+OBJ

"They have no common sense and no manners!—and she was disgusted.

Izh	di	bi	"Wil	sha"	zhonal:
BUT	SAY	XHON1	OPTV	HARMONY	SOUND+MANN=ALOUD
"Bóo	mesháad	nen	i		meláad."
REQ	PL+GO/COME	YOU6^	AND		PL+PERCEIVE

But aloud she said, "Please come and see."

Yide	áwithid	Zheshu	i	lili	be
BE-HUNGRY	BABY+MALE	JESUS	AND	BE-WET	X1
wi.	Nawée	be	i	náwée	be.
SELF-EVID	BEGIN+CRY	X1	AND	CONT+CRY	X1

As would be obvious to any thinking person, the Baby Jesus was hungry and wet. He started crying, and he kept on crying.

Éde	benem	mélhewith.	Lith
NEVERTHELESS	STAY	CROWD+PEJ	THINK
with	"Raláadá		menedebe!"
PERSON	NON+PERCEIVED+DOER		MANY

Nevertheless, the crowd stayed on. "What a lot of blind, deaf, dumb, thick-headed creatures!" the woman thought.

I	lámála	with	áwithideth	i
AND	CARESS	PERSON	BABY+MALE+OBJ	AND
náluth		beth.	Bíid	
CONT+ROCK		X1+OBJ	DECL+ANGER	

And she held the baby close and rocked him.

mesháad	hath	i	mesháad	hath.	Doól	di	with
PL+GO/COME	TIME	AND	PL+GO/COME	TIME	AT-LAST	SAY	PERSON

Time went by…and more time went by. At last the woman said

biyóodi,	"Bóo	melith	nen	woho!
XHONT+REFLX+GOAL	REQ	PL+THINK	YOU6^	ALL/EVERY

Bíi	ril		nen	
DECL	PRES		YOU6^	

to herself, "All of you, please think!

rathóo	wi!	Báa	melothel
NON+GUEST+IDENT	SELF-EVID	INTERR	PL+KNOW

nen	radaleth?
YOU6^	NON+THING=NOTHING+OBJ

You're not guests any longer, you're nothing but trouble!

Bíi	rilrili	meloláad	thul
DECL	HYPOTH	PL+PERCEIVE-INTERNAL	PARENT

nenetha	lhohoth."	I
YOU6^+POSS-BIRTH	SHAME+OBJ	AND

Don't you know anything? Your parents would be ashamed."

thib	with	i	bel	bi	áwitheth
STAND	PERSON	AND	TAKE	XHON1	BABY+OBJ

i	naya	bi	beth.
AND	CARE-FOR	XHON1	X1+OBJ

And she stood up and took the baby and took care of him.

Bíide	thi	with	zhath	Méri	wáa.
DECL + NARR	HAVE	PERSON	NAME + OBJ	MARY	TRUSTED

That woman's name was Mary.

Essays by Suzette Haden Elgin

Can a Language Be Owned?

I'VE SAID THAT the problems of IALs (International Auxiliary Languages), even IALs that are put together in ways that make them relatively easy to learn and use, have often been social rather than linguistic. IALs have tended to reflect the cultures of those who construct or choose them—as the evidence for the strong link between language and culture would predict—and therefore to bring along with them all the political problems associated with those cultures. Because IALs are a hobby limited to people with unusual interests, as compared to people interested in postage stamps or baseball or gardening, they've frequently been constructed with little regard for how difficult they might be to learn and use. [In science fiction constructed languages (or conlangs), for example, the emphasis tends to be more on how fancy the language is than on its usefulness for the ordinary person.] But the most counterproductive problem in terms of making a language successful in the real world is the problem of turf wars, which have been the downfall of IAL after IAL, and which need to be discussed separately because of their potential effects.

The turf war question is simply this: *Can a language be owned?* Nobody—no individual or group or corporation or government—owns English or Chinese or Farsi; the very idea is ridiculous. But what if someone sits down and creates a language (or a modified version of an existing language) in the same way that a person would write a novel or compose a symphony? Then what? Does that language belong to that individual?

The lengths that would-be Esperanto reformers went to in their attempts to get Ludwig Lejze Zamenhof to endorse their proposals boggle even the broadest mind. Without question, the coups and countercoups and Machiavellian intrigues of (and against) Esperantists, and their endless public wrangles over who controlled the language, caused the downfall of the movement as a whole. It all became so absurd that no rational adult wanted anything to do with it.

An organization for promotion of English internationally—the British Council—bought and still holds the rights to Basic English, which is the major example of a modified existing language proposed as an IAL. A company called the Science News Service bought the rights to Interlingua, a language constructed by the International Auxiliary Language Association under the direction of linguists André Martinet and Alexander Gode. James Cooke Brown constructed Loglan and claims copyright ownership and control for it; he was in court in the mid-1990s in a fight over whether a reform group now using the name Loglan can be legally prevented from using that name. (Loglan is described as a language specifically created as a mechanism for testing the linguistic relativity hypothesis.)

And then of course there's the matter of the Klingon language. According to Donald Harlow, Klingon's first few words were created by Scotty, chief engineer of the starship *Enterprise*. But when the Klingons caught the public imagination, and *Star Trek* episodes in which they appeared turned out to be wildly popular, Paramount sat up and took notice—and hired linguist Marc Okrand to create an entire Klingon language. The resulting *Klingon Dictionary* and its audio version and sequel have been smash best-sellers; the dictionary alone has sold hundreds of thousands of copies. There is a Klingon Language Institute housed at a university, with its own academic journal; there are two competing projects for translating the Bible into Klingon.

I'm exceedingly grateful to Klingon for the inroads it's made into the typical American loathing for foreign language learning. People who are multilingual because they know one natural language plus Klingon are more likely to be willing to learn yet another language, and I'm all for that. But I have major reservations about Klingon as an IAL, and I suspect that Marc Okrand would agree with me. For many and curious reasons, Klingon would be an inappropriate choice for "WorldSpeak" (that is, a worldwide Earth language). The idea of an allegedly extraterrestrial language being taught as the Terran IAL is bizarre enough all by itself. The idea of trying to run a world with a language specifically designed to express the perceptions of a warrior race is equally strange, despite its convenient fit with the Warrior metaphor that organizes so much of American life; a language designed for the Diplomat metaphor would be better suited to the task. In addition, Klingon has features that were linguistics in-jokes, and its writing system is difficult and inconvenient. Klingon is definitely a fixer-upper as an IAL. But anyone who decided to propose and publish an "improved" version of Klingon would be in far more serious trouble than IAL reformers have ever found themselves in up to now. They would be in court facing not just Marc Okrand but the corporate might of *Star Trek* and Paramount.

Láadan (like Klingon or Elvish) wasn't intended as an IAL, but nothing in principle would prevent it from serving as one. I didn't want any turf wars; I went out of my way to make it very clear that I didn't consider myself its owner or its chief of staff or anything of the kind. It was part of a scientific experiment that I took absolutely seriously, into which "marketing" would have introduced an impossibly wild variable, and so I made no effort to market it. I constructed it, and then I turned it loose and observed what happened, without interfering. But that's not the usual practice. People who "create" a language tend to take the position that they own it and have complete control over it.

It may be that as a philosophical matter this question is not only trivial but silly. So you whipped up a little hobby language during your summer vacation, and now you want to claim that it's yours alone and nobody else is allowed to play with it. So what? Who cares? So a giant media conglomerate won't let you play with its language, in the same way that McDonald's Corporation will sue you if you try to call your coffeeshop Cafe McDonald's. So what? Who cares if the squabbles of obscure language hobbyists result in a legal precedent that establishes as law the principle that a language can be owned in exactly the same way that a copyright or trademark or patent can be owned?

We would be wise to care. We would be wise to pay cautious attention to these developments, because ownership of WorldSpeak would be a gold mine. There would be textbooks and audio programs and videos and standardized tests and computer programs and libraries of original and translated literature. There would be magazines and newspapers and scholarly journals, both print and electronic. There would be WorldSpeak versions of every significant document in international government and trade and diplomacy. The money to be made in signs alone, to go up on streets and buildings and bridges all over the world, would be huge, as would the profit from the WorldSpeak instructions that would have to go into the boxes for every widget sold around the world. Every language item now used in international meetings and conferences would have to be republished or reproduced using WorldSpeak. Think of the money to be made from the licensing rights to put WorldSpeak slogans and catch phrases on toys and lunchboxes and bumper stickers and coffee mugs!

Anyone sharp enough to purchase the rights to an IAL that succeeded as WorldSpeak would be wealthy in a way that would make Bill Gates' fortune seem modest. And I would be very surprised if there are no investors right this minute busy buying up the rights to all the Internet domain names that might plausibly turn out to include the ultimate IAL, such as:

- http://www.worldspeak.com, or
- http://www.earthish.com, and
- http://www.terran.com

Just in case. I'd buy those domain names myself, right this minute, if I could afford it.

Suzette Haden Elgin, ©1999
From *The Language Imperative,* Perseus Books, 2000.

Láadan, the Constructed Language in "Native Tongue" Books

EVERYONE KNOWS ABOUT THE CONSTRUCTED LANGUAGES (conlangs) in Tolkien's writing (Elvish, for example); what is perhaps less well known is that Tolkien said he wrote his novels to provide a showcase for the languages. That sort of passion for language is unusual; it would be a shock to read that *Star Trek* had been created as a showcase for the Klingon language. Usually, as with Klingon (constructed by linguist Marc Okrand), the fiction comes first and the language is added later if it is added at all. Elvish and Klingon are famous conlangs; Klingon not only has a journal published by an institute located at a university, it has two competing Bible translation projects, it has a Shakespeare translation project, it has summer camps…. But there are also many little-known sf conlangs, among them Láadan, the language I put together for the novel *Native Tongue*.

Many science fiction stories and novels make references to fictional languages of one kind or another, and they usually include a handful of words or phrases from such languages. Some have glossaries in the back that expand the vocabulary and may include some additional information. But few writers feel a need to go beyond that and set up an entire constructed language (conlang). A conlang is a language put together with the intention that it should have enough grammar and vocabulary to make it possible for someone to use it to communicate, just as they would use an existing natural language. There are some very famous conlangs; Tolkien's Elvish tongues and Marc Okrand's Klingon come immediately to mind. There are also very obscure conlangs, like Láadan, the language that serves as a major plot element in the *Native Tongue* series. (If conlangs appeal to you, an Internet search with the words <international auxiliary language> as your search term will provide you with a lifetime's worth of fascinating material to read.)

When I put Láadan together, it was to serve two purposes. First, much of the plot for *Native Tongue* revolved around a group of women, all linguists, engaged in constructing a language specifically designed to express the perceptions of human women; because I'm a linguist and linguistics is the science in my novels, I felt obligated actually to construct the language before I wrote about it. Second, I wrote the novel as a thought experiment with the express goal of testing four interrelated hypotheses: (1) that the weak form of the linguistic relativity hypothesis is true (that is, that human languages structure human perceptions in significant ways); (2) that Goedel's Theorem applies to language, so that there are changes you could not introduce into a language without destroying it and languages you could not introduce into a culture without destroying it; (3) that change in language brings about social change, rather than the contrary; and (4) that if women were offered a women's language one of two things would happen—they would welcome and nurture it, or it would at minimum motivate them to replace it with a better women's language of their own construction. I set a ten-year time limit on the experiment—since the novel came out in 1984, that meant an end date of 1994—and I turned it loose. I didn't know in 1984 that the experiment would escape from the novel that was its lab, but in the long run I was glad that it did; it made the final results more interesting.

Constructing a language is formally easy, especially with today's computers. See "Language Construction 101," the next essay in this book. Any competent linguist can run up half a dozen in just a few hours or program the computer to spit them out at a fantastic rate. Making the language interesting, which is art rather than science, is much harder. Making it a living language, used by living human beings attached to a living culture, is enormously difficult. It's hard enough to keep natural languages alive, hard enough that we're losing them today by the hundreds; keeping a conlang alive is a quantum leap in difficulty. Nevertheless, there's a theory that women are distressed because existing human languages are inadequate to express their perceptions; if that theory has any validity, it would seem that women would welcome a language that better served that purpose. And suppose they did, what would happen? Finding at least one answer to that question was the point of constructing Láadan and putting it into a novel.

Now, what does it mean to say that a language expresses the perceptions of women, or that existing natural languages don't do that adequately? Let me stipulate immediately that I don't know all existing human languages or even a tiny percentage of them. It may be that there's one somewhere that, unknown to me, is the perfect medium for expressing women's perceptions. I don't know all women, either, or even a tiny percentage of them. The complaints around which the theory was constructed have come from women who are native speakers of well-known languages (especially English and languages in the same family as English); they were the research subjects for the experiment. With that constraint (which makes the experiment what scientists call a "pilot" experiment) stated, I can go on to tell you that I saw two major problems—for women—with English and its close linguistic relatives. (1) Those languages lacked vocabulary for many things that are extremely important to women, making it cumbersome and inconvenient to talk about them. (2) They lacked ways to express emotional information conveniently, so that—especially in English—much of that information had to be carried by body language and was almost entirely missing from written language. This characteristic (which makes English so well suited for business) left women vulnerable to hostile language followed by the ancient "But all I said was…" excuse; and it restricted women to the largely useless "It wasn't what you said, it was the way you said it!" defense against such hostility. In constructing Láadan, I focused on giving it features intended to repair those two deficiencies.

The results of this experiment were clear. For the first three hypotheses being tested—that the weak form of the linguistic relativity hypothesis is true, that Goedel's Theorem applies to language, and that change in language brings about social change—I ended up with nothing more than anecdotal information. The fourth hypothesis—that if women were offered a women's language they would either welcome and nurture it or would replace it with a better one—was proved false. (It was of course almost inevitable that if the fourth hypothesis failed I would learn nothing much about the other three, since they only begin to be tested if the fourth one succeeds.)

As I said…interesting. It was well worth the effort. Whether results would have been different if I'd given the experiment twenty years instead of ten, or if *Star Trek* had decided to present episodes about a war between a Láadan-speaking population and the Klingons, or any of a multitude of other modifications in conditions, is impossible to say; whether something different will happen when the reprint edition of *Native Tongue* comes out from Feminist Press is impossible to say. Experiments have to have limits or they have no scientific value.

Meanwhile, the Klingon language thrives—from which you are free to draw your own conclusions.

Suzette Haden Elgin, ©1999
From https://laadanlanguage.wordpress.com

Language Construction 101

YOU CAN OF COURSE CONSTRUCT AN ENTIRE LANGUAGE composed of just the item "A"; linguists torment students with that kind of thing routinely. But suppose you want to construct a language that might be of some practical use for communication in your fictional universe... Here's how it's done. It is *not* difficult.

STEP 1: Decide whether you want a *polysynthetic (or agglutinating) language* (one where you construct meanings by assembling lots of small meaningful pieces into larger chunks, as Navajo does) or an *isolating language* (one like English, where words are made up of only a *few* meaningful pieces and often of only a single piece). Polysynthetic (or agglutinating) is quicker, the way building stuff with a TinkerToy set is quicker; I recommend it.

STEP 2: Choose an order for verb, subject, and object. Only six are mathematically possible; English uses the order "Subject, then Verb, then Object." Pick one.

STEP 3: Choose the structure and assembly rules for your syllables (**pronounceable** chunks). For example, you could decide that all syllables of your language must contain a vowel; that none can begin with more than one consonant; that all can end with either a vowel or a consonant; that no double (long) vowels or consonants are allowed; and that no more than twelve syllables may be in a single word.

STEP 4: Choose a set of phonemes (that is, chunks of sound that change meaning). For English, the fact that we understand "bat" and "sat" as two different words proves that the sounds of "b" and "s" in those words are two different phonemes. Hawaiian has eleven phonemes, English has about thirty-five, seventy is roughly the upper limit, and all human languages choose from the same set. (You could pick sounds no human language uses, of course, if you're constructing a language for ETs, but you couldn't be sure that your human readers would be able to pronounce it in their heads as they read; it's not wise to annoy your readers that way.) Suppose we pick these twelve: /b/, /g/, /s/, /l/, /m/, /h/, /w/, /a/, /e/, /i/, /o/, /u/.

STEP 5: Set up an inventory of syllables that your rules will allow, either by hand or by computer. Like this…

a, e, i, o, u, ba, be, bi, bo, bu, bab, beb, bib, bob, bub, baba, bebe, bibi, bobo, bubu, bubab…

…and so on, till you've listed as many as you feel you need to get started with. By hand—which is how I did Láadan—this is tedious; a computer will whip the whole list out for you in a flash. The length of the flash is determined by what you did in Steps 3 and 4. Obviously, if you only allow three-syllable words in your language and you have only seven phonemes, the list will be shorter than if you're using ten syllables and twenty phonemes.

STEP 6: Decide how you want to handle your basic grammar markings. That is: How will you mark something as plural? As past (or other) tense? As completed or still going on? And how will you indicate whether something is the subject, the object, the possessive, etc.? Write the rules you need to do these things. Suppose you decide to mark these basics by adding syllables to your words. If you do that, you'll have rules like these: "Adding 'ba' at the end of a word makes it plural." "Adding 'ga' at the beginning of a verb makes it refer to past time." "Adding 'fa' at the end of a word marks it as the subject of your verb." And so on.

STEP 7: Start assigning meanings to your listed syllables, for your core vocabulary. That is, for words like "house, woman, child, man, tree, fire, make, eat, drink"… and words that are totally invented as well, if you need them because they're as basic to your fictional culture as "fire" is to human culture.

STEP 8: Make your basic decisions about syntax. That is: How will you indicate that a sentence is negative, or is a question, or is a command? And—very important—how will you combine two or more sentences into a single bigger sentence? Once again you could do this by using syllables. Like … "Adding 'fo' to the last word in a sentence indicates that it is a question." "Adding 'wa' at the end of the first word of a sentence indicates that it is embedded *inside* a larger sentence, as 'Mary is tired' is embedded inside 'I know Mary is tired' in English.' And so on. No human language does these things by repeating words, but for an ET language you could decide to do exactly that. You could have a rule that said "A sentence in which every word is repeated twice is a question." "A sentence in which every word is repeated three times is a command." And so on. Human beings would find that cumbersome, but your ETs might not; that's up to you.

STEP 9: Take some simple text—a short folktale is a good choice—and start translating it into your language. This serves as a diagnostic probe to let you know what you need to add or change. For the Láadan language, which was constructed to express the perceptions of women, I began by translating the Twenty-Third Psalm, because the King James Bible is one of the most masculine-perception-expressing books I know of and that psalm is the right size.

And there you are; this is how it's done. When you get through with these steps you will have a usable language, meeting all the specifications for a usable language. That's just the beginning, of course. Turning it into a *living* language would require native speakers. Using it to write great literature would require many years of additional elaboration, plus writing talent. Using it as part of a story or novel would require the construction of a culture to go with it. Turning it into a best-selling grammar and/or audio program would require a powerful media unit like the group behind the Klingon materials. Nevertheless, *you would have a whole language, constructed by you, to your personal specifications, to use for whatever purposes you like.*

Suzette Haden Elgin, ©1999
From https://laadanlanguage.wordpress.com

The Link Between Language and the Perception of Reality

> *Although all observers may be confronted by the same physical evidence in the form of experiential data and although they may be capable of "externally similar acts of observation," a person's "picture of the universe" or "view of the world" differs as a function of the particular language or languages that person knows.* (The Whorf Theory Complex: A Critical Reconstruction, 1996, by Penny Lee, page 87)

FIRST YOU HAVE TO CLAW YOUR WAY THROUGH the linguistic thicket created by the academic register in which that quotation is written. Why is it written like that? One of the rules of the Academic Regalian register is that the more you expect other academics to be *opposed* to what you're saying or wanting, the more extreme your use of the register has to be. This is unfortunate, because controversial subjects are also subjects about which it's important to be as clear as possible. But if the academic game is the game you're playing, clarity has to be sacrificed to this linguistic dominance display.

The translation process introduces a delay, certainly; but when you get to the end of it you will realize that you've come upon a concept so interesting that it grips the mind and won't let go. It's called "the linguistic relativity hypothesis" (also "the Sapir-Whorf hypothesis" and "the Whorf/Whorfian hypothesis"). Lee's quotation says that the way human beings perceive the world around them varies with the languages they know—even though they perceive the same things, in the same manner, using the same physical and mental "equipment." This will strike you either as common sense or *non-*sense, depending on your own personal convictions about the power of language.

Linguist Dan Moonhawk Alford offers the example of a Cheyenne parent who is sitting with a child on his knee when a ball suddenly bounces across the floor. An English-speaking parent would say to the child, "Look! Ball!" The Cheyenne parent, Alford tells us, would say, "Look! Bouncing!"[1] Both parents are perceiving the same stimulus, with the same sensory equipment. However, the way they express the perception—which *tells the child what it's important to pay attention* to—is not the same.

In 1958 Ace Books published Jack Vance's science fiction novel *The Languages of Pao*, in which a government tailored its population for specific roles in adulthood by controlling the language each person learned in infancy. One group of infants learned a native tongue that fitted them for life in the military, another group learned a language designed for business and trade, and so on. This worked very well—until the government was overthrown by a population that had secretly learned *more than one* of these designer tongues natively and had therefore grown up with more flexible perceptions of reality.

The Languages of Pao is a straightforward presentation of a fictional world having these three characteristics:

(A) The linguistic relativity hypothesis is valid and true.

(B) The hypothesis can be systematically applied to human life.

(c) The government has the power and resources to carry out that systematic application as a national policy, beginning with its population of infants.

Whether (A) and (B) are true in this nonfictional world that we all live in is a matter for fierce dispute; I am firmly convinced that they are. Because we know of no government in human history that has met the specifications for (c), it's difficult even to speculate about the truth or falsity of that proposition; in the novel, its truth is presupposed.

Suppose that the linguistic relativity hypothesis is true in the real world. Suppose we could prove that languages actually do have significant control over the worldviews of their speakers. What would that mean?

There are two major possibilities. If we assume that a multiplicity

---

[1] Anthony Della Flora, "Language and Experienced Reality," *Albuquerque Journal*, June, 1998.

of worldviews causes disunity in a society, it would mean that we could make a strong case for the proposition that multilingualism at a national level is dangerous and should be discouraged, even forbidden. (This idea is in many ways at the heart of the various "English Only" movements in the United States, although many of their proponents are unfamiliar with the linguistic relativity hypothesis.) On the other hand, we could assume that the more worldviews people have, the better; in that case, the validity of the linguistic relativity hypothesis would let us make a case for strong support of multilingualism. (This would be my personal choice.)

In addition, we would be able to make the case that letting a government decide which language or languages people will learn is dangerous, since that would mean that their government dictated their view of the world for them. Clearly, both life and government policy would be less complicated if we could be certain that the hypothesis is false.

The linguistic relativity hypothesis (LRH, from now on) is a source of controversy in many fields, including at least linguistics, anthropology and ethnology; philosophy, religion, political science and education. It's not a new idea; it goes back at least as far as Giambattista Vico, an Italian political philosopher who lived from 1668 to 1774. Today it's associated primarily with the work of linguists Edward Sapir and Benjamin Lee Whorf, especially Whorf. Linguists accuse one another of being "Whorfians," acknowledge (like me) that they are Whorfians, or deny ever having been Whorfians, all with an astonishing degree of passion.

Suzette Haden Elgin, ©1999
The Language Imperative, 2000

Frequently Asked Questions

Why did you construct the Láadan language?
I had four reasons....

1. I was writing a novel that had the construction of such a language as a major plot element. It was obvious to me that I'd be able to do a better job of portraying that process if I went through it myself. The women linguists in the novel were working as a group, and I had to work alone; still, I was better informed than if I had relied entirely on my imagination.

2. Science fiction is intended to have two parts: science, and fiction. When chemists or astronomers write sf novels, they're not expected to provide expert scientific information on geology (although they're expected to be accurate, if they include those fields in the book); they *are* expected to provide expert information about chemistry or astronomy. As a linguist writing sf, I have the same obligation regarding information about linguistics. I was less likely to include scientific errors about the linguistics of Láadan if I constructed it before writing about it.

3. Láadan was described as a language designed to express the perceptions of women. I had to find out what that *meant*; I had to find out what design elements could plausibly be included in such a project. (NOTE: Here, and in the material that follows, please understand that I'm referring to English-speaking women and to American English unless I specify otherwise; I'm not qualified to talk or write about women in their roles as native speakers of other languages.)

4. When I did teaching or "public speaking" about the problems women have with language, people would ask this question: "If women aren't satisfied with the language they have, how come they've never made up a language of their own? How come there aren't any languages constructed by women?" I was distressed by that question; I wasn't aware at that time of the

language constructed by Hildegard of Bingen[1], for example. It seemed to me that it would be useful for me to do a language, and specifically a language designed to express female perceptions—just so that I could say that it had been *done*.

The *Láadan Grammar & Dictionary* says that it's a "case grammar." What's a case grammar? And why did you do the grammar that way?

The word "case" in this context refers to the roles that nominals have in a sentence with respect to its predicate. That is, a case category in "The kids ate the pizza really fast on the porch last night" specifies who did the eating, what was eaten, where the eating happened and when, and how—in what way—the eating happened. Linguists analyze languages using a theoretical model; some of us prefer the case grammar model. I used the case grammar model for my dissertation on Navajo syntax, and I've always used it for any language that I was teaching (including English), and it has served me well. In my opinion, there is no *clearer* way to describe and discuss a language. (Case grammar in contemporary linguistics is usually associated with the work of Charles Fillmore.)

Is it hard to construct a language? Doesn't it take a very long time?

That depends on how you define "language" and "construct." By some definitions, a language could be made up of only A, B, and a "repeat" symbol; its utterances would be AB, ABB, ABBB, ABBBB, and so on. I could put together a dozen of those in five minutes, and nothing could be easier. If you're talking about something intended to be usable as a human language, it's more complicated—but not as complicated as looking at some constructed languages might lead you to believe. No law requires a constructed language to have seventy different meaningful sounds or fifty different personal pronouns or two hundred verb endings; the "constructors" may choose to provide all those things, but they don't have to. The set of things that human languages *must* include isn't very large; I could easily construct several languages in a single day. Any decent computer programmer could set up a computer to construct twenty-five of them in a single day.

---

[1] a German Benedictine abbess, 1098–1179.

Having said that, however, I have to explain a thing or two. It's one thing to construct something that *meets the definition* of a human language, in theoretical terms; that's not terribly difficult. But languages don't live because they meet a list of specifications. They live because they are used and loved and worked with and treasured; they live because they are associated with a culture. When Tolkien wrote *The Lord of the Rings* he was taking steps to provide his Elvish languages with a culture, so that they might become more than just squiggles on a page. Constructing a language that might become a living human language is like writing a novel or composing a symphony, with all that that entails. It's not just a matter of meeting technical specifications. It could take a lifetime. (If you're interested in looking at a lot of constructed languages, go to Google, type "constructed languages auxiliary languages artificial languages" in the search box, and follow the links.)

Is it possible to get permission to do things with Láadan? What if I want to write poetry in Láadan, for example, or fiction? What if I want to start a Láadan study group? What if I want to make some changes in the language?

No living human language is "owned" by anyone or anything. Since Láadan was launched as a scientific experiment, intended to live or die on its own like any other language, there was no way I could "own" it except in the sense of having copyrighted its original form. From the very beginning, every chance I got, I made it clear that I not only was willing to have other people do things with the language, I encouraged it. Nobody has to have my permission; nobody has to clear what they do with me, or report to me, or anything like that. People who want me to credit them for new Láadan words and materials in a future edition of the *Láadan Grammar & Dictionary* (and when I write or speak about the language) have to send me what they've done; there's no other way for me to know about it. But that's entirely up to them.

About making changes.... Adding new words, as long as they follow the rules of the Láadan sound system, is always fine; that's how real languages work. Adding new *rules* to the language—new grammar rules, new sound system rules, and so on—is different. Of course people can do that. But they need to know that what they have after they make the change is no longer Láadan—it's something else, the way "Esperanto Reformed" is no longer Esperanto. Rule changes certainly occur in living languages, but not because they are "decreed"; they happen gradually, over time, as a consensus develops about them among speakers of the language.

Right now, for example, English is losing the distinction between "may" and "might," so that younger people say "If he had known that, he may have left." For me (age sixty-six) that has to be "If he had known that, he might have left." The developing native-speaker consensus is that "might" as the past of "may" isn't needed, and its demise is inevitable. But the change is happening over decades, and it's happening in the living speech and writing of many thousands of English speakers; it's not happening because someone got up one morning and published a new rule.

I'm always interested in what's happening with Láadan, and I'm always more than willing to offer advice if it's asked for; I'm pleased when people tell me about their projects—but they don't have to. If some media mogul were to try to publish a Láadan grammar or use the language in a movie or anything of that kind without involving me I would fight that, on principle. But otherwise, Láadan is on its own.

Suzette Haden Elgin
2002

Láadan Made Easier —How It Works, part 1

RULE 1. A Láadan sentence begins with a SPEECH ACT MORPHEME, which is a chunk of language that explains what action—question, command, statement, request, promise, or warning—the speaker intends to carry out with that sentence. In connected speech or writing, the SPEECH ACT MORPHEME can often be deleted; however, a sentence headed by one is always acceptable—when in doubt, use one. The SPEECH ACT MORPHEMES we'll be using in this lesson are "**bíi**" (declarative statement) and "**báa**" (question).

RULE 2. A Láadan statement ends with an EVIDENCE MORPHEME, which is a chunk of language that explains on what basis the speaker claims the right to say what is being said. The EVIDENCE MORPHEME we'll be using in this lesson is "**wa**," which means "claimed to be true because the speaker has observed it with her or his own senses."

RULE 3. When a Láadan sentence is negative, the word "**ra**" comes immediately after the verb. (You'll notice that words that would be called "adjectives" in English or French or Spanish are verbs in Láadan.)

RULE 4. The "direct object" of a Láadan verb (that is, the creature or thing that an action is done *to*) carries the ending "**-th**" to mark it as object.

RULE 5. In Láadan sentences, the verb is before the subject and the object is after the subject. That is: If English had Láadan word order it would be correct to say "Ate Mary spaghetti" instead of "Mary ate spaghetti."

How it sounds

b, d, h, l, m, n, r, sh, w, and **y** are pronounced as in English; **th** is pronounced like the **th** of "think"; **zh** is pronounced like **s** in "pleasure." The vowels are **a** as in "calm," **e** as in "best," **i** as in "linguistics," **o** as in "home," and **u** as in "Susan" or "soothe."

When two identical vowels are side by side, one of them must take high tone. To get the high tone right, think of the difference between "convert" as in "to convert" and "convert" as in "the convert." In "the convert" the high tone would be on "con-"; in "to convert" the high tone would be on "-vert."

(Láadan has one more sound — the **lh** used to indicate negative meanings; we'll ignore it for now and come back to it in a later lesson.)

Examples

1. **Bíi ada with wa.**
   The woman laughs.

   Bíi ada ra with wa.
   The woman doesn't laugh.

   Báa ada with?
   Does the woman laugh?

Literally: **Bíi** (I-say-to-you-as-a-statement), or **Báa** (I-say-to-you-as-a-question); **ada** (laughs); **with** (woman); **wa** (true-because-I-observed-it-with-my-own-senses). Plus "**ra**," which means "no" or "not." NOTE: "The man" would be "**withid**"—"with" plus the masculine ending "-**id**.")

2. **Bíi lema with wa.**
   The woman is gentle.

   Bíi lema ra with wa.
   The woman isn't gentle.

   Báa lema with?
   Is the woman gentle?

3. **Bíi wida with yuth wa.**
   The woman carries the fruit. (Fruit = **yu**)

   Bíi wida ra with yuth wa.
   The woman doesn't carry the fruit.

   Báa wida with yuth?
   Does the woman carry the fruit?

4. **Bíi shulin ili wa.**
   The water overflows.

   Bíi shulin ra ili wa.
   The water doesn't overflow.

   Báa shulin ili?
   Does the water overflow?

Suzette Haden Elgin, ©2002
From https://laadanlanguage.wordpress.com

Láadan Made Easier, part 2

RULE 6. Láadan nouns have no plural form.

RULE 7. To make a Láadan verb plural, put the prefix "**me-**" at the beginning of the word.

Examples

1. **Bíi lema with wa.**
   The woman is gentle.

   Bíi melema with wa.
   The women are gentle.

   Báa melema with?
   Are the women gentle?

   Bíi melema ra with wa.
   The women are not gentle.

NOTE: Because Láadan words try to maintain a sound pattern in which consonants alternate with vowels, an "**h**" is inserted between "**me-**" and any word that starts with a vowel.

Examples

2. **Bíi ada with wa.**
   The woman laughs.

   Bíi mehada with wa
   The women laugh.

   Báa mehada with?
   Do the women laugh?

3. **Bíi en with wa.**
   The woman understands.

   Bíi mehen with wa.
   The women understand.

RULE 8. Láadan doesn't mark time on its verbs; it has no markers like the "-ed" MORPHEME that marks past time in English. Instead, it puts a TIME AUXILIARY right before the verb. Two of these auxiliaries are "**eril**" (past time) and "**aril**" (future time).

Examples

4. **Bíi aril ada with wa.**
   The woman will laugh.

   Bíi aril mehada with wa.
   The women will laugh.

5. **Bíi aril wida with yuth wa.**
   The woman will carry the fruit.

   Bíi eril wida with yuth wa.
   The woman carried the fruit.

   Bíi eril mewida with yuth wa.
   The women carried the fruit.

6. **Báa aril shulin ili?**
   Will the water overflow?

   Báa eril shulin ili?
   Did the water overflow?

RULE 9. Láadan has a set of suffixes that can be added to the SPEECH ACT MARKERS to carry additional information. Here are eight of them:

said in anger: **-d**
said in pain: **-th**
said in love: **-li**
said in celebration: **-lan**
said in jest, as a joke: **-da**
said in fear: **-ya**
said in narrative, as a story: **-de**
said in teaching: **-di**

Examples

7. **Bíi shóod le wa.**
   I'm busy.

   Bíid shóod le wa.
   I-say-to-you-in-anger, I'm busy!

   Bíida shóod le wa.
   I-say-to-you-in-jest, I'm busy!

NOTE: In English we rely on body language to express most emotional meanings when we speak. When I say, "I'm busy," you have to rely on such things as my tone of voice and the expression on my face to tell you whether I'm just stating a fact or am angry or joking. In written English, we rely on sequences such as "she said angrily." In Láadan, these emotional messages are lexicalized; they have a specific surface shape, whether they're spoken or written.

Suzette Haden Elgin, ©2003
From https://laadanlanguage.wordpress.com

Myths About Láadan

EVERY FEW MONTHS I DO A GOOGLE SEARCH for "Láadan language articles," just to see if anything new has turned up, and yesterday's search was productive—there were quite a few things I hadn't seen before, some of them composed mostly of words like "stupid" and a four-letter word I don't use. I'm accustomed to that, and to being misquoted, and to having the novels misquoted, and to reading criticisms that are based on the misquotations; I'm accustomed to the many well-justified complaints. All of that goes with the territory, and is to be expected; if I wasn't prepared for that, I should have gone into animal husbandry instead of into writing either fiction or nonfiction. But after reading for the n-th time that Láadan is a language intended only for women, I began to wonder if I had finally lost my mind. That is: I began to wonder if it was possible that somewhere in the *Native Tongue* trilogy I had actually *said* that Láadan was intended only for women. At which point I abandoned Google and went back to the novels to find out.

It turns out that I have not lost my mind. (Yet.)

For the record, therefore, here is an excerpt from pp. 355–356 of *The Judas Rose*, the second book in the trilogy, where a woman named Nazareth is lying in her bed thinking about things…

> *In a while, Láadan would move out among Protestant and other women as well as Catholic, because the easing of the prejudice against the "Lingoes" was at last beginning to heal the split between them and the rest of the world. Soon women of the Lines and other women would be mingling freely again, whether the government approved of that or not; soon, there would be non-linguist women coming to the Womanhouses as friends, and bringing their children along with them to be friends, too. They would hear Láadan spoken there, not just in church services and set pieces, but as common everyday language. And the little ones, both boys and girls, would pick up the language as effortlessly as they picked up any other language, and use it among themselves.*

Nazareth closed her eyes, thinking that after all she might sleep a little, and smiled at the ceiling. If she lived long enough, she would be so interested to see what they were going to be like—the first human men who had learned Láadan as infants and toddlers. It might make little difference, or no difference at all; on the other hand, it might make a difference worth rejoicing over, and the chances were good enough to make that the likely outcome.

We never dared teach our male children, she thought; it would have alerted the men to things they were better off not noticing. It was always "just for girls," and peer pressure has kept it that way without much effort on our part. But out in the world, and out in the colonies, it would be different. The little ones would be enchanted to have a "secret language" to play with and to share. Bless the children.

She wouldn't live long enough to see it all happen, but she didn't mind; it was enough to have lived to see it all begin.

I am reassured to know that I have not lost my mind. (Yet.)

It was never my intention that the language should be restricted to women, just as that was not the intention of my characters in the novel.

Suzette Haden Elgin, ©2006
From https://laadanlanguage.wordpress.com

Just One More Láadan Myth

MY FIRST POST ABOUT A LÁADAN MYTH had to do with a persistent misunderstanding, much of it my own fault. This one is a completely different sort of thing—but it is all too typical, and almost impossible to do anything about.

In 1991, Routledge (a London publisher) published an interesting and useful book edited by Lucie Armitt, titled *Where No Man Has Gone Before: Women and Science Fiction*. It included a chapter written by Armitt titled "Your Word Is My Command: The Structures of Language and Power in Women's Science Fiction," on pp. 123–138. In that chapter Armitt paid me the compliment of devoting a number of pages to *Native Tongue* and to Láadan; she had many positive things to say, and I thank her for every one of them. However, there's a problem.

On page 210 of *Native Tongue*, one of my characters says this:

> There's no particular reason to expect that nonhumanoid languages would have verbs, subjects, or objects, you see.

The quotation also appears on page 134 in Armitt's article. But notice what happens. Here is the section, exactly as it appears:

> Elgin's labelling of the linguist dynasty as the "Lines" is surely significant. She appears to sympathise with this critique of linearity, making clear the fact that in a women's language there would be "no particular reason to expect that ... languages would have verbs, subjects, or objects" (p. 210), the different grammatical classes of terms being the necessary foundation for a linear structure." She then goes on, on page 135, to give an example of a Láadan word and carefully prove that it is surely a verb, which "cuts across her position as noted above, and suggests a reassertion of the patrilinear form rather than a movement away from it.

That is: Armitt says that I first claimed in the novel that a women's language wouldn't have to have verbs, and that women reject the linearity that goes with dividing languages up into subject and verbs—but that when I tried to construct a women's language without verbs I failed and fell smack back into patriarchalism. It's neatly argued and articulately presented. But wait...

FIRST: The item she quoted from the novel said nothing at all about a women's language. The word "nonhumanoid" has simply been removed from the quotation. And Láadan, needless to say, is a humanoid language. (The italics that provide emphasis for the word "have" have also been removed.)

SECOND: No elaborate argument is necessary to prove that Láadan has verbs. You can just look at the Láadan glossary at the back of the British edition of *Native Tongue*, or at the Láadan grammar and dictionary published by SF^3; you'll find verbs everywhere, clearly labeled as verbs.

There's little or nothing that can be done about this after the fact; I have no way of reaching all the people who read the book, including the profs who use it as a textbook in their courses. All those people will read that in spite of my doctorate in linguistics I'm not capable even of recognizing that my own constructed language has verbs in it; they will read all that material about linearity and patriarchalism and how I undercut my own position in that context and reassert its opposite. They will quite rightly perceive me as incompetent, if not stupid—and they will have no reason whatsoever to go check the quotation on page 210 of the novel, where they would discover that it was a misquotation.

How could this happen? My guess is that Armitt saw the mutilated quotation somewhere else and re-quoted it without checking it for accuracy because she respected the author of the secondary source where she saw it and had no reason to think it contained an error. That's only a guess, but it's a guess based on the fact that it happens all the time in scholarly literature. I'm just sorry that she didn't contact me to ask me if I had any explanation to offer for the glaring inconsistency and contradiction.

People read other people's articles, take it as a given that the other person's quotations are accurate, and then go on to base arguments in their own work on those quotations; people even do this when their secondary source is only someone else's class notes. Noam Chomsky is notoriously the victim of this practice, with his students—who of course go on to become famous linguists—teaching from notes taken during his lectures, and their students teaching from notes taken during those lectures, and so on ad infinitum. Errors that creep into the quotations as they move through the generations of note-taking students then go into linguistics journals and textbooks and become fossilized. It truly does go with the territory; that makes it no less frustrating for the person it happens to.

Suzette Haden Elgin
LiveJournal, 2006

Teach Yourself Alien[1]

ONE THING THAT SEEMS TO BE characteristic of science fiction fans, no matter what their other differences, is their incredible and scrupulous fanaticism about scientific accuracy. You locate some minor star three feet from where it originally was—you realize, those stars you look at aren't *there* anymore—but you put that star three feet from where it used to be and you will be deluged with letters demanding to know just what kind of cockamamie science that's supposed to *represent*, anyway! Readers want their science up to date, preferably up to the minute, and they don't mind letting you know that.

Except—and here's an amazing contrast—except when it comes to linguistics, which is the scientific study of language. If you look at most SF dealing with language, you find that not only is it hundreds of years out of date, but nobody *cares*. I could put the most unutterable garbage into my own SF novels (which deal primarily with problems of communication and of language) and no one would say or write a single protesting word.

I think it comes partly from carelessness, and partly from the fact that although not everybody can fly a spaceship everybody can and does use language, thus becoming an expert through familiarity alone. And it comes from the fact that people are accustomed to thinking that Language (upper case) has nothing to do with Science (upper case). When linguists bill themselves as scientists, people chuckle.

The linguistics problems that should be dealt with in SF are as numerous as those in any other area, but they fall into four broad classifications, as follows:

1) Human-to-human communication through space.

2) Human-to-animal communication, anywhere.

3) Human-to-human communication on Earth.

4) Human-to-alien communication.

---

[1] Published in *Aurora*, whole number 19, Vol 7, No. 1, Summer 1981.

I'm not going to talk about the human-to-human through space problem because I've dealt with that in my books, and because it *is* basically technological.

I'm not going to talk about the human-to-animal problem, because that one is primarily ethical. We can communicate in a rough but adequate fashion with primates and whales, now. We aren't ready to discuss quantum mechanics with them yet, but we sure have the capability of ridding ourselves of all the shitwork problems that we have. We need only bring in the chimps and tell *them* to tote that bale, scrub that pan, clean that toilet, fire that rifle, etc. I'd be here a week if we took that up.

The human-to-human on Earth problem and the human-to-alien problem are the ones left over, and I had trouble choosing; so I left it to my students, who said: "Oh, talk about talking to the bug-eyed monsters!" I will defer to their judgment in this, as I do in many other things.

Now, how does most SF handle the matter of Terran/Alien communication? There are two basic choices made by our writers: (1) a machine that translates, like *Star Trek*'s "Universal Translator"; or (2) a human being that translates, like a linguist. The machine is a computer, or it's a helmet that you put on your head, or it's a Dick Tracy wrist radio device, or something of the kind; its effect is always the same. Whatever language you happen to be a native speaker of is the one you hear coming at you, no matter what language is actually being spoken. The linguist in SF is not what a linguist really is most of the time today, but a kind of glorified interpreter, who may also do translations and perhaps give language lessons to his or her colleagues.

Please keep in mind that both of these methods require a human being initially, because someone has got to analyze the language to provide the data to feed into the computer that *runs* the universal translator. More importantly, neither alternative would be likely to work.

I've got to do just a little linguistics here, to make all this clear. Although a *complete* analysis of a human language would not be easy it has never yet been done for any language. The sort of basic analysis intended by SF writers along this line would be a rather trivial task for a decently trained linguist. It would take three years also. But there's an excellent *reason* for that, which is: a linguist knows, in advance, what a human language is going to be like at the level of analysis we are considering here. The set of possible things that a human language can contain is extremely small, and it is very severely and rigidly constrained.

A linguist approaching a new human language knows it will have a way of asking questions, a way of giving commands, a way to indicate number and gender, and so on—this is predictable. The linguist knows what range of alternatives exists, to a pretty adequate degree; the task then is only a matter of eliminating those alternatives that the language being analyzed has not chosen from the universal set.

This didn't just happen by coincidence, by the way, although scientists who don't see any major difference between people and pigeons disagree with me. Linguists of my denomination will tell you that human languages are as they are because the set of things a human language can contain is part of the specifications—the biological specifications—of the human brain. The necessary equipment, the perceptual and cognitive equipment, for learning human languages, is innate in the human being in the same way that legs and lungs are.

Which is precisely why there is such a problem in writing about an alien language. My students, whether they come from the people-like-unto-pigeons disciplines or not, will agree with me for the sake of the argument; and then they say: "But then, what would an alien language be like?" And I have to tell them that if I could answer that question I would not have a human brain; there is no way I can step outside my humanness and imagine what an alien language might be like. About the best I can do is suggest what it probably would *not* be like.

Now, what does this mean for someone who wants to write about encounters between Terrans and aliens? There are a couple of immediate possibilities. You could make it a given that the only aliens to be encountered would be humanoid and of essentially the same proto-genetic stock that Terrans are—even many thousands of generations removed. If you do that, there is a minimal possibility that a skilled linguist with a good computer could do something useful. If, on the other hand, we run into life forms that are gaseous or crystalline or vegetable, the chances of a linguist being able to analyze their languages are miniscule. How do you suppose you would go *about* working with a language that has no subjects, no verbs, and no objects? Or a language that has no mechanism for asking questions or replying to them, or for making things negative? Or a language that lacks the concept of either word or sentence?

If you assume the latter situation, with the non-humanoid aliens, there is an alternative that is simply boring. That's the one where you say: we just accept it. We're never going to be able to communicate with these creatures—so be it. They're in the universe, we're in the universe; as we fly by each other, we'll wave something. Out of that would come the ultimately tedious tale of star-crossed lovers, the beautiful Terran and the handsome gas cloud. I don't see that as especially interesting.

A number of my students have pointed out that mathematics is alleged—by eminences like Asimov and Sagan, for example—to be universal. And they want to know if that couldn't be the basis for a logical system of communication. They have a point, and we could assuredly work out some kind of system for a stop sign between two cultures so that our space freighters wouldn't collide in space—that sort of thing could be worked out.

But that is about all such a system would get you, even if you are willing—and I am not—to accept as an absolute that in no universe could two and two ever equal more or less than four.

At which point you have to ask: then what do you do with this in writing science fiction? Without boring your readers out of their skulls? And that will lead us back into a tad more linguistics.

If you ask people how human infants learn their native languages, they will usually tell you that they learn them from their parents or the other people around them, by trial and error. Linguists of my denomination dispute that; remember, we are prepared to claim—and to prove—that the human infant is born with a set of innate perceptual and cognitive strategies that enable that infant to perform a specific task. And that task is: to extract the rules of their native language from the raw data in the environment around them. That's why very tiny children are able to acquire several languages simultaneously, without the slightest trace of an accent in any of them, with no sign of any significant difficulty, and with no help whatsoever from Berlitz. Adults *cannot do this*. It is a specific biologically innate characteristic of the human infant, which begins to decay somewhere around puberty, and which we in American education respond to by teaching foreign languages in the secondary schools and in college after that decay has already begun. The evidence for this is voluminous, and readily available.

And that gives the SF writer something interesting to do. The one possibility that might be productive, and not boring, is to hypothesize that what the human infant has is not just the innate specific capacity to learn human languages. Maybe, just maybe, it has the capacity to learn any language at all, including an alien one. You would have to make the additional assumption that the alien also understood the problem and was interested in cooperating to solve it. And you would have to construct an environment in your book that both the alien and the human infant could share, and still survive.

Let's assume that you've devised an alien willing to cooperate, and solved the technological problems of the shared environment, and that the Terran baby is beginning to talk not only in the human language it hears around it but also in the alien one. (It would have to hear *both*, as multilingual children hear both, or you would only have produced a Terran child that spoke only in Alien, which wouldn't be much help.) If all these things could be worked out, could we assume that we would be communicating with the aliens when the bilingual child interpreted for us?

I'd like you to consider an example from two Earth languages. Assume that we have a monolingual Navajo speaker, a monolingual English speaker, and an interpreter fluent in both languages. The Navajo says: "*Łį́į́'shiŁ naaldloosh nt'éé'.*" The interpreter turns to the English speaker and says: "I was riding a horse." Now the interpreter has indeed done what interpreters are expected to do; he or she has produced in English a sequence equivalent to the sequence in Navajo, in that they are what the two individuals would say in equivalent real-world situations. However, there is a very significant difference here. If you think about what it means in English to say "I was riding a horse," it means that you—the Master—were doing something *to* the horse. You have a power relationship to that horse, and it is the object of your action in the way that if you hit a table with a hammer, the table is the object of your action. The Navajo sentence isn't like that at all. What it says, in the most literal translation I can manage, is this: "The horse was animaling-about with me." There is no Master/Object relationship there. If there's *any* power involved, it belongs to the horse, because the verb in question is one that can only be carried out by animals...but if you ask a Navajo about it, you'll be told that the relationship is considered to be a matter of willing cooperation, not dominance.

And then there's the Navajo verb *sidá*. You have to translate it into English as "he (or she, or it) is sitting," but it's a past tense verb. Literally, it means in Navajo that someone has ceased to move about and has taken up a sitting position—and that's over and done with, so it's past. But the English equivalent is not only supposed to express present time, it's also what is traditionally called "progressive—that is, not over and done with yet—aspect". *Remember* that we have been discussing two Earth languages, now, and move the problem on out into space...At least it isn't boring.

There is one more thing that always comes up when I discuss this. Always, somebody says: "Oh well, the baby and the BEM would just use telepathy."

My personal opinion is that all of us are born telepathic and that our culture then systematically and unequivocally trains that out of us. But if we set my personal opinions aside and just *assume* telepathy to be possible, human-to-human and human-to-alien, under the conditions I have outlined above, would it help? We're talking about real telepathy now, not glorified mental Morse Code, which means that the moment the infant and the alien were telepathically in communication, they would share the *same set of perceptions*. I don't care to hazard a guess about what would happen to the alien, but my guess regarding the human infant is that it would—by our society's standards—go stark raving mad before the age of six months. As for an adult…there you would get instantaneous burn-out.

Maybe it could be set up so that the infant could, in the process of learning an alien language through its innate language-learning mechanisms boosted by its innate telepathic capacity, also learn to tolerate the different perceptual systems. (Whether this would involve automatic sacrifice of the sanity of the alien, the alien not being an infant, will have to wait for some other talk.) Perhaps the infant would be exposed in tiny flashes at first…just an instant at a time. It would be a gradual desensitization, much like that we are acquiring to violence and sex in the movies and television.

More interesting to me would be the idea of exposing the human infant from birth to powerful natural hallucinogens that would provide him or her with a more varied perceptual experience and teach the following principle: "Anything whatsoever may very well come along; and if it does, how very interesting." You could imagine a system in the future where—and this would please me greatly—linguists would be the most powerful individuals in the universe. Because they would be the only ones who knew how to pull this off, as well as the only ones sufficiently icy to use their own offspring in the way I've been describing. (The things linguists can do already would make your average human's blood run cold, by the way; everybody's worrying about genetic manipulation and mutated E. Coli, loose in the streets…ever wonder why you hear so little about linguists?)

So you see that there are some ways of writing good SF with good linguistic science included, despite the handicap that comes of having a human brain to work your plot out with. There are stacks of books to be written from the material I've been discussing, and if you want to write them, god bless you. *If* you do your homework. Otherwise, it's much like me deciding to write about a space warp, about which I know nothing at all. You know how I handle that? I use "asterisks": I write: "He got on the rocket ship." And then there's this space. And then: "He got off the rocket ship." I handle it just the way that sex was handled in Victorian novels for ladies.

What fascinates me is not that most SF writers know little or nothing about linguistics—why should they? What fascinates me is that they don't seem to let that hold them back at all from writing about linguistics in intricate and abominable detail. I wish they'd either get their facts straight or use asterisks, and I encourage readers to demand that they do one or the other.

Suzette Haden Elgin
Lesson, unknown venue, sometime before 1981

> A recording of "Teach Yourself Alien" is available to the public from the University of Oregon Libraries, Special Collections and University Archives, Sound cassette tape #48
> http://archiveswest.orbiscascade.org/ark:/80444/xv57659

Appendixes

Appendix 1

Rules of Láadan Grammar

A) **Auxiliaries**

Present	**ril**	Distant Past	**eríli**
Past	**eril**	Distant Future	**aríli**
Future	**aril**	Hypothetical	**rilrili**
Optative	**wil**		

B) **Case Markers**
   1. Subject   Ø
   2. Identifier   Ø
   3. Object   **-th**
   4. Source   **-de**
   5. Goal   **-di, -dim**
   6. Beneficiary
      - **-da**   voluntarily
      - **-dáa** obligatorily, as by duty
      - **-daá** accidentally
      - **-dá**   by force, against X's will
   7. Associate
      - **-den** neutral form
      - **-dan** with pleasure
   8. Time   **-ya**
   9. Place   **-ha, -sha**
   10. Manner   **-nal**
   11. Instrument   **-nan**

12. Cause
    - **-wan** — purpose; in order to
    - **-wáan** — reason; because of
13. Possessive
    - **-tha** — by reason of birth
    - **-thi** — by reason of chance
    - **-the** — for unknown or unacknowledged reasons
    - **-thu** — partitive (false possessive)
    - **-tho** — other (purchase, gift, law, custom, etc.)

NOTE: CASE MARKERS are attached to noun phrases; when no ambiguity is possible, they are optional—for example, in "I speak Láadan" no ambiguity can occur because languages cannot "speak" persons; therefore, the object marker of "Láadan" may be used or not, as the speaker wishes.

c) Degree Markers

Neutral Degree Markers

1.	to a trivial degree, slightly	-hel
2.	to a minor degree, rather	-hil
3.	to an ordinary degree	-Ø
4.	to an unusual degree, very	-hal
5.	to an extreme degree	-hul
6.	to an extraordinary degree	-háalish

Negative Degree Markers

7.	to a troublesome degree	-hele or -shéle
8.	to a severe degree	-hile or -shíle
9.	to an intolerable degree	-hule or -shúul
10.	special emergency form: unbearable to a degree that would cause catastrophic events such as suicide; a signal for immediate help	-shúle

Positive Degree Markers

11. to a pleasing degree; fine	**-théle**
12. to a more-than-pleasing degree; excellent	**-thíle**
13. to an extraordinarily pleasing degree; magnificent	**-thúul**
14. to the furthest degree of pleasingness possible; perfect	**-thúle**

D) Doer/Agent Marker

"-á" is the suffix for doer, agent; MORPHEME used to mark someone as the "do-er" of an action; like English "-er" in "baker" or "dancer."

E) Duration Markers

1. to start to Verb **na-**
2. to continue to Verb **ná-**
3. to repeat **ne-**
4. to finish, complete **no-**
5. to cease to Verb **nó-**

F) **Embedding Markers**

There are three of these in Láadan. To embed a sentential complement (like English "I know that she left," where "that she left" is embedded), the suffix "**-hé**" is used. To embed a relative clause (like English "I know the woman who is tired"), the suffix "**-háa**" is used. To embed a question (like English "I wonder whether/if she left"), the suffix "**-hée**" is used. The embedding markers are attached to the last element in the embedded clause.

- **-háa** — EMBEDDING MARKER: to embed a relative clause (like English "I know the woman who is tired") attached to the last element in the embedded clause (see also "**-hé**," "**-hée**")
- **-hée** — EMBEDDING MARKER: to embed a question (like English "I wonder whether/if she left") attached to the last element in the embedded clause (see also "**-hé**," "**-háa**")
- **-hé** — MORPHEME used to embed one statement inside another statement; EMBEDDING MARKER: to embed a sentential complement (like English "I know that she left") attached to the last element in the embedded clause (see also "**-háa**," "**-hée**")

When we want to put one English statement inside another one—a process called "embedding"—we can use the word "that" to mark the statement that is embedded. For example, "I know that science fiction conventions are fun," embeds the statement "science fiction conventions are fun" inside "I know (some other statement)," by putting "that" at the beginning of the embedded statement. Láadan embeds one statement in another by putting the morpheme "**-hé**" on the last word of the embedded statement. So, the statement "**radazhehul thod áabeth**"—"writing a book is very hard"—is marked as an embedded statement by adding "**-hé**" to "**áabeth**."

(Note: An EMBEDDING MORPHEME is the *only* morpheme that can follow a CASE-MARKING MORPHEME.)

g) Focus Marker

-hóo is a MORPHEME that is used to indicate special importance, or to give a word or phrase extra emphasis: **Bíi aril bilehóo buzh wa!** ("The convention will be *fun*!")

h) Pejorative Marker

lh- or **-lh** or **-lh-** connotes bad (intentionally). The pejorative element "**lh**" can always be added to a word to give it a negative connotation, so long as it precedes or follows a vowel and does not violate the rules of the Láadan sound system by creating a forbidden cluster. The addition of "**lh**" need not create an actual new word; for example, "**áwith** " means "baby"; to use instead "**lháwith**" (or "**áwithelh**") means only something like "the darned baby" and is ordinarily a temporary addition. But it is very handy indeed. We are indebted to the Navajo language for this device.

i) Plural Marker

"**me-**" is the plural marker (PLURAL MORPHEME) used at the beginning of verbs and words that correspond to English adjectives; always the first prefix in the word (beautiful women = **mewoháya wowith**)

J) **Evidence Morphemes**
1. **wa** known to X because perceived by X, externally or internally
2. **waálh** assumed false by speaker because source is not trusted and evil intent by source is assumed.
3. **wi** known to X because self-evident
4. **we** perceived by X in a dream
5. **wáa** assumed true by X because X trusts source
6. **waá** assumed false by X because X distrusts source; if evil intent is also assumed, the form is "**waálh**"
7. **wo** imagined or invented by X, hypothetical
8. **wóo** used to indicate that X states a total lack of knowledge as to the validity of the matter
9. **Ø** used when X makes no comment on validity, either because of personal preference or because no comment is needed (as in a series of sentences in connected discourse)

NOTE: These MORPHEMES are the final word in a Láadan sentence, and are used to make clear the basis upon which the utterance is offered. If none is used, and the context is not one in which the word would be redundant, the speaker is making an overt statement of refusal to supply these forms; that is allowed, but it cannot be easily overlooked. Note that these forms make direct contradiction (like English "I'm cold…" followed by "Oh, you are not," as a response) impossible.

K) **Repetition Morphemes**
　1. **bada**　　repeatedly, at random
　2. **badan**　repeatedly, in a pattern over which humans have no control
　3. **brada**[1]　repeatedly, in a pattern fixed arbitrarily by human beings
　4. **bradan**[1]　repeatedly, in a pattern fixed by humans by analogy to some phenomenon (such as the seasons)
　5. **bradá**[1]　repeatedly, in what appears to be a pattern but cannot be demonstrated or proved to be one

L) **Speech Act Morphemes**
　1. Declarative　**Bíi** (usually optional)
　2. Question　　**Báa**
　3. Command　　**Bó** (very rare, except to small children)
　4. Request　　**Bóo** (usual "command" form)
　5. Promise　　**Bé**
　6. Warning　　**Bée**

NOTE: These forms are the first word in a Láadan sentence. There is a set of suffixes which may be attached to them to further specify the speaker/writer's intentions, as follows:

---

[1] Exception to the regular Láadan morphology that does not permit adjacent consonants.

M) State of Consciousness Morphemes

1. **hahod** — to be in a state of
2. **hahodib** — deliberately shut off from all feelings, to be in a state of shut off
3. **hahodihed** — in shock, numb, to be in a state of numbness
4. **hahodimi** — in bewilderment/astonishment, positive
5. **hahodimilh** — in bewilderment/astonishment, negative
6. **hahoditha** — linked empathically with another, to be in a state of linked empathy
7. **hahodiyon** — ecstasy, to be in a state of ecstasy
8. **hahodo** — in meditation, to be in a state of meditation
9. **hahodóo** — in hypnotic trance, to be in a state of hypnotic trance

NOTE: The root for all these state of consiousness morphemes is **hahod**.

N) Other Speech Act Suffixes

- **-da** — "said in jest"
- **-lan** — "said in celebration"
- **-de** — "said in narrative"
- **-li** — "said in love"
- **-d** — "said in anger"
- **-di** — "said in teaching"
- **-du** — "said as poetry"
- **-th** — "said in pain"
- **-ya** — "said in fear"

o) Speech Acts
Anger

- **báad** in anger, I ask…; question speech act, in anger (**báa** = question speech act + **-d** = suffix "said in anger")
- **béd** in anger, I say as a promise…; promise speech act, in anger (**bé** = promise peech act + **-d** = suffix "said in anger")
- **béed** in anger, I say in warning…; warning speech act, in anger (**bée** = warning speech act + **-d** = suffix "said in anger")
- **bíid** in anger, I say…; declarative speech act, in anger (**bíi** = declarative speech act + **-d** = suffix "said in anger")
- **bód** in anger, I command…; command speech act, in anger (very rare except to small children) (**bó** = command speech act + **-d** = suffix "said in anger")
- **bóod** in anger, I request…; request speech act, in anger (**bóo** = request speech act + **-d** = suffix "said in anger")

Celebration

- **báalan** in celebration, I ask…; question speech act, in celebration (**báa** = question speech act + **-lan** = suffix "said in celebration")
- **béelan** in celebration, I say in warning…; warning speech act, in celebration (**bée** = warning speech act + **-lan** = suffix "said in celebration")
- **bélan** in celebration, I say as a promise…; promise speech act, in celebration (**bé** = promise speech act + **-lan** = suffix "said in celebration")
- **bíilan** in celebration, I say…; declarative speech act, in celebration (**bíi** = declarative speech act + **-lan** = suffix "said in celebration")
- **bólan** in celebration, I command…; command speech act, in celebration (very rare except to small children) (**bó** = command speech act + **-lan** = suffix "said in celebration")

    bóolan   in celebration, I request…; request speech act, in celebration (**bóo** = request speech act + **-lan** = suffix "said in celebration")

Fear

    báaya   in fear, I ask…; question speech act, in fear (**báa** = question speech act + **-ya** = suffix "said in fear")

    béeya   in fear, I say in warning…; warning speech act, in fear (**bée** = warning speech act + **-ya** = suffix "said in fear")

    béya   in fear, I say as a promise…; promise speech act, in fear (**bé** = promise speech act + **-ya** = suffix "said in fear")

    bíiya   in fear, I say…; declarative speech act, in fear (**bíi** = declarative speech act + **-ya** = suffix "said in fear")

    bóoya   in fear, I request…; request speech act, in fear (**bóo** = request speech act + **-ya** = suffix "said in fear")

    bóya   in fear, I command…; command speech act, in fear (very rare except to small children) (bó = command speech act + **-ya** = suffix "said in fear")Noun Declensions

Jest

    báada   in jest, I ask you…; question speech act, in jest (**báa** = question + **-da** = suffix "said in jest")

    béda   in jest, I say as a promise…; promise speech act, in jest (**bé** = promise speech act + **-da** = suffix "said in jest")

    béeda   in jest, I say in warning…; warning speech act, in jest (**bée** = warning speech act + **-da** = suffix "said in jest")

    bíida   in jest, I say…; declarative speech act, in jest (**bíi** = declarative speech act + **-da** = suffix "said in jest")

    bóda   in jest, I command…; command speech act, in jest (very rare except to small children) (**bó** = command speech act + **-da** = suffix "said in jest")

    bóoda   in jest, I request…; request speech act, in jest (**bóo** = request speech act + **-da** = suffix "said in jest")

Love

báali   in love, I ask…; question speech act, in love (**báa** = question speech act + **-li** = suffix "said in love")

béeli   in love, I say in warning…; warning speech act, in love (**bée** = warning speech act + **-li** = suffix "said in love")

béli   in love, I say as a promise…; promise speech act, in love (**bé** = promise speech act + **-li** = suffix "said in love")

bíili   in love, I say…; declarative speech act, in love (**bíi** = declarative speech act + **-li** = suffix "said in love")

bóli   in love, I command…; command speech act, in love (very rare except to small children) (**bó** = command speech act + **-li** = suffix "said in love")

bóoli   in love, I request…; request speech act, in love (**bóo** = request speech act + **-li** = suffix "said in love")

Pain

báath   in pain, I ask…; question speech act, in pain (**báa** = question speech act + **-th** = suffix "said in pain")

béeth   in pain, I say in warning…; warning speech act, in pain (**bée** = warning speech act + **-th** = suffix "said in pain")

béth   in pain, I say as a promise…; promise speech act, in pain (**bé** = promise speech act + **-th** = suffix "said in pain")

bíith   in pain, I say…; declarative speech act, in pain (**bíi** = declarative speech act + **-th** = suffix "said in pain")

bóoth   in pain, I request…; request speech act, in pain (**bóo** = request speech act + **-th** = suffix "said in pain")

bóth   in pain, I command…; command speech act, in pain (very rare except to small children) (**bó** = command speech act + **-th** = suffix "said in pain")

Poetry

báadu   as poetry, I ask...; question speech act, in poetry (**báa** = question speech act + **-du** = suffix "said as poetry")

bédu   as poetry, I say as a promise...; promise speech act, as poetry (**bé** = promise speech act + **-du** = suffix; "said as poetry")

béedu   in poetry, I say in warning...; warning speech act, as poetry (**bée** = warning speech act + **-du** = suffix "said as poetry")

bíidu   as a poem, I say...; declarative speech act, in poetry (**bíi** = declarative speech act + **-du** = suffix "said as poetry")

bódu   as poetry, I command...; command speech act, in poetry (very rare except to small children) (**bó** = command speech act + **-du** = suffix "said as poetry")

bóodu   as poetry, I request...; request speech act, in poetry (**bóo** = request speech act + **-du** = suffix "said as poetry")

Story

báade   as a story, I ask...; question speech act morpheme, in narrative (**báa** = question speech act + **-de** = suffix "said in narrative")

béde   as a story, I say as a promise...; promise speech act, in narrative (**bé** = promise speech act + **-de** = suffix "said in narrative")

béede   as a story, I say in warning...; warning speech act, in narrative (**bée** = warning speech act + **-de** = suffix "said in narrative")

bíide   as a story, I say...; declarative speech act, in narrative (**bíi** = declarative speech act + **-de** = suffix "said in narrative")

bóde   as a story, I command...; command speech act, in narrative (very rare except to small children) (**bó** = command speech act + **-de** = suffix "said in narrative")

bóode   as a story, I request...; request speech act, in narrative (**bóo** = request speech act + **-de** = suffix "said in narrative")

Teaching

báadi	in teaching, I ask…; question speech act, in teaching (**báa** = question speech act + **-di** = suffix "said in teaching")
bédi	in teaching, I say as a promise…; promise speech act, in teaching (**bé** = promise speech act + **-di** = suffix "said in teaching")
béedi	in teaching, I say in warning…; warning speech act, in teaching (**bée** = warning speech act + **-di** = suffix "said in teaching")
bíidi	in teaching, I say…; declarative speech act, in teaching (**bíi** = declarative speech act + **-di** = suffix "said in teaching")
bódi	in teaching, I command…; command speech act, in teaching (very rare except to small children) (**bó** = command speech act + **-di** = suffix "said in teaching")
bóodi	in teaching, I request…; request speech act, in teaching (**bóo** = request speech act + **-di** = suffix "said in teaching")

p) **Noun Declensions**

For those nouns which, like "grief" or "anger" or "joy," have numerous forms, there are two patterns.

FIRST DECLENSION (which always includes the affix "**-na**"):

for no reason	**-ina**
for good reason(s)	**-ena**
for foolish reason(s)	**-ona**
for bad reason(s)	**-una**
despite negative circumstances	**-ehena**

EXAMPLE: "joy" **thina, thena, thona, thuna, thehena**

SECOND DECLENSION (most easily presented as a matrix):

	-ara	-ala	-ama	-ana	-ina
Reason	+	+	+	+	−
Blame	+	+	−	−	−
Futility	+	−	+	−	−

EXAMPLE: "anger" **bara, bala, bama, bana, bina**

"**Bina**" would be an anger for which no reason can be offered, for which no blame can be attributed, but which is not futile anger because something can be done about the matter.

q) Word Order

For full details, see the "Lesson Set 1: Patterns." However, the basic order of a Láadan sentence is as follows: SPEECH ACT MORPHEME, followed optionally by an AUXILIARY, followed by a VERB, followed by one or more NOUN PHRASES— with Subject preceding Object— followed by an EVIDENCE MORPHEME. No distinction is made between "verbs" and "adjectives" in Láadan.

r) Morphology

This section does not provide all the regularly derived forms in the language. (Again, see the "Lesson Set 1: Patterns.") However, we have tried to present sufficiently numerous examples of regular processes or word formation to allow the reader to predict many additional forms. For example, sets like "**dan**" (language) with the prefix "**e-**" (science of) to form "linguistics" and the agentive suffix "**-á**" to form "linguist" are found throughout the Dictionary section. The negative prefix "**ra-**" will also be obvious. We want to point out that Láadan does not permit any consonant clusters, or any sequences of more than one vowel where neither vowel has a tone marker[1]; when combining morphemes would result in such a sequence, the language inserts "**h**" to break up forbidden vowel sequences, and "**e**" to break up forbidden consonant sequences. Thus "education" (from "**om**," "to learn") is not "**eom**" but "**ehom**."

---

[1] There are a few words beginning with br listed in Appendix K, repetition morphemes. They are footnoted.

s) **Adverbial Dependent Clauses**

Vocabulary

when	**widahath**	(carry + time)
where	**widahoth**	(carry + place)
why	**widahuth**	(carry + reason)
how	**widaweth**	(carry + way, path, road)

(NOTE: It would be reasonable to expect "how" to be either "**widaheth**" or "**widahith**." However, because so many languages don't make a distinction between the vowel "e" in "bed" and the vowel "i" in "bid," it is best not to use either of those forms.)

Examples

1. **Bíi lalom le widahath hal le wa.**
   I sing when I work.
2. **Bíi widahath hal le, lalom le wa.**
   When I work, I sing.
3. **Bíi widahoth ril yod rul, hadihad ina be wa.**
   Where the cat eats, she always sleeps.
4. **Bíi widahuth eril náhal with, lothel ra le wa.**
   Why the woman kept working, I don't know.
5. **Bíi widaweth aril mebedi háawith, lothel ra le wa.**
   How the children will learn, I don't know.

t) Grammar Facts About the Láadan Affixes

This is a work in progress and is not intended to be exhaustive. (For example, we still haven't added the degree markers and am not quite ready to do that yet, because of potential problems. And there are a lot of prefixes that aren't included yet, like "**e-**"/"science-of.")[1]

Verb/adjective affixes

- The plural prefix "**me-**" will always be the first morpheme in the word (which will correspond to an English verb or an English adjective).
- The "**-wo-**" affix goes between "**me-**" and the verb/adjective.
- The verb affixes go at the beginning of the verb/adjective but after "**me-**."

    1. "**du-**"
       to try to verb
    2. "**ná-**"
       continue to verb, keep verbing
    3. "**ne-**"
       to verb again
    4. "**no-**"
       to finish verbing
    5. "**nó-**"
       to stop verbing

- The agent suffix "**-á**" goes on the end of the word; it may be followed by a case-marker suffix.
- The masculine affix "**-id**" goes at the end of the word, but before the case-marker suffix.

Noun phrase affixes

- Possessive case markers always come before the case marker which marks the larger noun phrase that the possessed noun phrase is part of.
- Possessive markers can't go on proper names of people or other living things. A pronoun is added after the name to carry the case marker.
- The masculine affix "**-id**" goes at the end of the word, but before the case-marker suffix.

---

[1] More words have been added since Suzette Haden Elgin wrote this section, including degree markers (See Appendix 1-c) and prefixes like **e-** = science of (See Affixes).

Pronoun affixes

- Pronouns can take the "**-zh**" suffix (five or fewer) and the "**-n**" suffix (more than five).
- Interrogative pronouns (analogous to English who, what, where, when, why, how, which) take the "**-báa**" affix—which is a question marker, followed by the case-marker suffix.
- Indefinite pronouns (analogous to English "someone, somebody, somewhere," etc.) start as "**be-**," followed by the indefinite morpheme "**-ye-**," and can take the "**-zh**" and "**-n**" suffixes.
- The reflexive pronouns (analogous to English "myself, yourself," etc.) start with the appropriate pronoun form, which is followed by the reflexive morpheme "**-yóo-**," and then—if one is needed—by a case-marker suffix).

Examples

Bíi	den	le leyóoth	wa.
DECLTO HELP	I	I+ REFL + OBJ	MYPERC

I help myself.

Báa	hal	nezh	neyóozheda?
INTERR	TO WORK	YOU + 2-5	YOU + REFL + 2-5 + BENEF

Are you working for yourselves (2–5)?

Sentence-combining affixes

- The complementizer (the marker indicating that a sentence is embedded in a larger sentence) for statements is " **hé**"; the complementizer for questions is "**-hée.**" The embedding markers are the only affixes that can be added to a word after a case-marker suffix.
- The relative-clause embedding marker is "**-háa.**" (Except after the Place case-marker, or when the final syllable of the word is "**ha**," when it becomes "**-sháa.**")

Items that don't take affixes

(NOTE: The statements below are true except when the item mentioned is the last word in an embedded sentence. In that case, the sentence-combining affixes may be added.)

- Numerals and quantifiers (**menedebe**, many; **nedebe**, few/several; **woho**, all) never take affixes. They are stand-alone forms that follow their noun phrase.
- Postpositions (like "**obée**," during; and "**o**," around) never take affixes. They are stand-alone forms that follow their noun phrase.
- The EVIDENCE MORPHEMES never take affixes.

Miscellaneous

- The Speech Act affixes go at the end of the SPEECH ACT MORPHEMES. Nothing else can go there. (These affixes may also be added to "**lishid**" (to sign, as in ASL) and to "**dama**," to touch.)
- The pejorative—"**lh**"—can go anywhere in a Láadan word as long as putting it there doesn't violate a sound system rule.
- The focus marker "**-hóo**" goes after any morpheme or at the end of the word to indicate "this particular one" or to indicate emphatic stress.

u) The Láadan Passive

For English, we construct a passive sentence by switching the word order of the Agent subject noun phrase and the Object noun phrase, adding a form of "be" to the predicate, and putting the preposition "by" in front of the subject. Like this:

> The doctor examined the patient. (active sentence)
> The patient was examined by the doctor. (passive sentence)

To construct the passive in Láadan, there are 3 steps to follow.

STEP 1: Move the Agent subject noun phrase to Object position in the sentence, after the verb, and add to it the passive suffix "**-shub**."

STEP 2: Move the Object noun phrase, with its case marker, to a focus position immediately before the verb.

STEP 3: When no Agent is present in the sentence, attach the passive suffix to the verb.

Example

1. **Bíi eril bóodan háawith ruleth wa.**
   The child rescued the cat. (active sentence)

STEPS 1 AND 2:

2. **Bíi eril ruleth bóodan háawitheshub wa.**
   The cat was rescued by the child. (passive sentence)

STEP 3:

3. **Bíi eril ruleth bóodaneshub wa.**
   The cat was rescued. (passive sentence with no Agent present)

Discussion

Sentences (2) and (3), with the object placed in front of the verb, are very unusual constructions for Láadan—a language that ordinarily maintains verb, then subject, then object order.

This is deliberate. The goal is to signal immediately and unambiguously to the listener or reader that the sentence focuses significant importance on the object noun phrase.

v) Adjectives

The adjective marker, **wo-**, changes a verb to an adjective. It must be put on both verb and noun, after plural marker (beautiful woman = **woháya wowith**). Láadan has a form that is much like an English "adjective + noun" sequence, as in "green tree" or "small child." You can take any sequence of verb and subject (remembering that "adjectives" are only ordinary verbs in Láadan) and put the marker "**wo-**" at the beginning of each one. "Beautiful woman" is thus "**woháya wowith**." This is very useful, but it is a bit different from English, because it can only be used if you have just one verb. You cannot use this pattern to translate an English sequence like "little red brick wall." To make your descriptive phrase plural, you would put the plural marker "**me-**" at the beginning of the verb, as always. "Busy dragons" would be "**mewoshóod wohóowamid**."

w) Time Auxiliaries

aril	future (**aril** = later)
aríli	far future, long ahead (**aril** = later)
eril	past; a word used to indicate past time (**eri** = history)
eríli	far past, long ago (**eri** = history)
ril	present time, now
rilrili	hypothetical, would, might, let's suppose
wil	optative mode, indicating an option or wish

Appendix 2

Miscellaneous Additional Information

A) **Days of the Week, with English Equivalents**

Monday	**Heneshául**	East Day
Tuesday	**Honeshául**	West Day
Wednesday	**Huneshául**	North Day
Thursday	**Haneshául**	South Day
Friday	**Rayileshául**	Above Day
Saturday	**Yileshául**	Below Day
Sunday	**Hathameshául**	Center Day

B) **Months of the Year, with English Equivalents**[1]

MONTH	NAME	POETIC MONTH NAMES	
January (1)	**Anede**	**Alel**	Seaweed month
February (2)	**Ashin**	**Ayáanin**	Tree month
March (3)	**Aboó**	**Ahesh**	Grass month
April (4)	**Abin**	**Athil**	Vine month
May (5)	**Ashan**	**Amahina**	Flower month
June (6)	**Abath**	**Athesh**	Herb month
July (7)	**Ahum**	**Ameda**	Vegetable month
August (8)	**Anib**	**Adaletham**	Berry month
September (9)	**Abud**	**Ahede**	Grain month
October (10)	**Athad**	**Ayu**	Fruit month
November (11)	**Anedethab**	**Athon**	Seed month
December (12)	**Ashinethab**	**Adol**	Root month

---

[1] When Suzette Haden Elgin first formed Láadan words for the months of the year, she naturally chose poetic forms that conformed to the growing season. Regrettably, the growing season she chose was that of the northern hemisphere which begins in June, while it begins in December in the southern hemisphere.

c) Set of "Love" Nouns

áayáa	mysterious love, not yet known to be welcome or unwelcome
áazh	love for one sexually desired at one time, but not now
ab	love for one liked but not respected
ad	love for one respected but not liked
am	love for one related by blood
ashon	love for one not related by blood, but kin of the heart
aye	love that is unwelcome and a burden
azh	love for one sexually desired now
éeme	love for one neither liked nor respected
oham	love for that which is holy
sham	love for the child of one's body, presupposing neither liking nor respect nor their absence

D) Numbers, Numerals

1	nede		12	shinethab
2	shin		16	bathethab
3	boó		20	thabeshin
4	bim		21	thabeshin i nede
5	shan		30	thabeboó
6	bath		100	debe
7	um		101	debe i nede
8	nib		1000	thob
9	bud		1001	thob i nede
10	thab		1,000,000	rod
11	nedethab		1,000,000,000	merod

e) **Pronouns**

	Singular	Several	Many
1. 1st person neutral	le	lezh	len
beloved	la	lazh	lan
honored	li	lizh	lin
despised	lhele	lhelezh	lhelen
2. 2nd person neutral (and so on as above)	ne	nezh	nen
3. 3rd person neutral (and so on as above)	be	bezh	ben

NOTE: These are the base forms, to which the CASE MARKERS are added. Thus "I" is "**le**," "me" is "**leth**," and so on.

	Singular	Several	Many
4. Demonstratives	hi	hizh	hin
nearer (this, these)	**hithoma/ nuhi**	**hizhethoma/ nuhizh**	**hinethoma/ nuhin**
farther (that, those)	**hithed/ núuhi**	**hizhethed/ núuhizh**	**hineehed/ núuhin**

5. Indefinites:
use the base form, plus "**-ye-**," plus plural suffix, plus gender suffix, plus CASE MARKER.

6. Reflexives:[1]
use the base form, plus "**-yóo-**," plus plural suffix, plus gender suffix, plus CASE MARKER.

7. Interrogatives:
use the third person base form, plus "**-báa-**," plus plural suffix, plus CASE MARKER.

---

[1] Reflexive pronouns occur almost exclusively in non-subject case phrases, referring to the person/thing from the subject case phrase in a second case (object, goal, source, beneficiary, etc. Example: "Bíi eril naya Méri bayóo (hizhe)th wa" (Mary took care of her-beloved-self); clearly Mary and herself are the same person, but are being referred to in separate, differently-cased phrases.

Appendix 3

Notes on Adding to the Láadan Vocabulary[1]

NOW THAT THE LÁADAN WORKING GROUP HAS BEGUN putting substantial amounts of material for the language on the Internet, more and more proposed new words and morphemes are arriving. It seems, therefore, that it might be useful to have a brief overview available about adding new items to the vocabulary. I'll do my best to be brief without being obscure, and to define my terms as I go along. I'll try not to slip into LinguistSpeak (LS), but will provide the more common technical terms (in parentheses) so that they'll be familiar for those who may want to read further on the topic.

General Information

All living human languages have methods for adding new items to their vocabularies. Some of these methods are systematic and can be easily described; however, there is no rule forbidding native speakers of languages to simply make up new items from scratch. That is, no rule would prevent me from adding the new word "kappid" to English to mean "upper surface of the entire left thumb." Making that word succeed—so that people would say it and write it, and it would be added to the dictionary—is an entirely different matter. We don't know much about why a given newly-coined item does or doesn't "make it" in a language. A few things we do know are...

NOTE: If you are e-mailing a proposed new Láadan item and don't have convenient access to the accent mark, just substitute a capital letter for the vowel-plus-tone. In such a situation, Láadan would be written as "LAadan."

---

[1] This article was written to facilitate the evolution of the Láadan language via contributions from the community of Láadan scholars—using the Láadan website as the locus of this work. The Láadan website has been dormant since the early 2000s, but is now (2020) being revived, populated with much new material, including a ***70-Lesson Grammar Set***: Laadanlanguage.com

1. It helps if the item gets introduced in a movie or novel that's a smash hit and has a huge marketing budget behind it, or is introduced by an organization of scientists, or some such thing.

2. Items that violate the grammar rules of the language—for any part of the grammar—are unlikely to succeed. Consider my earlier example, "*kappid.*" If I tried to make that "*mkappid*" instead, native speakers of English would immediately reject it, because the part of English grammar that determines how the language sounds doesn't allow words to start with an "m" sound followed by a "k" sound. "M" and "k" are both meaningful English sounds and either one of them could be first in a word, but "mk" at the beginning of a word is unacceptable. The Láadan sound system has a rule that says there can never be a sequence of two identical vowel sounds inside a morpheme. (NOTE: "Working" is just one word, but it contains two morphemes: "work," which is a morpheme that can stand alone, and "-ing," which is a morpheme that can't stand alone.) This means that if there were native speakers of Láadan, and someone tried to introduce "maath" as a new morpheme, it would be rejected for violating that rule. Any time two identical vowels occur together, one of them has to have tone (in Láadan, a higher pitch, indicated by an accent marker). So, either "**máath**" or "**maáth**" would be acceptable, but just plain "**maath**" is unacceptable in Láadan just as "*mkappid*" is unacceptable in English.

3. It's much harder for a proposed new morpheme to succeed if it's part of a "closed class" of morphemes in a language. A proposed new English pronoun, for example, or a proposed new English tense ending, will inevitably face an uphill fight.

Because Láadan is a new language with no native speakers, its grammar isn't firmly set in the fashion that the grammar of English is, and many of the new items that have been proposed for it have been part of word-sets like the pronouns, the SPEECH ACT MORPHEMES, and the like. That's still possible for Láadan in a way that it's not possible for English or Cherokee or Japanese or Sign—the boundaries of "closed classes" haven't been established by centuries of speech and writing and signing—but it will nevertheless be harder to do than just adding a new noun or verb, and should be done with care. Once a class of words becomes closed, the language is essentially stuck with it; if that turns out to be awkward—the way not having a gender-neutral third person pronoun for English is awkward—it's not easy to fix.

How the Original Láadan Dictionary Was Constructed

My goal when I constructed Láadan was that it should be as easy to pronounce as possible—and its pronunciation as easy to understand as possible—no matter what the native language of the learner might be. Roughly speaking, the easiest linguistic structure for achieving that goal is sequences in which consonant sounds alternate with vowel sounds. How long or short the words and morphemes are isn't particularly important; some languages have very short words, some have words that are as long as a sizable English sentence. But the consonant sound/vowel sound alternation really matters. I therefore used a number of different strategies to preserve that structure as I put the language together.

NOTE: The reason I keep saying "consonant sound" and "vowel sound" is because English sometimes uses more than one consonant to write a single consonant sound and more than one vowel to write a single vowel sound. Linguists identify a phoneme—a single meaningful sound—by writing it between slashes—like /m/ and /sh/—so that it won't be mixed up with the letters of the English alphabet.

Another goal I had for Láadan was that it should be as easy as possible to figure out what a particular word or morpheme means just by looking at it. I wanted the language to work like a Tinkertoy set works, so that people could take the pieces and fit them together easily to make larger forms. For example: the Láadan word for "bee" is "**zhomid**"; that word is made from "**zho**"—the Láadan word for "sound"—and "**mid**"—the Láadan word for "creature." The meaning is transparent from the word's parts.

First, however, I had to construct the most basic elements of the language—the words/morphemes that are called "roots" and can't be taken apart into smaller meaningful pieces. When linguists begin working with a language for which no grammar or dictionary is available, they ordinarily start with a set of roughly 100 very basic words made up of items like "eat" and "sleep" and "food." I followed that practice, and began by constructing a core vocabulary of those basic words; when I had those done I began adding additional roots that I felt were needed. Sometimes I can explain to some extent how I chose a particular shape for one of those words; much of the time I can't.

For example… I can explain that I chose "**oódóo**" for "bridge" because when pronounced its tune makes the shape of a humpback bridge. I can explain that I chose "**rul**" for "cat" because the purring of a cat sounds to me like "rulrulrulrul…" But the choice of "**ana**" for "food" and "**ina**" for "sleep" was arbitrary; I have no explanation for those choices other than that I tried to give them a shape that could easily be combined with other morphemes. For any constructed language that isn't based on some existing language, the hardest part will always be putting together the inventory of roots.

The "Tinkertoy" strategy leads naturally to sets of words that people can easily recognize, even if they can't be certain of the exact meaning. When you see a Láadan word that includes "**mid**" as one of its morphemes, it should be the case that you can assume that the word is the name of an animal, even if you can't be sure precisely which one. (The word for "cat," because it's from the core vocabulary and is a root word—and all other animal names in the core vocabulary[1]—will be an exception; the assumption is that people will learn the core vocabulary first and then move on from there.) So: "**dithemid**" is "cow"—"**mid**" plus "**dith**," which means "voice"; "**lanemid**" is "dog"—"**mid**" plus "**lan**," which means "friend."

Just as Láadan doesn't allow two identical vowel sounds in a row inside a single morpheme, it forbids any two consonant sounds or two vowel sounds in a row both inside a morpheme and when you put morphemes together. (This is consistent with the strategy of trying to maintain consonant sound/vowel sound alternation at all times.) But obviously, when you start combining morphemes you're going to run into situations where you do have two consonant or

---

[1] For example, the word for "fox" is another core word **dumidal**.

vowel sounds in a row. Láadan has three rules that take care of this problem:

1. When adding one morpheme to another would give you a sequence of two vowel sounds, insert an "**h**" sound to prevent that.
2. When adding one morpheme to another would give you a sequence of two consonant sounds, insert an "**e**" sound (the vowel sound in English "bed") to prevent that.
3. When adding one morpheme to another would give you a sequence of two identical consonant sounds, you have two choices:
   A. Follow Rule 2 and insert the "**e**"; or
   B. Drop one of the two identical consonant sounds.

   For example, "**dom**"/"remember" combined with "**mid**"/"creature" to mean "elephant" would yield "**dommid**," which is not allowed. One choice, by Rule 3(a), is "**domemid**"; that choice was rejected. The other choice, by Rule 3(b), is to drop one of the two "**m**"s, which yields "**domid**"; that is the choice that was made. Either choice would have been acceptable.

The sound system of Láadan won't allow either "**dithmid**" for "cow" or "**lanmid**" for "dog"; instead, they become "**dithemid**" and "**lanemid**." Similarly, when I added the morpheme "**-á**" (which means "one who does") to "**bedi**"(which means "learn") to make the words "student" and "learner," I couldn't just make that word "**bediá**"; it had to become "**bedihá**." If I wanted to put the morpheme "**du-**" (which means "try to") at the beginning of a verb that starts with a vowel sound, I had to insert an "**h**" sound; so, "try to sell" (from the verb "**eb**") had to become "**duheb**."

This word-building process can result in some very long words. If my goal for Láadan had been that it should be composed as much as possible of short words, that would be a problem. If Láadan were a natural language, its speakers might decide over time that they didn't like long words, and they might start shortening them. That sort of thing happens in languages. However, there's a reasonable probability that the speakers of the language would try to preserve the two basic goals—ease of pronunciation based on consonant sound/vowel sound alternation, and ease of understanding based on the construction of words from already known morphemes. I don't claim that that's probable because it's "better" or "more logical" or "more esthetically pleasing" or anything of that kind. It's probable because when I constructed the language I built in many rules, at many levels of the grammar, that all work together to maintain those two goals.

Those rules could all be changed by native speakers, certainly, over generations; that happens with languages too. The end result would be a perfectly fine language, but it would be a very different language.

Additional Miscellaneous Word-Formation Rules and/or Constraints

1. There are four Láadan sounds that can't be used as the final consonant in a word or morpheme: /y/, /w/, /h/, and /r/. This isn't an arbitrary rule; it's part of the set of rules that work to maintain the consonant/vowel alternation mentioned above. Although it's traditional to put those four sounds into the class of consonants for the English alphabet, none of them is—in linguistics terms—a true consonant.

2. I've had many queries about the set of morphemes that contain the sequence "**br**," which includes "**bre… ébre**" ("if…then"), "**bre**" ("layer"), "**bremeda**" ("onion"), "**bróo**" ("because"), and the three REPETITION MORPHEMES "**brada, bradan, bradá.**" Since Láadan is said to have a rule forbidding consonant clusters, this set should not exist—but there it is. The explanation is very simple: I made a mistake during the construction of the language and added these items, which most certainly do violate that rule, and I apologize. There are several possible ways of handling this. (Deleting the anomalous items isn't one of them, because languages don't work that way; anomalies may die out over time because native speakers fail to use them, but "legislative" attempts to stamp out particular morphemes, even for very good reasons, are always a waste of time.) The possibilities are:

A. Say that these forms are a historical accident—which is true, that they should be treated as exceptions to the consonant cluster rule, and that no more items containing "**br**" should be added.

B. Rewrite the rule about consonant clusters to say that the only consonant cluster Láadan allows is "**br**." This would be simple, but it would open the vocabulary to many more forms containing "**br**."

Rewrite the rule about consonant clusters to say that Láadan allows no clusters of true consonants, rather than just no clusters of consonants. "**r**" (along with "**h**" and "**w**" and "**y**") is not a true consonant, which would mean that "**br**" is not a violation of the rule. However, doing this would suddenly open up the vocabulary to a large number of other sequences that would seriously complicate the sound system. It would be better not to do this.

My personal preference is for alternative (A), because it is simplest and introduces the fewest complications.

3. The consonant "**lh**" is a consonant like any other consonant, and it's entirely legitimate to use it to add new words. However, it's also a morpheme that has as its specific purpose the semantic information that the item it occurs in has a negative meaning. To use it in any other way would create misleading and ambiguous items. For example, the word for "apple" is "**doyu**"; one way to refer to a rotten apple, or an apple with a worm inside it, or an apple that is in some other way repugnant, is to call it "**doyulh**" instead of just "**doyu**." Doing that doesn't create a new word of Láadan meaning something like "nasty apple," it just uses "**lh**" the way English would use an adjective. On the other hand, there is the word for "rape," which is "**ralh**"; in that case, the negative meaning carried by "**lh**" is an inherent part of the word.

For either of these uses of "**lh**", the only rule is that "**lh**" must be added in such a way that the alternating consonant/vowel pattern is preserved and no other rule of the sound system is broken. For example, the word for food is "**ana**." If you wanted to say of some particular food that it was spoiled, or tasted awful, or anything of that kind, you could say either "**analh**" or "**lhana**"; both are acceptable and both would be understood to have that meaning. If you are constructing a new word of Láadan that has an inherently negative meaning you would follow the same rule, but your choice would be more final. It would be unlikely, and uneconomical, for the dictionary of Láadan to include both "**analh**" and "**lhana**."

Suzette Haden Elgin
From https://laadanlanguage.com

Appendix 4

Pattern Practice Answers

LESSON 1:
1. Bíi ril sháad óowamid **bethudedi** wa.
2. Bíi ril sháad óowamid **olinedi** wa.
3. Bíi ril sháad óowamid **miwithedi** wa.
4. Bíi ril sháad óowamid **yodi** wa.

LESSON 2:
1. Bíi ril thi Athid **áabeth** wa.
2. Bíi ril thi Athid **nith** wa.
3. Bíi ril thi Athid **dahaneth** wa.
4. Bíi ril thi Athid **webeth** wa.

LESSON 3:
1. Báa ril sháad ne **bothedi**?
2. Báa ril sháad ne **óoledi**?
3. Báa ril sháad ne **meladi**?
4. Báa ril sháad ne **shodedi**?

LESSON 4:
1. Bíi ril sháad be buzhedi **eshenan** wa.
2. Bíi ril sháad be buzhedi **memazhenan** wa.
3. Bíi ril sháad be buzhedi **zhazhenan** wa.

LESSON 5:
1. Bíi eril di Athid wa, "Báa ril sháad ne **sheshihothedi**?"
2. Bíi eril di Athid wa, "Báa ril sháad ne **wethedi**?"
3. Bíi eril di Athid wa, "Báa ril sháad ne **amedaradi**?"
4. Bíi eril di Athid wa, "Báa ril sháad ne **olinedi**?"

LESSON 6:
1. Bíi ril wida Athid **áabeth** wa.
2. Bíi ril wida Athid **ridademeth** wa.
3. Bíi ril wida Athid **ruleth** wa.
4. Bíi ril wida Athid **doyuth** wa.

LESSON 7:
1. Bíi ril merilin bezh **éebeth** wáa.
2. Bíi ril merilin bezh **laleth** wáa.
3. Bíi ril merilin bezh **zhuth** wáa.
4. Bíi ril merilin bezh **ilith** wáa.

LESSON 8:
1. Bíi ril néde le **rimáayoth** wa.
2. Bíi ril néde le **doneth** wa.
3. Bíi ril néde le **laleneth** wa.
4. Bíi ril néde le **lolineth** wa.

LESSON 9:
1. Bíi aril meheb lezh **esheth** menedebe wa.
2. Bíi aril meheb lezh **lulineth** menedebe wa.
3. Bíi aril meheb lezh **shinehaleth** menedebe wa.
4. Bíi aril meheb lezh **shidath** menedebe wa.

Appendix 5

Resources

Láadan website: **laadanlanguage.com**

70-Lesson Grammar Set by Amberwind Barnhart, posted to the Láadan website, **laadanlanguage.com**

Láadan-based music by Meteoric (Caitlin Pencarrick Hertzman) and Fallow Twin (Amos Hertzman). Their first album, Láadan, is a 45-minute ambient electronic "grammar lesson" between a wife and her husband. It is based on *Native Tongue* but set in a future in which women reach out to men to be allies. Their next album, *Earthsong*, based on the final book in the trilogy, will be an ambient set exploring resonance and sound nourishment. For more information, visit **laadanmusic.com**

Suzette Haden Elgin Papers. University of Oregon Libraries, Special Collections and University Archives Suzette Haden Elgin was known for her extensive scholarly work in linguistics, the development of a feminist language called Láadan, and numerous publications in science fiction and other genres. The collection includes original Láadan materials, correspondence, publications, academic work, biographical information, music, plays, poems, original artwork, and audiovisual recordings all pertaining to her life as a scholar and an artist in many mediums.
http://archiveswest.orbiscascade.org/ark:/80444/xv57659

About the Author

SUZETTE HADEN ELGIN (born Patricia Anne Wilkins; November 18, 1936–January 27, 2015) was a science fiction author and linguist. She founded the Science Fiction Poetry Association and is an important figure in the field of science fiction constructed languages. Her best-known non-fiction includes the *Gentle Art of Verbal Self-Defense* series.

Elgin was born in 1936 in Jefferson City, Missouri. She attended the University of California, San Diego (UCSD) in the 1960s, and began writing science fiction in order to pay tuition. She gained a PhD in linguistics, and was the first UCSD student ever to write two dissertations (on English and Navajo).

Photo by George Elgin

She created the constructed language Láadan for her *Native Tongue* science fiction series. A grammar and dictionary was edited by Diane Martin and published by by SF³ in 1985, and a second edition in 1988. She supported feminist science fiction, saying

Photo by George Elgin

> *Women need to realize that SF is the only genre of literature in which it's possible for a writer to explore the question of what this world would be like if you could get rid of [X], where [X] is filled*

in with any of the multitude of real world facts that constrain and oppress women. Women need to treasure and support science fiction.

Elgin was twice celebrated as guest of honor at the feminist science fiction convention, WisCon, in 1982 and 1986.

Overlying themes in her work include feminism, linguistics and the impact of proper language, and peaceful coexistence with nature. Many of her works also draw from her Ozark background and heritage.

Elgin became a professor at San Diego State University (SDSU). She retired in 1980 and lived in Arkansas with her second husband, George Elgin. She died at age 78 in 2015.

Suzette Haden Elgin founded the Science Fiction and Poetry Association (SFPA) in 1978, and also set up the Rhysling Awards and the SFPA newsletter, *Star*Line*. As a tribute, all proceeds from this book will be donated to SFPA. For more information, go to **SFPoetry.com**.

About this Book

THE FIRST DICTIONARY AND GRAMMAR OF LÁADAN (first and second editions) was edited by Diane Martin and published in 1985 and 1988 by SF³ (the Society for the Furtherance and Study of Fantasy and Science Fiction, Inc.). It has been long out of print. Sadly no electronic files exist for the book, which complicated the task of revising and reprinting *this* book. There was an additional complication: we discovered that a considerable amount of new work had been posted on the Láadan website by Elgin and other Láadan scholars: vocabulary, new lessons, exercises, plus Elgin's essays on constructing language. The website had been dormant for many years, but we are delighted to report that as of 2020, it has been revived. We decided that a new, third Láadan Dictionary should include all of the available material—the second edition book (1988), plus the original material from the website. And that is what you hold in your hands.

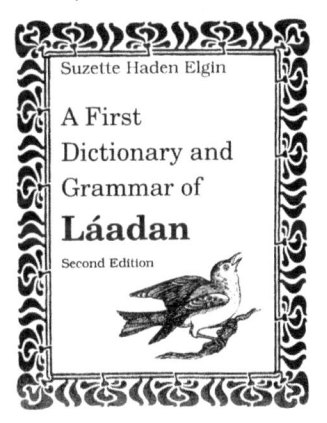

First of all we thank Suzette Haden Elgin for inventing the Láadan language. We hope to honor her memory by keeping the Láadan Dictionary available. Rebecca Haden granted us permission to publish material by her mother in this book and we are very pleased to include a preface by Ms. Haden.

We thank Karen Robinson for her extensive work in compiling the Láadan-to-English Dictionary for the first book; Toni Armstrong for permission to reprint the lessons originally appearing in *Hot Wire* magazine; and SF³ for sponsoring the first dictionary.

We are very grateful to Jackie Powers and Amberwind Barnhart, who shared with us their work from the Láadan website and on-going Láadan development. A considerable amount of the material added since the first and second editions, was developed by Jackie Powers and Amberwind Barnhart.

We also thank all those whose work we found on the Láadan website: Anne Hatzakis, Baer Gewanter, Carole Fontaine, Catriona Harrison, Julia Penelope (with her associates and students), M. Lynne Murphy, Rae Beno, Sharla Hardy, and Tina Black. We apologize to those whose initials we were unable to identify.

Suzette Haden Elgin at WisCon, 6, March 1982. Photo by Diane Martin.

Susanna Sturgis learned Láadan in the course of copyediting this book. We are filled with gratitude for her meticulous work.

The text type for this book is Adobe Caslon Pro, with titles in Salty.

All proceeds from the sale of this book will be donated to the Science Fiction and Fantasy Poetry Association, which was founded by Suzette Haden Elgin in 1978.

Jeanne Gomoll & Diane Martin
2020

About the Contributors

Amberwind Barnhart

When I entered college to study linguistics in the late '70s, San Diego State University was one option I explored; I missed actually studying under Suzette Haden Elgin by, as the TV show had it, "this much." When I married, my husband introduced me to Suzette Haden Elgin's science fiction, including the *Native Tongue* series. Láadan, the language devised by the women of the Lines, immediately fascinated me. Even so, it took almost 10 years to acquire a used copy of the *A First Dictionary and Grammar of Láadan*—but it was love at first read. I introduced myself to Suzette Haden Elgin via a lengthy email, attaching a database of all the vocabulary I could track down with a friendly user interface and a re-typeset version of the grammar that corrected some errata.

That was in 2006; Suzette and I then began an ongoing correspondence, with me doing my best to winkle out of her all the "bits and bobs" of Láadan that never made it into print. That very rewarding correspondence lasted well into 2010, when Suzette's declining health made it impossible to continue. During this time, my suggested edits for *A First Dictionary and Grammar* morphed into a much more ambitious project: a set of lessons designed to bring the student along, one step at a time. I have taught classes in Láadan to some friends—including one who taught high school; they greatly helped hone the teaching methods involved. Eventually, 70 lessons took the place of Suzette's original 14. At this writing, the lesson-set is complete and I'm converting it to html; I'll post that to **laadanlanguage.com** as soon as it's done. Next, I'll record voice snippets of the Láadan sequences and update the online lessons.

When Jeanne contacted me with the news that there was a third edition in the works, I was delighted! It has been my great pleasure to look over an early draft to contribute whatever expertise I may have.

Wil sha! (Let there be harmony!)

Jeanne Gomoll

Diane Martin and I have been friends for more than 40 years. We worked together on the feminist SF fanzines, *Janus* and *Aurora* and served on the first and several dozen subsequent WisCon convention committees. We worked for many years with the James Tiptree, Jr. Award/Otherwise Award. In 1980, Eileen Gunn gave me a tape recording one of Suzette Haden Suzette's lessons, titled, "Teach Yourself Alien." In this lesson Elgin offered advice to Science Fiction authors on how to deal with alien languages in their fiction. It was great. I shared it with Diane, and we immediately decided to contact Suzette and ask permission to reprint the text in our fanzine, *Aurora*, whole issue #19, Vol. 7, no. 1 (We've reprinted the lesson as an essay in this book; see page 281.) In 1982, WisCon invited Suzette to attend WisCon 6 and again in 1986 for WisCon 10 as guest of honor. Diane and I both loved and honored Suzette Haden Elgin as a friend, an advisor, and a brilliant scientist. We did not want to let the Láadan dictionary go out of print.

After working nearly 50 years as a professional graphic designer I retired in the Fall of 2018 but continued to design publications. I drew and published *The James Tiptree, Jr. Space Babe Coloring Book*. I wrote and published *TAFForensic Report* and edited and designed two other books: *Carl Brandon* and *Remembering Vonda*. This dictionary, *A Third Dictionary and Grammar of Láadan*, is special though: this project rescues a pre-electronic publication and thus keeps alive and celebrates the work of a phenomenal talent and dear friend, Suzette Haden Elgin. That it gave me the chance to work with my friend, Diane Martin, makes it an extraordinary gift.

Diane Martin

I "typeset" *A First Dictionary and Grammar* on an IBM Selectric. I don't recall the original draft material from Suzette (we're talking over 30 years here), but it was challenging. For the 1988 edition, I used an Apple computer. That was easier, but still a major PITA to do. And in the intervening years the files were lost. Luckily, Jeanne, who is a stellar graphic designer ran the pages through an OCR program to get us computer files once more.

I'm not a graphic designer or linguist, I earned my living as an accountant. But publishing has always been a hobby of mine. I dabbled in amateur newspapers (*FOFF, The Golden Nugget, The Alternative*) in grade school, high school, and college. And from the late 70s I worked with Jeanne and several other Madison, WI folks to publish the SF magazine *Janus*, which turned into *Aurora*, and also helped found WisCon, the first feminist science fiction convention.

Sometime in the mid-80s Jeanne got a cassette tape from Eileen Gunn of a lesson Suzette had recorded. That began a long wonderful relationship with Suzette. I'll let Jeanne tell you about that. The magazines ended about 1990, but the convention is now in its 41st year. I retired from my day job about five years ago, and coasted along gardening, petting my cats, and catching up on my reading. (Somehow recreational accounting did not appeal to me.) Jeanne retired in 2018, and immediately started on new publishing projects for herself. I'll let her tell you about that, too. Somehow she convinced me to work on the 3rd edition of the Láadan dictionary. So here we are. I'm so glad the work on Láadan will continue.

Jackie Powers

I read Suzette's *Native Tongue* books shortly after the second one was published and was immediately fascinated by the idea of Láadan. But between the challenges of work, kids and life in general, I never pursued it. But my fascination with Láadan remained.

On a whim in 2005, I emailed Suzette to ask how to buy a copy of the book, and shortly thereafter received *A First Dictionary and Grammar* and her Láadan cassette tape. As a technical writer, I quickly became frustrated with the inconsistencies in the book. But as I'm also a professional website developer, the solution seemed simple enough: I'd make a website for a corrected version of the dictionary and lessons. I broached the idea to Suzette, got her buy-in in late 2005, and worked extensively with her to clarify/correct words and add new ones. In mid-2006, we received SF[3] approval, and the website **www.laadanlanguage.com** was born.

Over the years, I worked off and on with Suzette and Amberwind, adding words and lessons to the website, as our busy schedules allowed. (I'm the inspiration for the "baby step" lessons on the website, because the steps in original lessons were just too big for me.) After Suzette passed, Amberwind and I continued her legacy (mostly Amberwind). The most recent iteration of the website is from when I was laid off in 2015, but after I returned to work in 2017, sadly, the website slid further and further down my priority list.

When I heard about Diane and Jeanne's project of *A Third Dictionary and Grammar of Láadan*, I was thrilled! And their project has inspired me to return to work on the Láadan website, this project of my heart. Diane and Jeanne, Thank you so much!

Susanna Sturgis

I came to F/SF late in life, like in my mid to late twenties. As a literarily inclined feminist, I couldn't help noticing that much of the most exciting feministically inclined writing was fantasy, science fiction, and/or (the term was coming into vogue at the time) speculative fiction. I was hooked. I loved Suzette's *Ozark* trilogy and I especially loved the *Native Tongue* series. Old women cast off by their patriarchal society, transforming the world by inventing a women's language? How could I resist? Thanks to *Janus→Aurora*, I discovered WisCon, and was an active participant through the '90s. Ironically enough, it was thanks to WisCon that I struck off in new directions: WisCon regular Marsha Valance had a hand in my becoming a born-again horsegirl, and being part of a world where writing was taken seriously told me it was time to take my own writing more seriously. Thanks to the FEM-SF email list and, a decade or so later, Facebook, I was able to keep up with the WisCon world and the people I'd known back when.

Funny thing: Over the decades I've learned that dropped stitches often don't stay dropped forever. Since 1999 I've been a full-time freelance editor and proofreader, and it was in that capacity that Jeanne Gomoll asked if I'd be interested in proofreading the third edition of the Láadan dictionary (whose very first edition and the accompanying cassette tape were still on my shelves). Well, yeah! It turned out to be the most challenging proofread of my career: the "manuscript" was in about ten parts that not infrequently contradicted each other. But it was a thrill to realize that others had kept Láadan, and with it Suzette's brilliance and vision, alive through the years, and an even greater thrill to play a small part in making it available in such handsome form to new fans and prospective speakers.

Lightning Source UK Ltd.
Milton Keynes UK
UKHW020630020821
388172UK00010B/842